RAGGED
CHAIN

RAGGED
CHAIN

To Shannon
Enjoy this taste of
the "Wet Coast"

A MYSTERY BY
Vivian Meyer

SUMACH
PRESS

Ragged Chain
By Vivian Meyer

First published in 2009 by Sumach Press, an imprint of Canadian Scholars' Press Inc.
180 Bloor Street West, Suite 801
Toronto, Ontario
M5S 2V6

www.cspi.org

Canadian Scholars' Press Inc./Sumach Press gratefully acknowledges financial support
for our publishing activities from the Ontario Arts Council, the Canada Council for the
Arts, the Government of Canada through the Book Publishing Industry Development
Program (BPIDP), and the Government of Ontario through the Ontario Book
Publishing Tax Credit Program.

Library and Archives Canada Cataloguing in Publication

Meyer, Vivian, 1958-
    Ragged chain : a Sumach mystery / Vivian Meyer.

ISBN 978-1-894549-84-4

    I. Title.

PS8626.E945R33 2009   C813'.6   C2009-904660-1

Text design based on design by Liz Martin.
Cover by Liz Martin.

09 10 11 12 13   5 4 3 2 1

Printed and bound in Canada by Marquis Book Printing Inc.

This book is dedicated to the threatened forests of the world.

CHAPTER 1

"WHAT'S THE MATTER, Anita?"

My friend looked over her shoulder furtively at the crowd standing around waiting for their luggage in the small Vancouver Island airport.

"Oh, Abby! I can't believe this. There's a guy over there who was in the house the night Dan was killed." Her fingers dug painfully into my arm. "If he recognizes me, I'm in big trouble. I've heard what some of those guys have done to keep people quiet!"

Anita had recently been a witness at a terrible crime scene in Toronto's Kensington Market area, and after a successful recovery process, the last thing she needed now was to be reminded of that trauma. "Are you sure it's him, Anita?" I asked doubtfully. "So far from home?"

She nodded, shrinking closer to me. "I'd recognize that face and that red hair anywhere."

"Jesus! Okay, wait, let me think." I hugged her, shielding her from the crowd. "Do you think he noticed you? Is he looking this way?"

Anita peered carefully around my shoulder and stiffened. "Abby, you're not going to believe this! He's actually talking with Andy. They're looking at the bikes."

I half turned and noticed that there was, indeed, a guy talking to my boyfriend. They were gesturing at the bikes still encased in transparent plastic airline bags. Andy seemed to be mostly listening, but that wouldn't last long. My Andy was a talker. I needed to get to him before he spilled out our life story and got Anita in trouble.

"Okay," I said grimly. "I want you to go to the bathroom down the hall behind you, Anita. It's the safest place for you to wait. I'm going to go over there and see what I can find out." I followed her to the doorway and looked her straight in the eye. "Will you be okay?" She nodded, and I squeezed her arm encouragingly. "I'll come get you as soon as it's safe. Hopefully, it won't be too long."

Anita smiled weakly, still pale and trembling. "I'll be okay," she said, and slipped into a stall.

I made my way back to the baggage carousel, furious. How could our holiday turn nasty so quickly? The last thing I had thought when I agreed to accompany Andy on this West Coast holiday was that, by taking Anita, she'd be exposed to new dangers. She had gone through so much and was doing so well. I was beginning to feel royally steamed.

I walked purposefully over to Andy Jaegar, a handsome surgeon I had met when recovering from wounds I incurred in a kidnapping incident, my introduction to amateur investigation. Andy shared my love of cycling, which brought us together while I was still in the hospital. We had brought our bikes and rack along, hoping to take advantage of the winding, hilly roads of the West Coast to get some exercise while enjoying our break at a luxurious hotel.

Andy and the thug were chatting amiably. Andy smiled when I walked up. "Hey, Abby. Where's—?" He looked at me curiously as I cut off his question with a silencing kiss to the lips and a warning squeeze to the arm.

"Our bags? I think they're just coming out now. Why don't you go get them while I watch over this stuff," I said, gesturing to the two road bikes and the bike rack.

Still looking a little puzzled, Andy said, "Okay, Ab. I'll be back in a jiff." He nodded to the young man and then wandered off looking for our bags.

I stepped back and held out my hand.

"Hi there."

He grinned affably. "Hi. I'm Brendon," he said as he shook my hand. "I saw your roadies and started telling your friend there about the best riding routes. You'll need mountain bikes for the trails, though. I live here in Bellweather. There are some great places to rent bikes in town."

"Oh, that's okay," I replied hastily.

He nodded. Then, switching gears, Brendon said, "So, you're from out east, from Toronto? I've been there a few times on business."

Nodding my head as he continued to talk, I could just imagine what kind of business he was in if he was hanging around Dan Burnett's the night of the murder. It had to be drugs, prostitution, organized crime or all three of the above. It was kind of creepy to know that behind this friendly exterior was a person who easily associated with violent criminals, if he wasn't one himself. I could only hope that Andy hadn't shared my name or mentioned Anita at all, otherwise we could be in big trouble.

"Toronto's a great city," I conceded, "but here, everything's so clean and green."

"True," he agreed. "That's why I live here. I'm just hoping I can build up my business with my partners from your city."

"Really?" I asked. "Well, I hope you'll be very successful. Small communities need some entrepreneurial spirit. What do you do, Brendon?"

Now he became a little more circumspect.

"Oh, um, importing," he said, "and we're in discussions about a small casino. We have lots of retirees moving into the area. In fact," he said, looking at his watch, "I'm expecting some visitors from your part of the world on the next flight in. They should be here any minute."

Suddenly, I was even more anxious to get us away from the airport. Any potential business partners of Brendon's might be too familiar with what went down in Kensington and might be interested in revenge if they knew we were here. I wasn't the most popular person with that crowd, seeing as I was responsible for several of them ending up in jail. I had to give him the brush-off quickly and get Andy moving. While we had been talking, Andy had added bags from the conveyor belt to our pile of stuff. He saved me having to make up excuses by walking up just then.

"Okay, Ab. We're all set. Help me get this stuff packed up, and we'll be on our way."

"Let me help," Brendon suggested as he leaned over to pick up a bag.

"No, no," I said, jumping to grab a pile of stuff. "We can handle it."

Andy smiled at Brendon. "Thanks anyway. It was nice meeting you."

"Yes," I said. "Maybe we'll see you around." I quickly followed Andy, both of us heavily laden as we made for the car parked just outside, at one end of the fifty-metre sidewalk along the front of the airport.

"That was weird, Abby," Andy said as we dumped the stuff under the protective overhang. It was still windy, but the heavy rain that had been falling during our landing had abated somewhat. "Why didn't you want me to talk with him? And where is Anita?"

"I'm sorry, Andy. I'll tell you once we get the hell out of here. Hey, listen, can you finish loading the car and then drive to the other end of the airport while I get Anita? And whatever you do, if you see that guy Brendon, don't even mention her name to him." I lifted the sweatshirt he had draped over his shoulders. "And can I borrow this? Anita was a little cold when I left her."

"Sure, Ab, but you're being more than a little strange." He shrugged. "I'll be five minutes or so, okay?"

I gave him a quick peck on the cheek. "That's fabulous, Andy. Thanks."

I stayed in the shelter of the overhang as I walked to the back entrance of the airport. During our landing, the rain had been falling sideways in sheets like grey laundry blowing on a line. I had peered out the window, questioning whether the holiday had been such a good idea. Out of my element and more than a little nervous, I had wondered whether we would get in any biking anyway, with the rain so intense.

Anita, however, had no such worries. She obviously found the landing thrilling and was excited to be going camping on Peregrine Island. Her enthusiasm had been contagious, and once the little turbo prop landed, I relaxed and was ready for adventure — until Brendon appeared to spoil the moment. Now I was worried about Anita, a familiar, uncomfortable feeling. There was no way that I was going to let anyone endanger her life again, I thought grimly.

Putting on a false front of calm for her sake, I entered and found her waiting in the far corner of the bathroom.

"Hey, Anita, I sussed out that guy. Brendon is his name. You're right. He does have some connection with Toronto. Fortunately, though, he lives here in Bellweather, so we probably won't run into him on Peregrine Island. He's waiting for some people from the East on the next plane. He said they're looking into partnering in some business venture here in Bellweather. If we keep a low profile, I think we'll be okay."

Surprisingly, Anita stuck out her chin bravely. "We'll just stay out of his way, like you say. Let's get going." She grinned at me, almost her old self again.

"Good girl," I said as I handed her Andy's hoodie. "Here, Anita, put this on just in case, and pull up the hood. Andy should be ready with the car now. I told him to wait at the entrance just past this washroom so we won't have to walk past the baggage area." Anita nodded, pulled on the hoodie and took a deep breath. We left the bathroom together, walking nonchalantly towards the exit where Andy was waiting with the engine running.

He was cool. "Hi, Anita," he said as he pulled out. "Abby hasn't filled me in yet on all this cloak-and-dagger stuff, but I'm glad to see you're in one piece." I quickly told him the details while Anita scrunched down in the back seat.

With the ever-competent Andy at the helm, we reached the ferry dock with only a few wrong turns. He pulled into the line to pay our fare, while I looked warily at the narrow channel we were about to cross. The island, dimly visible through the grey mist, was not far, but the water looked rough and forbidding. While the rain had lessened to a drizzle, the wind was still blowing hard from the south. I watched as the approaching ferry bobbed up and down over the waves.

"Are you sure we want to go out on that?" I asked nervously.

"They know what they're doing, Abby," Andy said. "I'm sure they wouldn't sail if it was dangerous."

"I guess you're right," was all I could mutter skeptically. It didn't help my nerves that twice during loading, they had to readjust the ramp because the ferry was bouncing around so much.

Once we had left the car safely loaded onto the car deck, Anita said, "Let's go inside and look around."

A diversion sounded good to me, so we navigated our way through the other vehicles and climbed the stairs to the ferry lounge. The seating area was in the centre of the ship, above the cars. Folks were lounging in padded chairs, chatting or reading, looking quite relaxed. I guessed this was a simple commute for the locals and relaxed a little while I looked over the bulletin board, which was covered with "for sale" notices, ads for jobs wanted or available, flyers for workshops and posters for community events.

As Andy and Anita went to the front windows to watch the ferry pull out, I stayed behind, scanning the board more carefully to get a sense of the place. The most intriguing notice had a large heading in red marker that said, "Stop the Rape of the Island!" It was an anti-logging poster announcing a community meeting, which had taken place a few days before. Someone had scrawled over the lower part of the poster, "Tree huggers kill jobs," along with a crude skull and crossbones. Looks like trouble, I thought, shaking my head.

Once the ferry pulled out, it started to rock more wildly in the open water, and I let out an involuntary "Whoa!" as I grabbed a rail. A fellow passenger, an old man who had also been looking over the ads, turned to me and smiled.

"This is nothin'. You ought to be here in the winter for the real gales. Why, last December, we had hurricane-force winds a few times. They even had to shut the ferry down for a run or two. This is just a little blow. Good weather coming, too, if you look down there." He gestured southwards.

He was right. Above the heaving horizon, pockets of blue sky and white cloud were replacing the grey mass above us.

"You wouldn't be from these parts, I guess," he said, taking in my nose rings, streaked blue and green hair (my variation on salt and pepper), and bright orange and red tight leggings. "I think you'll find Peregrine to be a right pretty island, for now, anyways. It might not stay that way if they log the whole darn thing at once, but for now it's real nice."

"We're booked at the Pinewood Lodge," I said conversationally as my heartbeat slowly returned to normal.

"Whoooee," he said, whistling. "Right nice place, but a little pricey. Hope you have a good time. Easy to f ind — just follow the signs when you get off this little boat."

"Um ... thanks," I said, holding out my hand. "My name's Abby. Is everyone so friendly on the island?"

He took my hand in a firm grasp. "Butler," he said. "Paul Butler. Well, you know, this ain't the city. We all pretty much know each other here. Can't afford to be too unfriendly. I guess you'll just have to find out for yourself, Ms. Abby. We're about to dock."

The ferry had rounded a point, and as it entered a protected bay, the waves subsided and the ship glided towards the dock.

"Thanks, again," I said before following Andy and Anita down to the car deck. He nodded, tipping an imaginary hat.

As I caught up with Andy, he said quietly, "Anita filled me in on what she saw the night of the murder. No wonder you're worried. I hope she'll be okay on Peregrine."

Nodding, I said, "Yeah. I'm so mad about this. If that guy makes one wrong move, I'm going after him."

Andy raised his eyebrows. "Let's talk about it later. The ferry's about to dock. At least Anita seems okay now," he said, nodding in her direction. She was leaning over the rail, looking excited again.

I smiled and went over to give her a big hug, and then we got back in the car and waited for our turn to disembark.

We found the lodge as easily as Paul Butler had said we would; the strategically placed small signs kept us to the correct turnoffs. The island already seemed big and wild by my citified standards. It was Emily Carr country, her early period, dark and green. Happily, the weather was changing quickly, and the sun began to flash through the trees. As we drove along, we saw the odd house here and there, amongst the never-ending rows of fir trees. The only other suggestions of habitation were little openings onto what I guessed were driveways. Not the clean, tarmacked kind, but long, muddy potholed ones.

"No wonder all those trucks with high suspension were on the ferry," I commented. "If I lived here, I'd need huge fenders and shocks for my bikes."

"I was thinking the same thing," grinned Andy.

"There's another sign!" Anita called from the back seat. This time the sign was larger and prettier, with the word "Pinewood" flanked by a pastoral image of trees and flowers burned into the huge wood plank. A more substantial rutted driveway led off to the left. We followed it until the trees suddenly gave way to a clearing, a gravel parking lot in front of a large, attractive wooden lodge with tennis courts to the side.

"Wow!" we said in unison.

The lodge stood at the edge a small cliff, beyond which lay the sparkling channel, then the mountains of Vancouver Island. Topped by blue sky, it was an incredible view. Just a few clouds lingered to remind us of the recent weather.

"Ahhh … This is more like it," Andy said as he parked. "Come on, you two, let's check in. I'm getting hungry, and it's almost dinnertime."

Anita hung back. "It's nicer out now. Maybe I should go to the campsite."

"Nah. Stay with us tonight, Anita," I said. "Our treat."

Andy nodded. "You can be alone soon enough. Tonight let's have a nice dinner enjoying this fabulous view."

Anita let herself be convinced. We started unloading the stuff while Andy checked us in, and then he came back to help us. We had rooms next to each other, facing the ocean. I surveyed ours with satisfaction. It was comfortable with nondescript furnishings; nature prints and pictures of fishing boats adorned the walls, but the lack of a TV kept the feel rustic.

The evening passed pleasantly, good food and good company alongside the murmur of the ocean below us. Andy played host with a light touch, jovial and liberal with the crisp, cool Chardonnay we had ordered. I allowed myself to relax, the anxieties of the day slipping away as I sat looking at the combined good view — the mountains against the twilight and my rather handsome boyfriend against the candlelight.

Even though the lodge catered to tourists, it became apparent there'd be no city-style carousing in this part of the world. Around 9:30, the staff began to hover, and we realized that we were the last ones in the dining room.

"I guess it's true. Country folk do go to bed with the sun," I said, smiling at the idea. We finished guiltily, but even an early ending was not enough to dispel the illusion that we were in paradise.

Before going to bed, I tapped on Anita's door to say good night. "Are you sure you're okay for now, my friend?"

"Absolutely, Abby," she said firmly. "I just have to get used to running into my past every now and then."

We hugged, and I closed her door, feeling a bit like a mother bear. Reassured by her confidence, I shook myself and walked thoughtfully to our room.

When we first started thinking about this trip, Andy had been hinting that I should commit further to our relationship, and possibly even consider settling down with him. I knew I liked him, but I have always been dubious about "settling down" with anyone. So I was a little conflicted, as it seemed he was looking at this holiday as a sort of trial at commitment. I wasn't sure I could rise to the occasion.

But Andy obviously had no such doubts. He treated me to a first-class massage, his fingers working out some of the kinks in my post-flight shoulder knots. Despite my languor, I found myself warming as he grew more exploratory, and as my mind released its tight hold on doubt, my body began to develop ideas of its own.

Bathed in the moonlight through the picture window, I gave myself up to his persuasions and then fell asleep thinking that the holiday with Andy might not be so bad after all. The following week might prove to be mutually stimulating.

I didn't realize then that I was going to get more stimulation than I had bargained for.

CHAPTER 2

SINCE I LIVE above a Kensington Market fish shop, I should be oblivious to strong odours. I certainly thought I was, but the first thing that hit me in the morning was *the reek*. I wrinkled my nose in disgust as it worked on every nerve in my body.

I nudged Andy, but he remained sound asleep beside me. He needs to catch whatever minutes of sleep he can, working in the hospital, and he seems programmed to stay snoozing unless there is a real emergency. It's tough to get him to wake up if he knows he's not on call. Now he just grunted and snuggled into his pillow. I gave up and walked over to the window where the sun grinned at me. The smell was definitely from outside, and I searched the view for evidence of some huge rotting carcass or vultures circling above a garbage dump.

Even this landlubber from the East was pretty sure that it wasn't an ocean smell. When my eyes started to water, I closed the window and resorted to one of the sacrifices to modern convenience: an air conditioner. While it worked on filtering the stench out of the air, I retreated to the shower, hoping that Pinewood had a very large hot water tank.

I relaxed until I felt my skin pruning up, enjoying some independence after the long period of enforced rest after my injuries. While recovering, I had often had to rely on the help of others, something that rubs me the wrong way. It was nice to feel like I had some time to myself.

As I emerged from the shower, Andy wandered into the bathroom sleepily. I urged him to close the door before all my hot air escaped.

"Abby," he asked plaintively, "why is it so cold in our room?"

"Sorry, hon," I said, much of my good humour slipping away as I remembered the reason. "It smelled so terrible outside I thought the filter would clean the stench."

"Hmm," he said, obviously not listening as his arms circled my warm and wet body. "Come back to bed and warm me up."

"Maybe later, pal." I tried to sound bright and cheery, not wanting to start the day on a sour note.

"Okay, no problem," he said, hanging his head in exaggerated disappointment, dog-like.

Laughing at his expression, I kissed his cheek and left him to his own devices in the bathroom. I guess I really was feeling the need to be my old independent self, because I dressed in the most unorthodox stuff I had brought with me.

Out came my bright pink "Call Girls Bike Couriers" T-shirt, my wildest courier bike-shorts combo — tight, black, knee-length pants over which I pulled my tie-dyed cut-offs — red socks, two-toed bike sandals, earrings, two nose rings, a studded collar and a matching belt. When Andy emerged from the bathroom, his eyebrows rose. But I think he figured out I wasn't in the mood for games and wisely said nothing as we went to breakfast. Unfortunately, the dining room doors were wide open.

"Ugh, I smell what you mean," said Andy. "What is it? It smells like a massive dose of chlorine gas."

"Yeah, that and a brewery and dead animals all rolled into one," I said.

It was quiet in the restaurant, probably because we were up later than most people. A waitress asked if we wanted to sit outside in the sun.

"No thanks," I said, my nose rebelling at the thought.

"What is that awful smell?" Andy ventured.

"What smell?" She looked at us blankly and then smiled in understanding. "Oh, you mean the mill. That's the pulp mill in Bellweather across the way." She pointed Vancouver Island way, towards a clump of trees — strategically left standing, I imagined, to hide the offending sight.

"Sometimes we get it over here, when the wind blows the right way," she said.

More like the wrong way, I thought.

"Most of us don't notice it anymore. Don't worry, you'll get used to it," she said brightly. "The wind will probably turn soon. It usually goes right down the channel or more in the direction of Bellweather."

"I hope she's right," I said grumpily as she went to get us coffee. The smell had put a damper on our appetites as well as my mood, so we'd just ordered coffee and toast.

"Do you think Anita is up?" mused Andy as we tried to distract ourselves with the marvellous view.

"Probably sleeping," I said. "She's a bit like you, sleeps whenever she gets a chance. Tell you what, Andy — let's get ready for a ride. Sunny said he would direct us to some good trails."

Sunny is an old courier friend who gave up on the city to move out to Peregrine, but has kept in touch. He had been encouraging me to come out and try the coastal trails for years, so when Andy and I decided to take a holiday together, I thought it might be fun to see Sunny's island hideaway.

I said to Andy, "Let's blow the lodge for the day, take Anita to the campsite, find Sunny and get outside. It's a big island. Maybe we can escape this foul odour."

"Sounds good. You go ahead and rouse that sleepyhead. I'll settle up here."

As I headed towards our rooms, I was surprised to see Anita coming into the lodge through the main doors. She looked fully awake, healthy and happy, and appeared not to be bothered by any smells.

"Oh, hi, Abby," she said. "I've just been for a walk by the ocean; a bit of a climb, but it's worth it. The tide is out. Did you know there are petroglyphs along the coast here? One of the waitresses told me there's a book about them. It's so cool."

Then almost as an afterthought, she added, "But Abby, did you notice that smell? When I was on the beach, I saw smoke pouring from huge smokestacks across the channel. Someone on the grounds told me that it's a pulp mill. Isn't it gross?"

"You said it, Anita. I'm glad to see you're already having a good time, though."

"I think I really need it. But what about you, Abby?" Her glance took in my outfit. "You're looking pretty Queen Street today. You're supposed to be on holiday, too."

"Maybe I *have* overdone it a little." I smiled. "Listen, we're thinking of getting going for the day. Will it take you long to get ready?"

"I'm already packed," Anita said eagerly. "I can't wait to get to the campground." She bit her lip. "I hope it doesn't smell there, too. This island is so beautiful. It's a drag they have to deal with that."

"We've been told it might veer offshore soon," I said mildly. "But it is disgusting *and* pretty serious if it can put me off my breakfast."

Anita nodded, and then she glanced behind me. "Hi, Andy," she said, smiling.

I looked up. Sure enough, there was Andy looking pleased with himself, carrying a large paper bag.

"Good morning, Anita. Abby thought you were sleeping, but you look like you're ready to go."

"Absolutely," she said.

"What's in the bag, Andy?" I asked, my usual curious self. As he grinned boyishly, I had to admit to myself that his smile always melted me a little. Maybe the studded collar could come off.

As if reading my thoughts, he grinned again. "It's a little surprise for later. Come on, Ab. Let's get ready, too. We'll meet you outside in ten minutes, Anita."

Once on the road, we decided to go to the campground first. All traces of the previous day's rain had vanished. In fact, it was starting to look pretty dry in the open areas. The gravel roadway at the lodge even kicked up some dust as we drove along. We motored through what was becoming familiar landscape — tall, majestic firs punctuated by little openings suggestive of dwellings. There was very little traffic, but most drivers who passed us waved. This is a friendly island, I thought again, waving back.

We were driving along a ridge or plateau, which was the high part of the south end of the island. The name Peregrine came from its distinctive outline on a map, reminiscent of the bird diving. From the little hotel map, it seemed that the bulk of the human habitation was in the southern end, the head of the bird. Except for little pockets along the coast, the northern half of the island was unpopulated.

The campground was located on one side of the bird's beak. As we approached, the road began to descend, and by the time we reached the campsite turnoff, we were almost at sea level. The trees had thinned, and we could see the shimmering emerald water sparkling in the sunshine. Anita checked in at the office, which also housed a snack bar, and then we drove to her campsite right on the beach.

"Pretty nice, Anita," I said admiringly as we stretched our car legs. "Just about paradise." The tide was still far out, so the beach stretched away into the bay. The bay was sheltered by a spit, which extended away from the campsite. The glistening jewel-like water was dotted here and there by yachts and dinghies. The smell of wet sand and drying seaweed filled the air, strong but welcome after the morning's cloying mill odour.

"Gee," I said. "They could make a scratch-and-sniff brochure to introduce you to this island. My olfactories are getting quite a workout."

"Missing your fish shop?" Andy asked, with his usual winning smile. He plumped down Anita's luggage: tent, sleeping bags, clothes, and a preponderance of paper and books.

"Did you bring any food, or are you planning to fast?" I asked.

"Well," said Anita, "I have some dried fruit and nuts, but I thought I would eat out or shop later. Lots of people seem to be hitchhiking around here, so I shouldn't have any trouble getting around."

I nodded. We had seen a few thumbs on the way.

"Be careful, Anita, now that we know there might be some unpleasant people around," I cautioned.

She smiled. "You know I won't do anything dumb, Abby."

I shrugged. "Okay, we'll check in later, to see how you're doing. If you need anything, leave a message at the lodge. Maybe we'll find some extra bikes at Sunny's and go for a ride together sometime."

"Maybe. I want to get started on the reading list for my course this fall. But don't worry, I'll relax lots, too." She breathed deeply and flung out her arms to the view. "Who couldn't relax amidst all this?"

"Come on, mother hen," called Andy from the car. "She can take care of herself."

"Of course, she can," I said, slightly irritated. "I know that. I'm just trying to help."

Andy was hitting my nerves today, it seemed.

"Sorry, Anita. Have fun!" I glowered at the back of Andy's head when he turned the other way to talk to Anita as she leaned in at the driver's side.

She saw the glower and raised her eyebrows, but said simply, "Abby, you know I love you. I couldn't ask for a better friend." She pecked Andy on the cheek. "I am really spoiled. Thanks for the luxury evening, you two. I'm glad I didn't get my first taste of this paradise in the rain." She waved as we took off.

Andy drove along, oblivious to my sour mood as he chattered on. "Good thing the road network on this island is so straightforward with the roads radiating off east and west from the main one. It sure makes finding things easy," he said. "It's pleasant driving with no traffic, too." He waved at an oncoming car, already in the habit of the locals. "And people are friendly. I could get used to this!"

"Dammit, Andy," I said. "Do you always have to be so cheerful?"

"Why not, Abby?" he said, still clueless. "Beautiful day, good company, bike trails waiting … what could be wrong?" He briefly turned to me and grinned. "Relax," he said, leaning over to rub my shoulders with one hand. I thawed a bit more. "Let's have fun, huh, Ab?"

Perhaps, with the tension I always seem to carry around, the way to my heart *is* through my shoulders. I began purring as he drove, while he one-handedly worked my tension away.

By the time we reached Sunny's place, I had almost decided to have a good time. We spotted a little sandwich board at his driveway. The stylized sun, which transformed into a spoked wheel halfway around, announced "Sunny's Bicycles: Sales, Rentals and Repairs" on the outside in bold, black letters. Tacked to the main sign was an additional small rectangular board, which made the claim "Recumbents a Specialty."

I've never really been a mountain bike rider, but Andy often waxed rapturous about wilderness trails. I was skeptical, but we had struck a deal that we would do a bit of both road riding and trail riding. We had packed our two second-best roadies, a Trek 2300 and a Trek 2100. Sunny had said he would lend us mountain bikes for the trails. My anxiety about the idea of riding on a bumpy trail after my injuries was making me touchier than usual.

We turned in and immediately slowed to negotiate a massive pothole, a kind of reverse speed bump. Our progress was further hampered by a gaggle of peafowl wandering aimlessly around. The rutted drive gave way to a clearing with a small house and a large garage-cum-bike shop — and Sunny.

There he was, overall-clad, more than six feet tall and heavily bearded. As we emerged from the car, he looked up from his work at a bike stand and hastily wiped his hands on a rag that hung from his pocket. Judging from the colour of the rag, this was an oft-repeated activity.

"Well, look who's here," he said with the slight country drawl I remembered so well. "Welcome to my humble abode. Watch the puddles now. That was a right pretty storm we had yesterday, but it should dry up fast this time of year. It's been dry as the desert most of the summer." We shook hands as he clapped me heartily on my bad shoulder and then enfolded me in a great big bear hug. I guess I was truly on the road to recovery, because I hardly winced.

"Hey, Sunny," I said. "It's so good to see you." I turned to Andy, who hovered nearby. "This is the friend I told you about, Andy Jaegar, a fellow bike junkie."

"Pleased to meet you," Sunny said, smiling as he pumped Andy's arm. "Come see this baby I'm workin' on right now. It's a classy little number, for a mountain bike. Most of the guys around here go for some crazy trails. They like steep stuff covered in rocks and roots. But as they get older, those who can afford it want a cushier ride, so they get this kinda bike. Front and rear shocks, lightweight frame, the best components. This belongs to a local teacher — they seem to have the dough. The rest of us just try to ride easier."

"You're sounding more like a country boy than ever," I teased as he led us into the shop.

"Island life has a way of doing that to folks," he grinned, exaggerating his drawl. "Hey, Abby, have you tried one of these yet?" He pointed at a recumbent, an eccentric-looking bike with the seat down at around knee height. "I seem to recall that speed is your thing — Abby, the demon of downtown. These go real fast."

"I've seen a few around, Sunny, but I've never tried one. They look kind of silly, like Harley-Davidson road hog bicycles."

"Yeah, I know what you mean, but if you just give it a chance, you'll be amazed. I'll loan you one sometime this week."

As we emerged back into the sun, Sunny said, "Y'know, guys, I've got a lot of work to do. Everyone wants his bike fixed yesterday for no money. I'd really like to visit, but it will have to wait till later today. But I reckon you'd like to get out riding. Here, take this trail map."

He reached for a map from a holder on the wall. "You could try the Deer Lake trail first. It's real pretty and not too tough, a good starter for you soft city folk." He poked a finger into my stomach. "And there's a few nice spots to take a break along the lake." He chuckled. "Besides, it's one of the few you can find easily by yourself, being that it's actually well marked. Just drive on up the main road north. First you'll hit gravel — watch out for the logging trucks. Get stuck behind one of those, you could be eating dust for miles. Keep on going until you see the sign on the left that says 'Deer Lake Trail.' There's usually a car or two parked along the side of the road."

"Sounds good," I said, looking at Andy for agreement.

He nodded, glancing at the map. "I think we can handle that."

"Okay," Sunny continued as he pointed to our road bikes on the car rack. "Leave those here for me to tune up, and you can borrow a couple of my rental bikes for the trail." He ran his hands over our nice little Trek roadies. "I'll fix you up with something more service-able. You can take a spin on the main road with yours sometime soon," he said.

Sunny busied himself preparing two sturdy mountain bikes for us.

"You'll find the hills fun, Abby. These bikes have got lots of gears for the uphill. Hey, by the way, have you got bathing suits with you?"

We nodded. We had thrown our suits and a couple of hotel towels in the back in case we wanted to swim at Anita's beach.

"Deer Lake water is silky and real warm this time of year. As I said, you'll find a coupla nice spots along the trails. Just be sure and rub yourself down well when you get out. There's a kind of bug in that water that causes what we call 'swimmer's itch.'"

"Bugs in the water, even," I said. "Might be too much wildlife all around for me.

"You'll get used to it, Ab." Sunny laughed.

I grimaced as we helped Sunny exchange the roadies for the other bikes. "I can't wait to shake myself silly on the woodland trails."

"No worries," said Sunny. "This trail is tame, and there are good shocks on these bikes. You'll like it — Sunny's guarantee."

We walked to the car, and the guys shook hands. "Thanks Sunny," said Andy. "We'll drop in on our way back."

Chapter 3

MOUNTAIN BIKES LOADED, we drove off in companionable silence. After the first turnoff for the north end of the island, the main road hugged the coast for a while. Small bays flashed by, barely visible through breaks in the trees, except where landowners preferred the tree-free manicured-lawn look. There was no doubt that this country was beautiful *and* rugged. Further out, we could see the Strait of Georgia, which stretched out a Caribbean blue-green, giving a tropical feel to the scenery. Layers of sharply serrated mountains on the horizon separated ocean from clear blue sky.

Soon the going became more circuitous, until the road gave way abruptly to gravel and the car started climbing a steep hill. Andy slowed, intent on the job of driving. The coastline disappeared as more tall dark trees loomed on either side of the road. As we drove slowly down another particularly steep hill, we met a large logging truck labouring up the opposite side of the road. It kicked up copious dust, so we hastily rolled up our windows. The logs weighing down the rear of the truck were a phenomenal four to five feet in diameter at their base.

I felt sad to see such magnificent trees cut but struggled to remain objective, figuring it was my East Coast liberal guilt combined with my characteristic righteous attitude that fuelled my feelings. Who was I to criticize the Westerners' need to make a living?

The sight of the actual clear-cut that the trees had come from blew all my careful, silent thinking away. It hit us in the face as we crested the next hill — a desecrated valley, barren save for stumps and debris and scarred by switchback logging roads. The area was flanked by the remaining forest, which even then was being cut back by busy machines, their diesel smoke lending the scene the image of a battlefield.

"Holy shit!" I swore.

"Wow," said Andy, aghast.

We fell into a shocked silence at the sight of all that devastation for the sake of paper and furniture. It didn't take long, however, to be surrounded by trees again and to have the illusion that clear-cuts did not dominate.

A few minutes later, we spotted two cars at the side of the road. As we drew closer, there was the little marker announcing the Deer Lake trail. We could have easily missed it, if it hadn't been for Sunny mentioning there'd be cars at the side of the road. We pulled in behind the second one and stepped out.

The silence reverberated loudly in my ears. I am so citified that I find country silence a little unnerving; it seems to echo. I always think there should at least be bird sound, but though my ears were wide open, quiet prevailed. Back in the trees, even the machinery a quarter mile back was beyond my hearing. Maybe I've just blown my eardrums at too many punk clubs, or maybe I would hear more acutely if I stayed still longer.

We made up for the silence by creating plenty of noise unloading the bikes and packing for the ride. A little rumble in my stomach triggered its usual imperative, and with a sinking sensation, I realized that food was far away. Andy laughed at the audible growl in my stomach.

"I can't believe I didn't think about food for this trip," I moaned.

Shrugging boyishly with a little grin, he leaned far into the back of the car. This view triggered my second-most automatic response. Something about his cute butt in close fitting pants always turned me on. It made me want to slip my arms around his waist and murmur suggestive endearments in his ear, but before I could act on my impulse, he emerged triumphantly, holding up the same brown paper bag I had seen in his hands not long ago, at the lodge.

"Voila!" he said, and with a flourish, he handed it to me.

I looked inside while he proudly recited the contents from memory: "smoked salmon and goat cheese on rye, one mango, two oranges, carrots and celery sticks, two bottles of apple cherry juice and two almond croissants for a little snack." He reached back and produced a small thermos. "I don't know how good it is, but here's a little coffee, too — beans fresh from the island's own roasteria." Andy proved that he knew my appetites.

"Wow! You're a genius, Doctor!"

"True, true," he said, bowing with a flourish. "We can have these now," he said, handing me the croissants and coffee, "and save the rest for later." We sat on the back of the car, drinking and munching companionably, and once my primary appetite was sated, the secondary one returned rather persistently.

"Thanks bud, I am disarmed," I said, giving him a suggestive kiss. "Now that my little stomach rumble is gone, I have to say that you look very dashing in your bike gear." He had on his new bike shirt and those tight black Louis Garneau bike shorts.

"Why, thank you, ma'am," he said with a smile, a little swelling adding to the style of the shorts. "You're looking pretty, uh, bikerly yourself in a punk kind of way ... but lovely, of course. The studded wristband is a particularly appropriate addition for the woods. Never know if you'll have to fight off an errant cougar."

"It's not cougars I'm worried about," I said ruefully. "But I guess you're right. The armour might be a bit much. I *am* feeling a little warm." I removed the studded bracelet and tossed it in the back.

Since I was clearly letting down my guard, Andy began to practise a little of his privately honed bedside manner. He leaned over unabashedly, and we kissed, making up for earlier tensions. Despite the sense that we were all alone in the silent forest, we decided to move into the hatchback. This cramped version of adolescent exploration was fun as long as we were actively engaged.

The tight fit and the smell of clean sweat intermingling with the odour of new car interior were only pleasant until our pheromones subsided. I was happily oblivious for a few minutes; then I became conscious of bumps, debris and cramped knees. A loud mosquito spurred me to reassemble my clothing.

"Andy," I said, feeling a little foolish as the flush subsided, "I'm getting too old for this."

"Nah," he said, with a winning grin. "You mess around like a spring chicken. Come on; give me another little peck or two." He tried to sit up for another kiss but hit his head on the car ceiling in his haste.

"Ow!" he said, shaking his head. "Okay, maybe you're right. We do need a little more space. Next time, I'll rent a van with a bed."

"Agreed," I laughed. "Now let's not waste any more time. It's a beautiful day, and I have to face this trail riding business sometime."

"Sure thing," said Andy, rubbing his head.

We quickly donned our clothes and our hydration packs and helmets, locked the car and crossed the road to the trail. It looked well used and only a little damp from the rain. A few bike tracks showed in the mud, which was drying up so fast that it was hard to tell if they were recent.

Andy took the lead, and with a whoop, he was off. We'd agreed that he would ride ahead. I didn't want to feel like I was holding him up, and I was sure it would take me a few minutes to get used to the strange bike. Sunny had been right; the trail would have been hard on my nice roadie. I wondered now why we'd bothered to bring them if trail riding was the goal. As I cautiously bumped along, I resolved to take Sunny's suggestion and do a road ride later.

Miraculously, despite the rutted trail, I began to enjoy myself. The forest was undeniably beautiful, a jungle of trees, fallen logs and giant ferns, the winding trail bulging with roots. I was as far away from downtown Toronto as I could get, mentally and physically. My arm wasn't hurting, so I began to relax, and pedalling a little harder, I soon came upon Andy. He had stopped at a fork in the trail and was sipping from his hydration pack while he waited for me.

"Isn't this great?" he enthused as I stopped. "Incredibly lush. You can practically feel the humus decomposing in the ground."

Nodding my agreement, I took a more careful look around. There were a variety of trees, even the odd large maple was starting to show colour already. The dead trees lying haphazardly on the ground were rotting, acting as nurse logs for new growth. The cycle of death and regrowth was being played out everywhere I looked. Uncharacteristically hushed into reverential silence by the immense beauty of it all, I felt as if I was in a huge natural cathedral.

Andy looked up from his map. "According to this, we should go to the left. The other trail leads up a mountain. It might be a bit much for our first ride, but there's supposed to be a great view up there. We'll have to try it if we get time later. Ready?"

I nodded again, and we continued our ride. Now at home on the trail, which was admittedly pretty easy as long as I watched out for stray tree roots, I kept up most of the time. About an hour later, we reached the lake. It stretched out before us, silently reflecting the treed slopes surrounding it on all sides. The trail continued above the trees that crowded to the edge of the water.

We rode until we found a rocky outcrop that opened access down to the lake. Our perch had clearly been used as a rest spot before. There were traces of campfires, and unfortunately a couple of crumpled beer cans and empty candy wrappers had been left behind.

Once we gathered up the garbage and temporarily stashed it behind a rock, we enjoyed the illusion that we were alone in the vast wilderness, even though we knew that the occupants of the cars must be around somewhere. There wasn't a sound other than the splash of a fish or the occasional call of an eagle or raven. We leaned the bikes against a tree, and Andy pulled a blanket out of his pack for us to sit on. He was like a Mary Poppins of the forest as he continued, with flourishes, removing towels, cups, juice and chips from his pack.

As we ate, we talked about Anita. "She dealt pretty well with the scene at the airport yesterday," Andy remarked.

"Yeah," I replied, mouth half full. I swallowed and continued. "I can't believe how resilient she's become despite all that she's gone through. I'm so impressed. But I'm worried, too."

He nodded. "I know. It's pretty freaky, that guy showing up. And I'm worried about you, as well. You really stuck your neck out for her with those people."

"But that's how I met you, Doctor. We've had some fun, haven't we?"

He gave me his boyish grin. "Yeah, Ab, but will you be able to stick with me? I know your track record." He looked at me sideways.

"I feel bad, Andy, but I'm not a guarantee girl. I have to be honest and say that I might not be able to stick this out."

"Ouch," he said. Then he seemed to decide to enjoy the moment. "Well, it's not like you haven't told me this before, and you're still here. So let's just concentrate on having some fun and see how it goes. That's enough of the serious stuff for me now."

"Suits me," I replied, leaning over to give him a light kiss.

As Andy finished the last chip, he winked and said, "Why don't we cool down with a swim? Sunny said the water was silky. Let's try it."

"Soon," I said, doubting I would get up the courage to dip into unknown water. "Go ahead. Don't wait for me."

"Okay," he said, stripping down. "I'm going to dispense with the suit ... no one here anyhow." He walked to the edge of the rock and looked down into the clear water. Encouraged by his eagerness, I decided to be more courageous and go in after all, so I stripped down, too, and gingerly sat to slide my feet into the water.

It was warm, not quite my preferred hot shower temperature, but warm enough, and inviting after the hard ride. As I was slowly working my way in, Andy took a running leap and jumped in, splashy cannonball style, so for all intents and purposes, I was in, too. So I just submerged, and enjoyed the amazingly soft water.

We swam a bit and then climbed out, quickly towelling off as instructed against swimmer's itch, and then let the sun-drenched rock warm us. We passed a couple of lazy hours eating, sunning, and swimming until around 2:30, then we decided to pack up, wanting to see about evening plans. With care, we cleaned up our site before we left, remembering to collect the extra garbage and put it in our packs.

CHAPTER 4

THOROUGHLY MELLOWED OUT, we rode at a relaxed pace, meandering quietly along the return trail. I was so relaxed that it came as an extra shock when our peace was shattered by a horde of upwards of ten thundering bicycle hyenas. The leader of the group rode a very obviously high-tech blue mountain bike. It looked similar to the one Sunny had been working on.

He was yelping some kind of parody of a Tarzan yodel as he thundered down on us. They all obviously had too much testosterone, leaping their bikes in the air and yowling. We pulled off the trail, but not quickly enough to suit them. The loudmouthed leader yelled, "Coming through! Out of the way before I run you over!"

I have a rather instinctive switch that is triggered by the sound of threats, real or imagined. It erupted full force this time with a string of invectives that got Andy raising his eyebrows in admiration. My courier's protective urge, I guess. Of course, most of the horde was past us by then, but loudmouth must have heard me because he actually turned in mid-air a little further along the trail.

In my fervour, I must have made a reference to the desecration of the beautiful forest or something because he yelled angrily, "You talking to me, lady?" He made a move as if he was going to ride back. "You're not another one of those city tree huggers, are you? Because we have ways to deal with you!"

In reaction to the threat, I yelled back, "Is that right, loudmouth? Where do you get off acting like you own this trail?" I was about to yell some more when I stopped and peered more closely at the helmeted man, a few wisps of his curly red hair showing.

Oh my God! It was Brendon.

His buddies must have had cooler heads because they started to cajole him, telling him not to bother with us. He and I just continued to stare at each other in hostility.

Andy played the jovial peacemaker. "Forget it — we were just a little surprised by the noise, that's all."

I guess Brendon's friends finally got through, or maybe it dawned on him that we had met before, because he became more conciliatory.

"Okay," he said, relenting. "No problem, folks!" With a couple more war whoops, he and his buds were off down the trail.

I must have had too much testosterone, too, because I was still steaming while Andy tried to rub my raised shoulders. I shook him off as he said, "Well, that was a different side of that Brendon."

I nodded, my anger slowly settling down.

"Let's just move on. We still have a bit of a ways to go."

"I guess you're right, Andy, but I'm so mad, I'd like to give that guy a lesson or two." Then I realized the implications of his being on the island. "And what do we do now about Anita?"

A look of consternation crossed Andy's face. Now we had something to think about.

I remounted my bike. "I'm going to ride off my steam for a bit. See you at the car," I yelled.

I released my anger and adrenaline in a fast ride down the rest of the trail. I even jumped once or twice over a root, which was trail riding progress, I guess. Arriving at the car flushed, with most of the energy worked out, I felt tired the moment that I stopped. Oh, my poor, overworked adrenals.

The car in front was gone, replaced by two large 4x4s with huge tires. Must belong to them, I thought, mentally spitting at the tires. On the side of one truck was a business name, "Armstrong Lumber," with a logo of a log and a chainsaw in a cross over a bent arm, all encompassed in a big circle.

I filed a mental memory of that bit of info as Andy came walking his bike out of the forest. I looked up questioningly. "What's up?"

He shrugged. "I must have something in the chain. It started running ragged a few minutes ago. It's a good thing it happened at the

end of the ride," he said as he lifted it onto the bike rack. "I thought
we could take a quick look at it out here in the light. It was too dark
in the woods."

"Good idea," I said, opening my tool kit. I got out an Allen key
and watched the chain as Andy turned the crank. He came to a spot
where the chain was all kinked up. "Look Andy, here's the problem."
I carefully poked at some debris that had worked its way into the
chain.

Andy helped work out some damp bark and a few leaves and tried
to turn the crank again. "That's better. It's running more freely now.
At least we won't have to take a gummed up chain back to Sunny."

"We'd better suggest he look it over before the bike goes out
again."

Andy nodded as we secured the bikes and our packs. Working on
the bike had temporarily taken my mind off Brendon's obnoxious-
ness. Now memory flooded back in, and I fretted about Anita while
I mulled over his behaviour.

CHAPTER 5

I WAS STILL thinking when Sunny ambled out of the darkness of his shop.

"Hey, you two. Did y'all have a good time at the lake?"

Andy was full of good cheer. "Very nice, Sunny. Thanks for the loan of the bikes," he said, smiling as he took his off the rack. "By the way, the chain on this one was running a bit ragged near the end. Ab and I cleaned it out, but you might want to check it more carefully." Sunny nodded.

"I'll do that, thanks. I'm glad you had a good time."

"Yeah, it was fabulous until these souped-up maniacs practically ran us over on the trail on the way back," I grumbled as I wheeled one bike back into the shop. Andy and I had agreed that we wouldn't share my worries about Anita's safety yet, so we didn't let on we knew who the leader of the pack of yahoos was.

"Maniacs, huh?" Sunny commented. "Some of the local guys like to ride hard, but they all know to take it easy on that trail, on account of the tourist traffic there."

"Maybe we should tell somebody about it. There were a couple of high riding 4x4s parked by the road when we got out. One had an 'Armstrong Lumber' logo."

Sunny knit his eyebrows together, and his eyes became hooded. "Hard riders, you say?" He shook his head. "Sounds like that SOB Brendon Armstrong. His daddy runs a private lumber company and owns huge swatches of the island. Young Brendon tries to lord it over the islanders, how we should be grateful for his father's largesse."

He shook his head. "Most of us hate the old man's guts because he logs with total disregard for the community, and it galls us that there's little we can do about it. Brendon's a spoiled pain in the butt and a troublemaker, too. Drugs, brawls at the pub, and there's word he's always fighting with his father."

Sunny's usually calm exterior had given way to an angry flush and more words in a row than I usually heard from him. But just as he was getting on a roll, he seemed to remember his relaxed island persona and stopped himself.

"Sorry about that. The whole logging thing always gets me heated up. There's nothing uglier than a clear-cut."

"I know exactly what you mean, Sunny," I said comfortingly. "We saw one off the road not too far from the trail. Is that one of Armstrong's sites?"

"Nah. There's another big company, High Timber, also has licences here. There are supposed to be some controls in the amount they cut, but it seems the forester in town just okays any application for cutting that crosses his desk. The new laws around forest practices have fewer teeth than a worn out saw. Of course, they need logs over there at the mill to keep making their darn paper. Crazy, eh? Big old logs to make paper when you could use hemp or recycling."

He shook his head. "It's a total drag that this is happening here. But," he said sarcastically, "everyone says you gotta keep the economy going."

"How do people around here feel about it, Sunny?"

"Well, folks are split. It has provided a livelihood for some, especially in the town across the way. But I have a few friends who are real fed up with the archaic logging practices. Hey, that reminds me. We're having a potluck tonight to try to help take my friend Jan's mind off the upcoming anniversary of her son's death. Maybe you'd like to meet her. Armstrong just logged most of the land near her place at the north end. She is so mad, she could spit. You guys can come along, if you like. You'll get to meet some real island folks."

"That sounds like good fun," said Andy before I could say anything.

"I don't know," I said hastily. "What would we bring?"

Sunny grinned as he said, "Just hop down to the store near the ferry. You can get all sorts of dips and such at the deli in the grocery store. You'll be surprised. The plan is to meet at the park just past the campsite around 6:00. Gives you one and a half hours. What do you say, Abby? I already was thinking that we should give the road ride a rest till tomorrow. After your first real mountain bike ride, you've probably had enough for the one day. We could go early tomorrow, instead, before I open the shop — say, 8:00?"

"How could I say no?" I asked, giving in to the two eager faces. "Should we just leave our own bikes here, then?"

"Sure thing. I'd be happy to babysit those beauts. They can commune with mine while we're out. A little party for all."

I turned to Andy. "Let's check on Anita before we go to the store. Maybe she'd like to join us. It's okay, isn't it Sunny, if we bring along our friend?" Privately, I thought it would be a way to keep her near me, to know she was safe.

"Sure! The more the merrier," he said, smiling. "It's going to be a beautiful evening."

Another car wobbled along his rutted drive, and Sunny's attention was diverted.

"Well, duty calls. Looks like tourists. I'll see you guys at the beach, six-ish. You'll see my recumbent and a bunch of folks at the picnic tables by the last parking lot. Do me a favour, guys?" he said as we turned to go. "Flip the Open sign over to Closed at the top of my signboard. I need time to make something for tonight."

"My mouth is watering," I said. "I just remembered what a great cook you are, Sun."

"We'll be there with bells on," Andy chimed in. Sunny shook Andy's hand quickly and then turned his ample charm on to the newcomers.

"Howdy, folks. What can I do for you today?" he said as we got into our car.

We bumped our way to the road, flipped the sign over as requested and coasted downhill to the campground. No one was there. Anita had set up her little tent, and her books and papers were stacked on the picnic table. A solitary crow poked around, looking in vain for food. It must have figured out that Anita eats like a sparrow as it hopped off in disgust.

"She must be out exploring," I said hopefully as I hastily scrawled a note.

> Hi Anita —
> Hope you're having fun. We survived our first trail ride and are planning to meet some people at a potluck down at the beach tonight. We'll pick up enough food for you, too. Come and join us after 6:00, at the picnic tables, last parking lot in the park. See you.
> Love, Abby.

I found a rock to hold down the note on the picnic table. As I climbed in the car, Andy said, "Let's go see what we can find at the store. Do you need to go back to the hotel to change or anything?"

"Nah," I said. "I have a sweatshirt in the car, and we have our suits if we want to swim again, so I'm ready." I stopped, still feeling a little anxious for Anita.

"Andy, do you think we should wait and warn Anita?"

He thought for a few seconds and then said, "She's probably safe here at the beach, Abby. Brendon won't be looking for her. He doesn't even know she's here."

"You're right," I relented.

We drove back to the village where the ferry had come in the night before. There we found an amazingly well-stocked grocery store with fresh foods. They had a whole range of ethnic goodies — Indian pappadums, Thai rice rolls, Mexican *refritos* and Japanese sushi. There was also a liquor section and, as Sunny had promised, a deli full of colourful salads and cheeses and sandwich fillings. We had fun deciding what to buy and settled on an eclectic mix of organic peaches, sushi, corn chips with a sun-dried tomato dip and a nice organic Chardonnay. On our way to the cash, we couldn't resist adding smoked salmon, and Andy grabbed a couple of bottles of mango juice and mineral water.

"I think we have more than enough, don't you?" Andy said, gesturing at the mounting pile.

"Yeah," I said, feeling the glow on my face that comes from the thought of good food.

Finally, we treated ourselves to two bike magazines from the impressively laden shelves of the magazine rack.

"From the look of this place," said Andy, "these islanders are literate gourmands."

"Sounds like my kind of place," I replied, laughing, as we walked out of the store, laden with packages.

Just then another 4x4 pulled up beside our little rental car. It also bore the Armstrong logo, and its jacked-up body towered over our vehicle. I readied myself to respond to any taunt, but the driver turned out to be a young woman with a troubled frown etched on her forehead. She opened the door, almost knocking me off my feet. My yelp brought her out of her preoccupied state.

"Oh, I'm sorry," she breathed shyly, eyes averted, straight blonde hair hanging over her face. "I didn't see you."

"No harm done," I said, peering at her curiously. The girl scooted away to the store like a scared animal.

Is that little mouse related to Brendon? I mused. I'd have to remember to ask someone later.

"Hey, Andy," I said after we put our stuff in the car, "there's a café next to the store. Do you want to have a coffee before we go to the beach?"

"Sure, I'm up for it," he said, "but I spotted the local roasteria up the road. Let's go there. I'd like to find a decent cappuccino, if possible."

It felt strange to be driving everywhere. We could have easily walked the distance but had quickly fallen into the predominant mode of travel on the island — automobile. In the city, I walk or ride almost everywhere.

CHAPTER 6

"HERE WE ARE," Andy said airily as we pulled into a little plaza with a gift shop and a cute café proudly proclaiming itself the home of Peregrine's roasted coffee. The "Peregrine Coffee Co." sign was adorned with a stylized, crow-like bird, wings circling a cup of steaming coffee.

The day was still glorious, and folks were chatting and drinking coffee, seated outside at small round tables. One table was crowded with somewhat unkempt teenagers. They'd be right at home in Kensington Market, I thought as I observed three or four dogs at their feet and barefoot toddlers playing nearby. The local hippies, I guessed. They were not too concerned about the activities of their children, who clearly felt right at home on the concrete patio.

I studied the notices posted on the walls and windows, while Andy ordered us each a cappuccino. One poster announced a country dance at the community centre; another, a vegan potluck dinner on Vancouver Island. I thought Anita might be interested in the evening of poetry readings coming up at Peregrine Café, so I took down the phone number. I sat down at an inside table just as Andy arrived with our coffees and a scrumptious-looking piece of peach pie.

"I hope we still have room for dinner," I said, taking a sip of the delicious cappuccino.

"No problem, Abby. I've yet to see your appetite falter when good food is available."

"True," I said, not even bothering to be offended as I tucked into the pie. "Mmm ... delicious. It must be the fresh air. Everything tastes so good." I sniffed. "Hey, I just noticed. The mill smell is gone."

"You're right," he said. "What a relief!"

"Oh, look." I pointed to a low table nearby on which a pile of magazines and newspapers were scattered. The top paper was called the *Bellweather Bulletin.* "Can you pass me that paper? I'd like to get a taste of the local news."

Andy handed me the paper and grabbed a tattered mountain bike magazine for himself, courtesy of Sunny's shop, I noticed.

The paper was folded to the sports section, showing a long piece about a local youth group sports tournament, accompanied by pictures of wholesome kids holding their medals proudly. There was also a detailed article about the sport fishery that supports the lodges along the coast, and a list of fish in season along with where and when the big ones were caught. A huge ad for a lodge called The Discovery announced the standard sport fishing and luxurious accommodation, and also offered ecotourism, including kayaking, whale watching and wilderness hiking. Accompanying the descriptions were colour pictures of fish jumping in a golden sunset, kayaks set against mountains under a full moon and a pod of whales dotting a pancake-flat ocean. No clear-cuts, mills or motorboats in sight.

I turned the last page of the sports section to reveal the front page of the paper, where a headline blared "Armstrong Catches Peregrine Off Guard." This was the third time in as many hours that name had leapt at me. I read with interest how the head of Armstrong Lumber, a man named Jack Armstrong, had begun marking off lots to be logged at the south end of the island, right next to the village, in the heart of Peregrine Island's residential area. The company had owned the forested land for such a long time that most of the locals had simply forgotten the potential threat. Only now that the felling was about to start were people up in arms.

In the article, an islander named Janice Field was quoted as saying that Armstrong had gotten away with too much for too long. "Now he is going to rip the heart right out of the community. It's time," she said, "for people on Peregrine to take a stand — to stop the man once and for all."

The article went on to report that a spokesperson for Armstrong Lumber said the company had the right to do what it wanted with its property. Good old Mr. Armstrong himself was willing, as always, to meet with stakeholders to discuss options. Some islanders interviewed focused on the fact that logging provided employment, while others talked of holding prayers in the woods, a sort of spiritual resistance to the coming carnage. One or two others echoed Field's comments that they should do whatever it took to stop the logging.

"Andy, look at this," I said. "This map shows that Armstrong has just started to log a large area right up the hill from here. How gross." I noticed as I spoke that someone had scrawled along the margin of the paper, "Death to Armstrong" along with a caricature of a man's head in a noose, his tongue lolling out. I raised my eyebrows.

"I'm going to ask if I can take this. The place is about to close, and the paper is two days old, anyway," I said.

"Go ahead, Abby. That way, I can look at it later." He looked at his watch. "It's past six. We'd better get going."

As we exited the café, paper snugly under my arm, I noticed another large, handmade anti-logging poster on the inside of the door. This one was not marked up. The words "Save Peregrine Island" with three exclamation marks circled a photo of a clear-cut pasted in the centre. "Community meeting to discuss strategies, Wed. Aug. 29th, 7:00 p.m. sharp, Community Hall. Come with your ideas. Child care provided at the daycare centre 6:30 to 8:30."

"Look, Andy," I said. "There was a poster like this on the ferry, too. I wonder if Sunny went to that meeting. It doesn't sound like it went well for the anti-logging activists."

"Maybe they'll talk about it tonight, Ab. But we'd better not bring it up if this party is supposed to support Sunny's friend. Let's just see how it goes."

I nodded as I thought about what I had read. Today was August 31st. The meeting had been held two nights ago. I wondered what solutions, if any, had been found. Sunny certainly hadn't seemed happy. I hoped I would have an opportunity to talk with him that evening.

"That coffee was a boost," I said, feeling pleasantly buzzed as we cruised back to the beach. "I think we've already done a lot for our first day out."

Andy nodded as he bobbed his head along to the music on the radio. "But that's good, don't you think — as far removed as possible from the hospital."

"Andy, you always seem so happy."

"Possibly, Abby," he mused. "But maybe you just don't know me well enough yet. I'm still working on charming your pants off whenever I can."

"You had an unfair advantage, Andy. I wasn't wearing pants when you first met me."

"I'm just a fool for biker girls," he quipped.

I saved any retort for the time being. We were entering the provincial park, which lay on the spit that created a natural harbour. We were momentarily silenced by the spectacular view. On one side, the serene little bay was dotted with yachts, knots of people lolling on the beach and swimmers, mostly kids, in the water. On the other side was the open ocean, again flanked to the east by the razor-edged mountains of the mainland. A few islands lay closer in front of the mountains.

As we continued to motor along the spit, our view was obscured by a patch of forest. The end of the road opened into a parking lot, beyond which lay a clearing with picnic tables on the harbour side and the odd tree to the east. Further on were more trees. Presumably, one could walk the rest of the distance to the end of the spit. Many of the picnic tables were in use by people having or preparing for dinner. Although we were late, we caught Sunny just dismounting his recumbent. As he unstrapped a pannier from the rear, we found a spot to park and walked over to him.

Chapter 7

"HI, Y'ALL," he said. "Glad to see you're already slippin' into island time. I was a little worried you'd be here wondering where I was."

"We're not late, then?" Andy asked.

"Nah. Now let's see if the others are here. They're usually at the far end, where there's a good grouping of tables." We left the stuff in the car and followed Sunny.

Sure enough, as we neared the end of the clearing, someone waved and called out, "Hey, Sunny, we're over here."

We walked over to a group of six people, some of whom were drinking beer at a table while three women prepared a nearby table. A floral tablecloth was spread with drinks, chips, various covered dishes and even a small vase of flowers — little sweet peas that smelled beautiful, even out in the open.

"Hey, all," said Sunny. "This is my friend Abby from Toronto and her pal, Andy. I hope you don't mind that I invited them along for a taste of Peregrine hospitality."

"Welcome, Abby," said a composed woman with a strong British accent. "I'm Janice. You're more than welcome. I must say that you don't look like most of the people we meet from Toronto," she said, taking in my hair, nose rings and leggings.

"No, probably not," I said. "Andy fits the bill, though, don't you think?"

"I suppose," she said pleasantly. "Make yourself at home on our beautiful spit. This is our living room in the summer, especially for those of us without beachfront."

"Thanks," I said. "I'm blown away by how nice almost everyone has been to us since we arrived." I turned to Andy. "Maybe we'd better get our stuff from the car."

But Andy interjected, "Sit down and chat, Abby. I'll get it."

"I'll help," said Sunny, and the two ambled off while I sat down to talk with Janice.

"Now, dear," said the amiable, motherly woman. "Sunny mentioned that you used to work with him as a courier. That must be demanding work."

"Well, it suits me," I said. "It provides autonomy and speed, both necessities in my life. I'm starting to mix it up, though, doing some investigative work on the side." That sparked some interest around the table, and we chatted along until our conversation was interrupted by Andy and Sunny's return.

"Here you go, Jan, some more goodies for tonight's feast," Sunny drawled as they unloaded our contribution. "C'mon, Andy," he continued in his cheeriest buddy-like tones. "I'll point out a few of the spit sights."

I got up to join them, but Janice said, "Oh, let them go off on their own. We'll just chat while I finish setting things up here." I sank down again. Andy gave me a proprietary kiss, and then my old buddy went off with my present lover. I surprised myself by feeling an odd tug of conflicted emotion that I thought had been safely discarded with my adolescent daydreams. Where did that come from? I wondered.

Rattled, I turned to Janice. "Can I help?" I asked.

"No, no, everything is just fine. You must just enjoy being a guest. Would you like a glass of wine?"

"That would be wonderful," I replied.

After Janice had finished setting up the food, she sat across from me at the picnic table and we chatted about the island, my tentative beginnings at detective work for emerging Toronto lawyer Juaneva Martin, and Sunny's comfort with island life.

While she seemed vibrant and interested, there was a look about Janice that didn't match her tone. For all her energy and smiles, her eyes never seemed to light up. I remembered what Sunny had said about the anniversary of her son's death and wondered if she would talk about it.

"You know, Abby," she said, "I'm glad Sunny has settled in here so nicely. We needed some of that get-things-done Eastern energy here. Many islanders are so complacent about the logging devastation, but Sunny has become very involved in our local Sierra Club."

"Really? Sunny seems awfully laid-back to me."

"Yes, well, it's all relative, isn't it?" she said. "Compared to the speed of life in Toronto, I suppose he is. But Sunny's been very active in our latest campaign against Armstrong. That man has already decimated the area I live in. Now he's planning to log out the heart of the southern community." Her eyes woke up for the first time, flashing fire.

"I read about that today," I said. "And, funnily enough, I had a run-in with the son, Brendon I think his name was."

Her anger shifted to scorn. "He's a spoiled brat," she said. "He's rude and acts superior all the time. He's deeply into drugs and hangs out with unsavoury types who deal heroin over in Bellweather. The only good thing about Brendon is that he causes his father a great deal of grief. That family is such a disaster — but it doesn't stop them from demolishing forests up and down the coast. It's got to be stopped."

She was so angry and upset that I was a bit at a loss for what to say. So we sat quietly for a few minutes.

My mind was ticking over about Brendon as a potential threat. I just had to hope I wouldn't cross paths with him again and that he wouldn't find out I was Abby Faria. If he was connected to the murder in Kensington, he probably knew I had helped to ferret out the organizers. And if he knew Anita was here and could point her out to his cronies, we were in big trouble.

Finally, Janice took a deep breath and seemed to give herself a metaphysical shake.

"Perhaps I'm just so angry because my son, Jon, died at an Armstrong logging site." She sighed.

Wanting to comfort the grieving woman, I nodded. "I heard that from Sunny, Jan. I'm so sorry. I don't want to pry, but I'm happy to listen if you want to talk about it."

Jan's partner, Mike, came over and sat beside her. Jan smiled sadly.

"I'd like that, Abby. The others are kind, but they've heard the story. I don't want to bother them, but I keep hoping if I talk about it enough, I can let him go." Mike put his arm around her as she began to open up.

She had been a single mom, working hard at menial jobs to provide Jon with opportunity. They had relied on each other, and he had fulfilled her hopes by doing well in high school and earning a scholarship in environmental studies at the University of Victoria. They had begun to grow distant when he became involved in Earth First!, an environmental group that believes in what she then viewed as extreme measures to protect the forests. At the time, Jan felt that they had led Jon astray, that they were too radical and he was spoiling his chances for success in school.

"To this day, I kick myself," she said, tears wetting her eyes, "for being angry with him. I betrayed Jon with my lack of trust in his good sense and a lack of faith in his commitment." Mike leaned over to put his arm around Jan's shoulders.

"He was a wonderful person," she said, a smile lingering about her lips. "He cared deeply about nature, even when he was a child — always bringing home injured animals and literally hugging trees, even then. As a four-year-old, he would go up to trees in the park and put his arms around them. He said he could hear their hearts beating." Her smile widened, her tears flowing freely now as we sat silently, allowing her to be with her little boy once more.

Eventually, Jan took a breath, straightened her shoulders and sniffed.

"I should have known then that his commitment would hold steady. I was just so afraid he would get hurt or in trouble. The last time I saw Jon, he and I argued. He was so angry and hurt that I couldn't understand what he was doing. He yelled at me that I should open my eyes. I told him that he could call me when he calmed down, and he slammed out of my house." She paused.

I imagined how hard it would be to live with her painful memories as I waited for Jan to continue.

She looked up at me and grimaced. "A week later, he was dead. They said he was monkey-wrenching — trying to sabotage vehicles at a logging site on Vancouver Island near Ucluelet, on the West Coast. They called it 'death by misadventure,' said that a tractor had rolled back over him, or some such story, while he was pouring sand in its oil tank."

"How horrible that must have been for you, Jan," I said sympathetically.

She nodded. "I was broken up for a long time. He was my whole life." She sighed. "A few months later, Mike came to my door and introduced himself as a friend of Jonathan's. He said he had met him at a convention of environmental groups and had been impressed by Jon's commitment and intelligence. Remembering my son's last words to me — to open my eyes — I invited him in to talk."

Mike patted her hand as she continued. "We talked about Jon and his work. Mike told me about the devastation of the forests and the different players — the companies, the work of the government, the environmental groups."

She looked up at me.

"This time, I was ready to listen. He said he was surprised by Jon's 'accident' because he had seemed a sensible, cautious youth. He also said that Jon had told him that he was doing research on non-violent methods to halt logging, including lobbying, public relations and media campaigns — even working with the loggers and companies to try to find alternatives. He had seemed very excited about his findings."

"That must have made you very proud," I said encouragingly.

"Yes," she said, her eyes welling again.

"Mike asked if I had Jon's work from school, because he was interested in the research. Everything was in boxes in the storage locker of the co-op I lived in. I hadn't had the heart to look through it, but I thought, with his help, I might be ready."

She stopped again to compose herself and continued with a weak smile.

"When we met the next day to go through the boxes, he told me more about the Sierra Club and invited me to their next meeting and slide show. He told me about the company Jon had been fighting, Armstrong Lumber, and about the dirty tricks private logging companies use to get around opposition. The useless Forest Protection Act does not apply to private land, so they can get away with almost anything. I was grateful as Mike chattered on while I sorted through Jon's papers, but in the end, we didn't find the research he had been looking for."

She smiled again, an unguarded warmth coming into her eyes for the first time.

"Well, the rest is history, as they say. I opened my eyes and became involved in the fight to save the forests, and I began to feel a little better. I feel closer to Jon as I continue to fight his fight, and my cloud had one silver lining," she sighed again. "I have Mike."

They smiled at each other.

"Despite the changes, there were still too many ghosts for me in Victoria, and Mike was ready to retire and try something new. We decided to move up to Peregrine, still beautifully treed, though not immune from logging, and to set up a little farm and summer vacation spot here. It was a challenge for us, but most of the people here have been so kind, and we have made some headway."

She tilted her head thoughtfully. "You know, we were in a kind of subsistence paradise until last year, when my nemesis, Armstrong, appeared. The problem was, we didn't do our research carefully enough. It turns out that he owned great tracts of land on the island and had just been waiting for the right time to slash and develop."

Jan shook her head sadly.

"It was like opening a large wound when we heard that he was going to cut a hundred acres of beautiful forest just one lot over from us. It was so close to home — a travesty. At that point, Jon's spirit rose in me full force, and we have been fighting ever since. Not terribly successfully, I might add. That is the worst of it. I can't even avenge my son's death. She slumped again and stared at her hands.

After a lengthy silence, she looked up at me. "Thanks for listening to my story, Abby. I hope I haven't spoiled your evening."

"No, no," I said reassuringly. "I feel honoured that you shared with me. It must be very hard for you."

"It is," she said simply. "I keep hoping it will get easier. At least I have Mike, and the farm keeps us busy." She gave herself a little shake and stood up. "Now, enough about the past; it's time to eat. The boys are back," she said as Andy and Sunny ambled up companionably. Giving them a quick wave, she called out to the others, who had gone down to the beach to walk in the surf and throw sticks for the dogs. "Is everyone hungry?"

"I sure am," Sunny said, rubbing his hands together as the others came up.

The air was warm, the sun still high and everyone seemed ready to party. The wine was doing its job, and I felt myself mellowing, too. It was hard to be moody in paradise.

The bay sparkled, tempting children into the water, their calls echoing up and down the beach. The smoky odour of picnic fires mixed with that of the kelpy ocean and the thick scent of the conifers that towered above us. We talked with Janice's partner, Mike, and the other couples: Sandra and Dave, and Uta and Stan. Sunny was the only single person there, but he seemed as comfortable as always, cracking jokes in his long drawl. Andy was enjoying himself, too, and he knew me well enough to avoid hovering too closely. His respectful distance worked like a charm to draw me nearer. Once we had collected food from the astonishing array of delicacies, I sat close to him, feeling his warmth emanate along my side.

"This is wonderful!" he said enthusiastically. "Your friend Sunny's a great guy. He seems to really love it here, and I can understand why," he said as he swept his arm out towards the view.

"Hmm," I said, distracted. "Andy, look at all this food! I feel so stingy with our meagre offerings. These people went all out."

There were garlic-and-nut-stuffed mushrooms, and two salmon — one cooked to a delicate pink and served cold with a lovely lemony hollandaise sauce, and Sunny's, still warm and covered in a garlic butter glaze. Alongside that were a Caesar salad, a plate of candied carrots, and a bowl of curried baked tofu. To top it all off, there were fruit salad and homemade chocolate chip cookies for dessert. Of course, I tried some of everything. The wine and the day's exercise made it easy to stuff down more than I should have. I resisted being a complete pig only because I was still mildly interested in people's good opinion of me.

Once I had got beyond concentrating only on food, I looked up at the others. Janice seemed happy enough, given her story, as she talked amiably with Uta, her neighbour from the north end. When the first rush for food was over and I could talk again, I turned to chat with Mike. He was starting to tell me more about their farm when I felt cool fingers slide over my eyes, obscuring my vision.

I waited it out for a second or two before grabbing the thin wrists connected to the fingers. My guess was confirmed by the sound of a tinkling laugh. When I turned, there was Anita, looking fresh and happy.

"Anita! I was about to track you down! I'm so glad to see you."

"Me too, Abby," she replied, smiling at me, one hand on her hip.

I introduced her to the others while Janice spirited another plate and some cutlery out of her large hamper and set Anita to collecting food for herself. She shepherded her to a seat at another table, chatting away while Anita tucked into the food. It really did feel like this was an extension of Janice's living room. She acted the hostess with aplomb. Perhaps the diversion of entertaining kept her mind off her unhappiness.

I felt momentarily adrift, not wanting to be overly mothering, but dying to ask Anita about her day. Finally, I decided to leave her in Janice's capable hands. Heading back to my seat to continue my conversation with Mike, I saw that my wine glass had been miraculously refilled in my brief absence.

As the sun began to drop nearer to the horizon, Mike sighed. "What a difference from yesterday's weather. Peregrine's been a bit changeable this year. We usually have long pleasant summers and early springs. Still," he sighed, "we'll have to pack up soon. It gets dark early now that fall is arriving."

He was a rough and ready kind of guy who seemed more stereotypically suited to the homesteading life he described, compared to his outwardly cultured partner.

Sunny ambled up. "Hey, Ab — maybe you and I can go for a short stroll before packing it in for the night. Gotta work tomorrow, y'know."

I looked around. Andy was happily absorbed in talking with Stan and Uta, and Janice was in deep conversation with Anita.

Mike smiled and said, "Good idea. I'm going to clean up here a little. You leave food around unattended at the spit and those blasted crows will be upon it in seconds." I offered to help, but he waved me away. "Go on, enjoy yourself."

So I agreed. "Let's go, Sunny. We can plan our cycling for the next few days."

Chapter 8

ACTUALLY I WAS happy to go off with my old buddy Sunny. After a brief romantic liaison, we had always been close, cycling together often and hanging out in the same punk clubs. His transformation on the island was a bit startling, but we had corresponded enough through the years to remain friends. Even so, I was feeling self-conscious, like I had stood still — still opinionated, nosy, and in a hurry.

Since introspection is not much fun, I resisted the notion that I was stuck in a rut and scooted along at Sunny's side — one and a half strides for every one of his. We walked silently for a while, just enjoying each other's company. The sun was starting to settle on the edge of the hills to the west, softening the light and cooling the air only slightly. I yawned.

"Are you still into a ride in the mornin', Ab? I mean, you are on holiday and all. Maybe early's not your thing."

"Oh, I think we can handle it, Sunny. We've had a pretty full first day here, but we're still on T.O. time, so we should be able to get up. Besides, after the mountain bike experience, pleasant as it was, I'd like a spin on the road. I'm still trying to get back in shape after my 'accident,' you know."

"Yeah, you wrote me about that mess in Kensington. That's when you helped Anita out, right?" I nodded. "She looks good. You'd never guess she'd been in such rough shape by looking at her now." He laughed lightly as he continued. "And you, Ab, you haven't changed much at all, still a little edgy. I'm glad to see that some old thugs couldn't scare you into normality."

"Now what's that supposed to mean?" I said, feeling mildly challenged to defend myself.

"Now, now. No offense, Ab. It's your edge that I love. Makes you a fast rider. Besides, you usually have a little dash of common sense, too."

"I hope that last point is true. What about you, Sunny? You don't miss the city? You seem to have perfected your drawl since you moved here." I gave him a poke.

"I love it here," he grinned, "but sometimes, Ab, when I get tired of everybody knowin' my business, I need a break. Most of the time, though, I know this is the place for me. I have some good friends, get to tinker with my bikes and enjoy the beauty of the island. When the winter rain gets to me, I do what the other islanders do if they can. I leave — go to the Baja for a cycle or somethin'."

"This *is* such a beautiful place, Sunny. Doesn't the logging stuff drive you crazy? Janice certainly seems angry about it."

"Yeah, we're tryin' to fight it, but the islanders don't all get it — that they are being manipulated by big loggin' concerns. You know the old tactic: divide and rule. Those old boys just go laughin' to the bank as we bicker."

I linked my arm with his, and we walked quietly for a minute before I said, "I really like Janice. It sucks about her son."

He nodded. "I actually got the story second-hand from Mike. Janice was pretty upset by the whole business. She never believed it was just an accident, but nobody could prove anything. She and Mike finally decided to move from Victoria, to start fresh, to try to leave that pain behind them."

"I know," I said. "She told me about it when you went off with Andy."

He shook his head. "When Armstrong began loggin' a big swatch of land on the road near them, it was like a knife digging into a raw wound for her. I guess she thinks she has nothing to lose, so she's going after this guy whole hog this time." He continued soberly, "I wish I could help her, Ab, but there's nothin' I can do but perhaps help her fight for the trees."

I squeezed his arm.

By this time, we had nearly completed the loop that circled the end of the spit. The sun was down, the sky releasing a mix of magenta, blue and gold.

Sunny collected himself. "So, your bikes, Ab. How many do you have in your collection now?"

"I still have ten. My best Trek was involuntarily retired last year. But I got a Rocky Mountain beauty in return."

We were nearing the picnic site, and some people in our group were seated around the firepit. It had cooled down a little, and the others were packing up. Andy was helping, so I said, "Maybe we can talk shop some more tomorrow."

"Nice guy," Sunny said, nodding at Andy. "He knows his bikes." This was a high compliment from Sunny.

"Yes," I said. "That's how we connected, by talking about bikes while I was in the hospital."

"He seems quite devoted to you, Abby."

"I'm not sure that's a good thing, Sunny. You know my bad habits — wanting what I can't have, disdaining what comes too easily. He is so nice and very easy on the eyes, too. But I think he wants to settle down, and I don't. I'm feeling bad about it, but I'm too used to answering only to myself. This trip is a kind of test, which I'm already failing."

As if on cue, Andy waved us over. "Hey, there," he said, taking my hand. "We missed you. Catching up on old times?" he asked.

"Something like that," I said as I turned back to smile at my old friend. "Thanks, Sunny. That was nice. Hey, Andy, are you still up for a ride in the morning?"

"You bet," he said. "Is 8:00 still okay? Just name your time, Sunny. We'll be there."

"How about 7:30 instead? It won't take more than an hour to do the circle and then you can come in for a bite. I can still get to work by 9:00, 9:30. Not much business starts till 10:00."

"Perfect," I said as I looked around. "Where's Anita, Andy?"

"She headed back to the campsite about ten minutes ago. She said she wanted to get settled in before it gets too dark. I offered her a ride, but she seemed happy to walk. She said to say good night to you and tell you not to worry, she's having a great time. It sure looks like it, too," he said. "She was smiling away at dinner, and completely relaxed."

"She deserves happiness," I said. "I hope Brendon Armstrong and his buddies stay out of her way."

He nodded, stifling a yawn. "Well, what do you say, Abby? Should we go home? I'm feeling the day a little."

Just then, Janice joined our little group. "I'm glad you're back," she said brightly to Sunny and me. "We have a bit of a drive ahead, and I wanted to say goodbye to you, Abby. Would you like us to throw your contraption in the pickup, Sunny? Save you the ride up the hill?"

"No, that's okay, Janice. My little baby is comfy and fast, and I need a ride after all that good food." He patted his stomach

Janice, ever the graceful host, turned to us and said, "It was a pleasure to meet you both. I hope you enjoyed our little dinner."

"It was wonderful," I answered. "And I'm thrilled to see that Sunny has found such good friends. Of course, the downside is that we'll never get him back East now."

"No, I think he is truly an islander," she smiled. "Listen, I hope we'll meet up again before you leave the island. Perhaps you can visit us up at our end. There are some beautiful places to swim up there." She nodded, making up her mind. "Yes, I'm going to arrange something through Sunny, and you will have to bring Anita with you. I really enjoyed talking with her this evening."

"That would be a pleasure," I said, and Andy nodded.

"We look forward to it," he said, taking her hand.

Instant friends, she and I gave each other a quick hug. Her eyes were still quiet as she said softly, "Thank you for listening, Abby."

I smiled. "I had a wonderful time."

We said quick goodbyes to the others, and then made our way to the car.

The drive home was quiet and harmonious, and by the time we reached the lodge, it was pitch dark outside. In the city, with all the lights reflecting off the sky, it never truly gets dark, and the night sky is generally quite dull. But here, tonight, away from the urban light pollution, the dark sky was filled with myriad little pinprick stars. With my rudimentary knowledge of constellations, even I could pick out a few.

As we walked towards the lodge, Andy cautiously slipped his arm around my waist. "It's been a great day, Abby. How about a nightcap to top it off?"

"Great idea, Andy. It's just after 8:30, so we've got plenty of time."

We were in luck — *our* table by the window was free, the beautiful view filled with sparkles: the stars in the sky bouncing off the ocean accompanied by the twinkling lights on the coast of Vancouver Island. It was easy to relax, to slide into a comfortable abyss of temporary ignorance; to imagine that only such beauty filled the world.

The momentary drift on my own personal ocean of bliss was further enhanced by a superb little bottle of Ontario ice wine, along with a plate of local blackberries and blueberries, candied salmon (my latest bliss), a little wedge of chévre and some nice crusty French bread freshly made on the island.

We sat side by side, holding hands, a little hiatus in Abby's war with her feelings. The white flag was up, and when we finally made the languorous move to our room, it was natural to make my surrender complete. As Andy helped me undress, I felt a little shiver of delight penetrate what was left of my armour. We fell into a comfortable slow release, too full from the events of the day to do more than give and take in a rhythmic, familiar way.

When the last wave of pleasure flowed away, the only thought that surfaced before succumbing to the depths of a peaceful sleep was that just maybe I could get used to such a partnership, something comfortable, calm and familiar. Maybe I was ready for a chance to wear away a bit of my edge. Perhaps that sort of leap of faith was what I needed, but could I do it?

Chapter 9

INSTEAD OF THE persistent chirp of the alarm on my watch, I was shocked out of sleep by hammers in the middle of paradise. Initially, I thought I was back in Kensington Market and some jerk was digging up the road first thing in the morning. Then the thought filtered through that maybe it was all in my head, the beginning of a massive hangover. My one open eye adjusted to the dawn's light to see Andy snoozing away, oblivious to the noise. How did he do that? The banging continued, and my head wasn't throbbing, so I opened my other eye reluctantly, raised myself on one elbow and glanced at my watch. 6:00 a.m.!

I heard a loud whisper. "Abby! Open the door. It's me, Sunny!"

That finally got my attention. What was Sunny doing at our door at such an ungodly hour? I stumbled out of bed, threw on a long T-shirt and underwear, and blinked my way to the door.

Sunny looked grim, dishevelled, even for him, and very short on his usual casual demeanour. I threw open the door, blinking at him, and he stepped into the room, running a hand through his hair.

"Gee, Abby," he said, taking a look at the sleeping bundle on the bed that was Andy. "I'm sorry to bug you, but something awful has happened. Janice has been arrested."

That woke me up completely.

"What? Why? Everything seemed fine last night."

He just stood there looking as confused as I felt. He seemed lost now that he had gained entry to the room.

"Give me a minute, Sunny," I said, motioning to the armchair by the window. Grabbing some more clothes, I dashed into the washroom, splashed water on my face and dressed quickly. I returned to the room, took Sunny by the hand and dragged him to the dining room for a much-needed cup of coffee and the lowdown on Janice's arrest. I knew it would be open already to cater to the early morning fishing buffs.

My table was available, but now Sunny occupied Andy's chair. I liked seeing him there, but had no time to dwell on what that meant as a tired-looking waitress brought a stack of toast to our table and filled our coffee cups.

"Okay, Sunny," I said more briskly than I felt. "Fill me in. What happened?"

His big frame hunched over the steaming coffee as he looked at me, his beautiful eyes glinting as if tears were about to fall. "Damn it, she's had such a hard time, and now she's arrested in the middle of the night … for … for murder."

"Murder!" I cried, evidently a little more loudly than I should have, as a few heads turned our way. "Who was murdered? And what did Janice have to do with it?"

"Well, Abby, that's just it. I just don't believe she could kill anybody. But that bastard Jack Armstrong was killed last night, and lots of people know how angry she was at him."

"Jesus. But half the island is angry at Jack Armstrong."

"I know, Ab, and anyone who really knows her would say that Janice would be incapable of killing someone. But most people here don't know her well, but what they do know is her fiery anger about Armstrong and the logging."

"Okay," I said, patting his hand as the cogs in my head turned. "Tell me what happened, exactly as you found out yourself."

"Well, I actually don't know a lot. Mike called me in a state about 4:30 this morning. He said that the police came by their place at about 2:00, woke them up and arrested Janice. He was upset by the charge, of course, but also by how roughly she was treated. Mike said it was real traumatic for Janice because they wouldn't even tell her what had happened — only that she was charged with Armstrong's murder.

"Mike followed them to the local station, which was in a chaotic state. I'm sure murders are few and far between on this island, so they're not exactly set up for dealing with it. Anyway, Mike called the Sierra Club's attorney, Andrew Martin, for help. Andrew said it wasn't what he was used to doing, but he would step in until a criminal attorney could be found to defend her."

"I don't understand, Sunny." My mind was ticking over. "We were with Janice last night. When was she supposed to have killed this man? And where was he killed?" I paused. "Does he even live on the island?"

"No, but here's the thing. Mike said that after they left us last night, Jan suggested they take the long route around and look at the prayer flags."

"The what?"

"Oh, well, a while back some of the locals made prayer flags, like the Buddhists do, and put them in the areas slated to be logged. It was a gesture, a kind of gentle spiritual protest in the woods. Jan just wanted to go there and, you know, commune with the trees and remember her son, I guess. So they went there, and who should they meet but Armstrong. Mike said it looked like maybe he was checking out the site for the next round of cutting, as some machinery had been moved in. When Janice and Mike got to the site, Armstrong was pulling one of the flags off a tree. He must have already removed a few, because Mike said they were lying around on the ground near Armstrong's feet.

"That got to Jan — some of those flags had been made by the local kids who had been really hopeful about saving their forest. She bent over to pick them up, Mike said, when Armstrong told her she was trespassing and made some crack about whether she had come to say goodbye to her precious trees."

"No wonder she was upset," I said, horrified.

He nodded sombrely. "Apparently, he laughed right in her face, and Jan lost it, shouting that she would stop him somehow."

Sunny sighed. "Mike says Armstrong wiped his hands on a flag and told her to accept defeat. His men had the machinery in place to start the next day. By that point, a few of Armstrong's workers had gathered around to watch the interaction, so when Janice lunged at Armstrong, they grabbed her and held her back. Armstrong laughed again and walked away. Jan was spitting fire. She told him he'd be sorry and walked away with Mike.

"He says that it was only when they were well away that her stiff resolve melted. He said that Jan sobbed uncontrollably all the way home. She had trouble settling down so she took a couple of sleeping pills, but even so, she still tossed and turned. They had just finally quieted down to a fitful sleep at two in the morning when the police arrived."

Sunny paused to take a long slurp of his coffee before continuing. "Apparently, a watchman found Armstrong in that same forest just before midnight. Someone stays out there because of the potential for sabotage to the machinery. He had been one of those on site during Janice's altercation with Armstrong, so he made the assumption that she had snuck back to do damage to the machinery. A string of prayer flags was wrapped around the old man's neck. He had been strangled.

"They came after Jan because the watchman who witnessed the earlier altercation said he thought he saw Mike's truck speeding down the road when he was on his way back to the site."

"Strangled by prayer flags ... that is ironically gruesome," I said. "I wonder why Armstrong was out there so late at night?"

"Yeah," said Sunny, looking miserable.

"Well, Sun, I'm sure the police will release Jan soon enough. They'll need more concrete evidence before they can keep her. Once a criminal lawyer comes into the picture, they'll probably let her out on bail."

I had a thought. "Sun, nobody knows me here, so if you want, maybe I can ask some questions without getting anyone's guard up. I'll take the nose rings out first, I promise."

In fact, I was kind of excited to have a little challenge dropped in my lap, especially one to do with the Armstrong family. Brendon had a history of violence and could be a more likely suspect than Jan. Maybe I could do some quiet nosing around and see if he had anything to do with it. If he did, and if I could prove it, that would be one way to get him out of Anita's way. Not that I was prejudiced one way or the other, I grinned to myself.

I reached over to pat Sunny again; he looked so disconsolate.

Maybe it was just the thought of trying to solve a mystery that energized me, but I felt a definite thrill as we touched. I shoved the feeling
to the back of my mind and focused on the issue at hand instead.

"So?" I asked enthusiastically. "What do you think?"

For my efforts, I was rewarded with a weak smile from my old
friend.

"That would be great, Abby. What would you do first?" he asked,
taking a last swig of his coffee.

"Well, Sun, first I should talk to Janice, if I can."

"We can call Mike. Maybe he has a lawyer now."

I nodded. "That's a good idea. And it would be good to talk to
that watchmen and see the site, if I can get in there. And maybe later,
talk to Armstrong's family." Though, thinking rapidly, I decided I
wanted to put that off to avoid tweaking Brendon's antennae for a
while.

I paused. "I'd love to have your help, Sunny, but I should do this
as anonymously as I can, at least for now. No one's going to answer
questions if they know I'm connected to Janice. Or to you, for that
matter. Besides," I said, "you've got to work, too."

"You're probably right." He sighed. "This is still a busy part of the
season. There's not as much business when the tourists are gone. But
Ab, how are you going to get those other people to talk to you?"

"Leave that to me, Sunny." Silently, I wondered the same thing.
I didn't want to worry Sunny about the Toronto connection with
Brendon, and I was going to have to try very hard to avoid helping
Brendon figure out who I was. He was dangerous.

We sat quietly for a few more minutes until our silence was interrupted by a sleepy voice. "I thought we were meeting you at your
place." I stopped patting Sunny's hand and leaned back somewhat
guiltily. Andy looked half asleep and didn't seem to notice.

"Oh, hi, Andy. Sunny showed up early this morning with some
bad news, and he has asked for our help." I continued, "I'll tell you
about it in a minute." I looked at my watch — 7:00. Time had passed
quickly.

Turning to my old friend, I said. "Listen Sunny, why don't you go
home? You can call Mike and find out what's happening. I'll explain

everything to Andy, get us organized and be over to see you soon. Try to find out if I can see Janice, okay?"

"Thanks again, Abby," he said. He gave me a little hug and shook Andy's hand. "See you folks later, I guess." He still looked a little lost as he ambled out without another word.

"What was that all about?" asked Andy as he slipped into the chair Sunny had warmed. "Sunny looked awful."

"Janice was arrested for murder last night," I replied soberly.

"What?" he responded with predictable surprise, waking up more fully.

"I'll fill you in in a sec," I said as the waitress approached to replace Sunny's dishes with a clean set and take our order. I was awash in coffee and toast, so I opted for fresh fruit, while Andy ordered a more spirited breakfast, a smoked salmon omelette, coffee and orange juice. Once the waitress was away with our order, I filled Andy in on Janice's situation.

"So you see," I said as I finished the tale, "I'd like to help them if I can."

Andy took my hand. "I don't know, Abby. I'm concerned about these people too, but what can you do? This isn't really your territory, and maybe you're too emotionally involved given Anita's connection to Brendon. Besides," he said slowly, "to be honest, I'm disappointed. I wanted this to be a chance for us to spend more time together."

I took a breath. "Andy, this is part of my life, and I need you to accept that about me."

"I know that, hon," he replied with a tone that revealed his ambivalence, "but we're on holiday."

"You're right," I said. "And I feel badly about spoiling your break, but if someone had an accident right in front of you, even while you were on holiday, wouldn't you feel you had to use your special skills to help them, if you could?"

I gave his hand an affectionate squeeze. "It probably won't take long, a couple of days, tops, to see if I can make any difference. We'll still have some time, I'm sure." I wasn't sure I believed that myself.

Andy gave in, shrugging. "Okay, Abby. Please yourself. I can explore the island for a while by myself. Or maybe," he added hopefully, "I can help you out a bit."

"Really?" I said happily. "That would be fantastic!"

We halted our conversation while the waitress delivered our food. As Andy tucked in, I said carefully, "Thanks for the offer, Andy. You're a stranger here too, so nobody will associate you with the investigation. You might be able to help me play a role or two along the way."

Looking satisfied, he said, "That sounds like fun."

"Just remember," I said "let me call the shots. I've done this before."

"Yes, ma'am," he agreed, and we completed the meal in relative peace, talking about my plans and how much we would share with Anita. I wanted to protect her from knowing what was going on, but Andy convinced me that we should alert her. We both thought it likely that Brendon would be too busy to run into her, but Andy agreed to call the campsite and leave a message for her to call us at Sunny's.

Chapter 10

AS WE GOT ready, I found myself questioning my behaviour with Andy. He was such a good guy; I wondered why I couldn't relax with him for any extended period of time. Despite the fact that I often told him I wasn't able to stick things out for the long term, I wasn't sure he believed me. And maybe I wasn't exactly being overly convincing. Was I using him, in some subconscious way? We had to have a serious talk once we finished helping Jan.

We headed towards Sunny's place on reasonably good terms. The next step for me depended on what Sunny had learned, and Andy was coming along to see if he could help. I set myself to thinking about how to approach Brendon Armstrong. I didn't relish exposing myself to him, but he seemed a likely lead: He was notorious for troubling his father, and I had already witnessed his hot head in action.

I knew nothing about the mother or the sister. As a matter of fact, some more information about the whole family would be useful. It's common knowledge that foul play is often tied to family or business, or a combination of the two. I'd be wise to keep that little factoid in mind.

Jack Armstrong had probably made enemies up and down the coast with his cut-and-run method of logging and his in-your-face way of dealing with communities who suffered the consequences. There was sure to be more than one likely suspect. I hoped the police would look further than Jan. There had been so many cases in the news lately of people who had been wrongly accused and spent many years in jail before the truth came out. I didn't want this to happen to my new friend just because the police got gung-ho with her as a "sure-fire" suspect.

I shook my head clear. It was another beautiful day, blue sky, sunshine, mild and calm. I wondered how anyone could think of murder in such a paradise, as Sunny's unmistakable sign came into view. We steeled ourselves over the potholes, and eventually the car rolled to a stop at the open shop door where Sunny was already at work. He came out of the shop, wiping his hands on his well-worn apron. Behind him on his work stand was a familiar-looking blue high-tech mountain bike, complete with front and rear rock shocks and a mangled front wheel.

"Hi there," he said affably enough, although knowing him as I did, I could tell he was still somewhat on edge. "You'll never guess who showed up this morning, wanting his bike fixed 'right away.'" He waved his hand towards the blue bike on the stand. "Ol' Brendon Armstrong. He hasn't changed one iota, that kid. Still demanding, still rude. In fact, he seemed so unfazed I wondered whether he'd even heard about his daddy's death."

"He didn't say anything about it?"

"Not a peep. Like it hadn't happened. I even hinted around, asked him if he had heard anything, but he wasn't even interested in anything but getting his bike fixed *right away*. I'm seriously thinking maybe he hasn't even heard the news. So I just shut up and told him his bike might take a coupla days if I don't have a spare wheel. He wasn't too pleased, said something about having to ride an old clunker. Then he had the gall to point at *my* mountain bike and said he might as well rent that one. I told him to think again. I just don't like that kid. Finally, he took the best rental in the shop, complaining all the while. I don't trust him, so I took a large credit card deposit and tried once more to suggest he phone home as he drove off."

"I wonder if Brendon spends much time at home?" I speculated.

"Well, maybe not, but he's supposed to. I heard he's on a kind of open custody for some drug charge or other, and there's some talk of him being connected to incoming gang activity. I think his mother took on a legal obligation to know where he is at all times in order to get him released after the drug charge. That shows what privilege can buy. You or me on that kind of charge, we'd be coolin' our heels, but not Brendon. He's out makin' life miserable for the rest of us." He shook his head.

"Well," I said, "we'll get to Brendon later. I'd love to know where he was last night, though. Did he say what happened to his wheel?"

"I did ask him because it's quite a nasty bend, but he either didn't figure I was worth explainin' it to or he didn't want to tell, 'cause he told me it was none of my business and just to fix it fast."

"What a brat. Hey, have you had time to call Mike, by the way?" I asked as we walked over to the bike on the stand.

"Oh, yeah, much to Master Brendon's annoyance. The kid was here waitin' when I got back this mornin'. He was annoyed that I made him wait some more while I made the call. As a matter of fact, I have to admit," he said with a hint of a smile, "the more he complained, the slower I went. I took quite a while to put away my truck and finish my call inside, away from his ears. I let the guy stew out here for a while.

"Anyway, Mike has a cellphone, so I got him right away. He's on the mainland. They moved the proceedings over there, and they're just waitin' for a judge to decide about bail. The lawyer's hoping that Jan's lack of a previous record will stand her in good stead, providing she promises to stay put on the farm. Mike said he'd call as soon as they know. He appreciates your offer to help, and he's going to talk to Jan about it."

We gathered around the bike, which was already on the work stand.

"What are you going to do with it?" I asked.

"Well, I have other bikes ahead of his, so despite His Lordship's insistence, I'm goin' to finish up with those first. I might get to it this afternoon, but I doubt it."

"Maybe we can look at it together," Andy suggested.

Sunny nodded. "Sure, unless I get everything done quicker than expected and am looking for work to do." He winked.

"Cool," I said. "Meanwhile, while we're waiting for Mike to call, how about we help with the other bikes?"

Sunny smiled wickedly. "That'd be fun, a nice diversion."

He threw me a rag and handed me some soapy water in a bucket.

"Why don't you wash that dirty clunker there," he said, pointing at a well-used hybrid leaning against the shop near a hose.

"And Andy can true that wheel." He pointed to a somewhat tacoed wheel mounted on the truing stand.

I laughed. "Oh, I see. I get the dirty work. We wouldn't want to strain the surgeon's fingers, would we?"

"That's not it, Ab." Sunny grinned. "It's just that he has to put up with so much from you that I thought he needed a break."

The two men laughed at my expense while I rolled my eyes dolefully, and then we settled to work in companionable silence.

We were interrupted by the simultaneous ringing of the telephone and the sound of car springs suffering along the rutted driveway. Sunny answered the phone, leaving us to greet the arrival of a station wagon loaded with kids, bikes, a dog and two tired-looking adults. Everyone piled out, creating instant chaos.

"We were sent up from the campground," said the woman, hauling a kid's bike off the rack. "They said you could fix a flat for us."

"Well," I said, "I probably could, but I think you're looking for Sunny. He'll be right out."

I wasn't ready for a pile of kids and all the noise they created, so I slid away to the garden, leaving Andy to make small talk and Sunny to deal with the bikes. When it seemed peaceful again, I ventured back. The horde of noisemakers was indeed gone, and Sunny was back at work on a tune-up, talking to Andy, who was lending a hand.

"Oh, there you are," they said in unison.

Sunny was looking a little happier. "It was Mike who called," he said. "Jan's been released, and the two are on their way back to the island. They'll drop in here on their way home, and then you and Andy can follow them up to their place."

"That's great news, Sunny," I said enthusiastically, and Andy nodded in agreement.

"I'm going to stay here and get some work done. Maybe you can call here later and let me know what's happening."

"Sounds good," I said. "Sunny, while we're waiting, I'm going to go for a little walk to do some thinking."

Andy looked up from cleaning a chain.

"Do you want me to come along?" he asked, looking anxious lest I tear him away from the alluring smell of Varsol.

"No, Andy," I chuckled. "I'll be fine."

Sunny pointed down the side of his property, away from the road. "There's a trail over there. It's a nice walk, about a half-hour each way and pretty flat, with a nice view at the end. I made it for the bikers to hook up with the north road trail, so look out for cyclists."

"No problem," I said. I left them chatting happily about bikes, acting like best buds.

I'm like a fish out of water in the countryside, and I feel sure that all of bounteous nature knows it. I had trouble relaxing along the sylvan trail because I was sure that the rustling bushes were whispering to their tall neighbours about my nerves as I passed. I felt foolishly afraid that unknown critters could be lurking in the underbrush ready to leap out at any moment and eat me alive. Of course, all I saw were a few birds in the trees and a chipmunk that scurried across the trail.

Ironically, I have no hesitation whatsoever of taking on the toughest opponent in the city, though naturally I know that the human animal is far more dangerous than any deer or raccoon. I suppose it all had to do with the familiar versus the unknown. Treading on the balls of my feet, I was pumped with the adrenalin I was generating, partly from imagining a bear or a cougar on the trail, but also, I had to admit it, from the scent of a mystery. I decided to divert myself from my little wildlife fears with a dissection of what I knew so far of the murder.

From the little I had gathered so far, we had three possible places to look for suspects: someone local, like Janice, who opposed the logging; someone close to Armstrong, like family, particularly Brendon, or his friends if he had any; or anybody more distant who had been affected by other Armstrong business dealings.

While there may have been other possibilities, I thought I would start with the first two categories and see where that took me. I realized that Andy might come in handy. His bedside manner could open doors better than my direct approach, in some circumstances. And with him by my side, I could just be his sidekick. Then I stopped in my tracks for a moment. Given my growing emotional ambivalence, I shouldn't be thinking about him in terms of how useful he could be. I liked myself less for what was happening between Andy and me, and I was beginning to feel more and more like a user.

I left these thoughts unresolved as I had come almost to the end of the trail. There was a small bend ahead where the trail narrowed and picked itself around two large rock outcroppings. An old, gnarled arbutus, red-barked and leafy, seemed to be the only thing between cliff edge and space. I inched my way up the hill to the arbutus, wondering what kind of drop accompanied the view I had been promised.

The sky was a pale blue, and as I looked west, I was greeted by a breathtaking vision of the Vancouver Island Ranges across the channel. An eagle was wheeling in an updraft. A dizzying distance away, the water sparkled, producing jewels far more impressive to me than diamonds. I could see the ferry working its way towards Peregrine, the wide wake behind it severed a couple of times by criss-cross trails of barges heading south. Sunny's trail meandered off to the left, where the slope was more gradual. I lost track of it but assumed it would join the road below that he had mentioned.

From my perspective, there were still many trees on the island, but a large gash to my left must have been Armstrong's latest cut. I looked at the mountains to the west. There, in the distance, was evidence of a great deal of forest activity, from light green squares showing the beginnings of new growth on an old cut, to large brown patches, evidence of new cuts.

Armstrong was probably just one pawn in a large logging chess game, but what I saw helped strengthen my resolve to help Janice so that she could continue her fight for the forests.

Chapter 11

JAN AND MIKE had arrived by the time I got back. Mike was talking with Sunny and Andy by the bike repair stand, but Janice remained in their little pickup. Although I had met her only once, she was visibly altered since our last encounter, slumped in her seat, shoulders practically above her bent head. The face she turned to me was an awful, greyish colour, her eyes completely without shine as she greeted me with a wan attempt at a smile.

"Oh, my dear," she said. "It is so kind of you to offer to help. I'm afraid this is not quite the visit to my house that I had in mind last night."

"No matter," I said. "I can't promise I'll be much help, but maybe fresh eyes and ears will be useful. Are you up to talking today?"

"Oh, yes. I want to straighten this out as soon as possible."

The men approached and Mike shook my hand. He looked worn as well, but worry was the predominant emotion etched in his face as he said shortly, "Good of you to try to help us out."

"I just hope it will make a difference," I said. "I'm a stranger here. Perhaps I'll do more harm than good."

"Everyone on this island is too involved to see straight. Things look pretty bad for Jan right now," he said, "but I'm certain that something will come up to give us a better picture."

Sunny spoke up. "Abby here is very good at unearthing facts, and she isn't too worried about ruffling feathers."

"Now Sunny," I said, "that's a backhanded compliment, but I truly don't go out of my way to bother people."

"Whatever you say, Ab." He smiled. I silently wished I shared his confidence in my abilities, but I pushed that thought aside and decided I should just get started. "I'm ready," I said as I turned to the couple, "if you two are. If you want to lead the way, Andy and I will follow in our car."

"Right," Mike said.

As we walked to the car, I called back to Sunny, "We'll keep you posted. Oh, and Sun," I said, suddenly remembering our message to Anita. "If Anita calls, can you fill her in and ask her to be careful, but not to worry, please?"

"Sure Ab," he said, looking confused about my message. He gave a little wave as we drove off.

Initially, the route was familiar, as it was the same road we had taken to the Deer Lake trail. Before we reached the bike trail, however, Mike took a cut-off that led farther up the island. The road was unpaved and rutted. The tedious reminders of logging were everywhere, from signs warning of logging trucks or announcing "tree farms" to the more obvious stumped landscapes that peeked from behind trees. The noise of the gravel road and the concentration required to peer through the dust kicked up by the car ahead of us discouraged conversation, so we travelled in the company of our own thoughts.

After about twenty minutes of driving, we reached yet another clear-cut, this time on a slope that bordered a small lake, little cottages dotting its shores. As we continued on through the heart of the devastation, I got the occasional extra pang at the sight of the odd tree left standing at the edge of the road, sad against the stark backdrop.

The truck ahead slowed as it reached a driveway. Surprisingly, there were four or five vehicles parked on either side of the road near it.

"Uh-oh," I said. As Mike and Jan's truck slowed, people began emerging from the cars. Some had still cameras; one held a video camera. "Looks like the press has got wind of what has happened. I hope those two have the sense to just drive right through."

It appeared that they would have liked to, but the nearest car — a sporty BMW — pulled into their path. By the time we had pulled up behind them, we could see the person who had emerged from the car screaming at Janice through the window. As the media hounds hotly crowded in at the scent of a kill, I wanted to jump from the car and help. But I knew I had to stay out of the media's eye for my sake and Anita's.

"Andy, I can't stand having to sit and watch this."

He nodded understandingly. "Jumping into the fray is much more your style, Ab," he said as he undid his seatbelt. "Let me see what I can do. I'm used to handling this kind of feeding frenzy in the emergency ward." With that, he got out of the car and walked over to the scene. I opened my window to hear what was going on.

The woman sounded drunk as she called out repeatedly, "Let me get at you! You murderer! You killed my husband!" From this tirade, I assumed she was Armstrong's wife. She was a mess; brittle, dyed-blonde hair piled on top of her head and heavily made up with a red slash extending beyond the lips, bright blue eye shadow on her eyes and thick black mascara running down her cheeks — a caricature of a clown. It was hard to tell with all that makeup, but something about the uneven coverage on one side of her face suggested she had tried to cover up a bruised eye.

Mike stood by helplessly, not able to interfere in the woman's grief, but I knew Andy's kind manner would be helpful. He gently took Mrs. Armstrong by the arm and began talking quietly in her ear. She must have been used to his kind of solicitous doctor talk because she quickly became quite docile. He nodded to me as he walked her towards the passenger side of her car. I noticed smugly that he had his personal first aid kit with him. So much for leaving work behind!

As the media folk milled about, shooting pictures, Mike returned to the truck. I could see him trying to comfort Janice, who now looked even more shaken and pale.

Andy helped Mrs. Armstrong into her car and then walked over to speak to me. He dropped our car keys into my hand through the open window.

"I'm going to take Mrs. Armstrong to some friends she says live near the ferry dock. I'll see if someone can give me a ride so I can come back to get you later."

I nodded. "Thanks, Andy. Are you sure you can find your way?"

"No problem. I can always ask if I get lost. Looks like our new friend is already an item," he said, nodding at the reporters and then at Jan.

"I guess this is pretty big news on the island," I said heavily. "Still, I hate the way the media pick on the carcass of crime."

He nodded. "I see them all the time, sifting for a good story."

"I'm glad you were here to help. I'm sorry to have spoiled the second day of your vacation."

"I'll get you to make up for it later." He grinned boyishly.

"Watch this," he said, and then he walked over and climbed into the BMW. He moved it out of the way of Mike's van and gestured to Mike to drive in. After the truck disappeared amongst the trees along the twisty driveway, Andy approached the reporters, and I heard him say firmly, "Ms. Field has nothing to say at this time, and I will remind you that this is private property. Please respect the privacy of these people. Perhaps they will provide a statement at a later time."

They clamoured, yelling questions for a few minutes, but Andy simply stood silently with his arms folded. The local press must be of a gentler type than their urban cousins, or they had gotten enough exciting footage, because they soon turned and slunk off to their waiting vehicles. Andy winked at me, and I drove in past him with a wave, marvelling at his performance on the road. I still had the feeling that the worst was not behind us, but maybe at least the reporters were off our backs.

Chapter 12

I DROVE SLOWLY up the grassy drive, the trees giving way to a rough-hewn pastoral scene surrounding a large weathered, lovingly cared-for farmhouse that spoke instantly of home. Sheep grazed in one fenced-in area, while closer to the house, geese and ducks meandered around at a little pond. I could hear the gentle clucking of chickens in a coop to my left. Near the house was another fenced area with a vegetable garden and fruit trees, and a brook ran alongside the road. Tall firs on three sides and a sheer cliff towering above on the fourth side enclosed the property.

Again, I was struck by the contrast of the perfect outward picture with the circumstances being played out within. It was hard to believe that any strife could exist in such a setting. After I parked beside the van and approached the main gate, a German shepherd came bounding up, barking. A woman I recognized as Uta from the night before came out of the house and grabbed the dog by its collar. Once the dog had done its sniffing-to-get-to-know-you routine, she let him go and greeted me.

"Hi, we live right next door," she said, waving vaguely in the direction of trees. "I came over to help out as soon as I heard what happened." She shook her head. "Jan looks pretty bad." Uta opened the gate, and we walked to the house.

I said only, "They're lucky to have friends like you to help out."

"Oh," she said, "living up here, we learn to rely on one another. You can get pretty lonesome otherwise." She tilted her head a little. "Then again, some people like it that way. Come on in. We're just having tea."

There it was. Tea — the cure-all, the ritual invocation of normalcy, the routine. I've used the convention of the tea ritual a few times myself to ease a situation.

Inside, the house was finished in warm wood. A large wood stove occupied a central space in an open-concept living, dining and kitchen area. Jan was sitting close to Mike on a small sofa. Uta gave me a tray with teapot, mugs, sugar and milk, while she carried a plate of cookies and a handful of napkins.

"Abby's here, just in time for tea," she said brightly, as if I was a chance visitor on a social occasion. "Just set the tray there, Abby," she said, pointing to a glass-topped coffee table in the centre of a grouping of couches and chairs. I looked around appreciatively, impressed by the collection of stunning West Coast Native prints and some nicely framed colour photos of landscapes. On a narrow wall above the wood stove was a suite of what looked like family photos. A large bookshelf against a wall was jammed with books. The house was very clean and tidy. Janice looked up as I sat in a nearby chair, and she smiled another weak smile.

"Thank you —" she paused. Picking up her thought, Mike finished for her: "— for helping out there at the road."

"We were lucky to have Andy's expertise," I said. "That woman seemed completely over the edge!"

Mike nodded gravely. "She's had a shock, of course, but the rumours are that there was little love lost between her and Armstrong. Did you see the black eye she was trying to cover up with all that makeup? And the few times I've seen her in public, she's been pretty bombed."

"You can't always tell from outward appearances what's really going on," I said. "As far as I'm concerned, anyone could be a suspect until they're ruled out. That performance out there could have been an act, for all we know. I'll try to talk to her later. What is her name?"

"Mabel," said Mike. "Mabel Armstrong."

"Abby, you don't think she killed him, do you?" asked Jan, a little colour returning to her cheeks as she sipped Uta's tea. I had silently approved when I saw Uta mix the tea: mostly milk and three spoons of sugar, a useful combination for someone in shock.

"Who knows?" I replied. "I'm just looking for any likely suspects.

Family conflict can be a cause for murderous thoughts. By the way, you've had quite a shock yourself. Do you need anything to help you calm down?"

She shook her head. "No, no, I'll be fine. I'm still woozy from the sleeping pills Mike gave me last night after that dreadful encounter with Armstrong at the logging site. They really knocked me out, and I want to keep my wits about me while this is going on. Besides, if I need anything, I have a cupboard full of stuff they gave me when Jon died." She grimaced. "I was a wreck for a while."

"Well then, do you think you're up to talking?" I asked solicitously. "I'd like to hear your story and any ideas you have to get me started on a plan of investigation." The afternoon sun filtered through the windows of the cozy room. Mike sat near her supportively, but he seemed restless as she spoke, his eyes darting about. I wondered what that was all about.

Jan nodded. "I want to talk," she said.

"Did they tell you anything at the police station about the circumstances of Armstrong's death?"

Mike spoke up. "Not much. Apparently, he was found at the site we visited last night. They believe he was hit on the head with something heavy, and then, while unconscious, he was strangled with a string of prayer flags. Their main reason for suspecting Jan is that she had been there earlier that night and that the watchman thought he saw our truck later. They didn't seem to care that there was no way the watchman could have been sure in the dark whose truck it was, that it could have been anyone's."

"Or that I really had nothing to gain from murdering him," Jan said with a little of her earlier fervour. "Armstrong's death doesn't change anything. Many of the trees are long gone, and more are slated to fall. The man was just one worm in the wood."

We were silent for a few moments. Wanting to ease the pressure, I commented, "You have a beautiful home, Jan." I gestured to the photos above the wood stove. "Is that your son?" I asked.

Jan nodded, seemingly relieved at the distraction. "Yes," she said as she got up and walked over to the pictures. "It's a kind of memory wall for me."

I got up to look closer as she pointed them out. The first two were small shots of Jan and a young boy who looked into the camera with a calm and open but serious expression. In the next few shots, he was older, still unsmiling, but the same open, direct gaze met me in picture after picture.

A change occurred in the three pictures from college. There was the same sweet face, but added to it was a somewhat angry glare. I guess if I were to read into it from Jan's story, I would say that it had something to do with his work with Earth First! and his fight to protect the forest. His mother was not in the college shots, but a variety of other students appeared. It seemed that Jon was popular, ever in the centre of a mixed crowd of young men and women.

"Did Jon have any one special friend?" I asked.

Jan shook her head. "He said he didn't want to tie himself down or get too involved until he was finished his studies."

The largest picture on the wall was a fairly formal shot of a younger Mike Porter, along with Jon and some of his friends seated around a table in what looked like the patio of a restaurant. A couple of tables could be seen on the periphery of the shot, and flowers in hanging baskets filled in the upper edges of the picture frame. Mike explained that this was a group that had gathered at the conference where he had met Jon. They had all planned a dinner on the last night, and Mike had gone along because he had wanted to talk more with Jon about his research.

"Did you know any of the other people in the group?" I asked.

"No. I gathered that most were Jon's environmental group, but I think some were just his friends from school. He seemed to be easy with everyone, although I wasn't paying much attention. In fact, I think he and I might have been pretty rude, talking shop the whole time. A couple of young women seemed pretty attentive, not that he seemed to notice. Jon was very popular."

"It seems like he was a person to be very proud of," I said as we returned to our chairs.

"He was," Jan agreed. "As I said last night, I so regret not realizing it at the time. It's never easy, thinking about that, talking about it all. I loved him so much."

I cleared my throat. "I can only imagine how you feel. I have just a little of that feeling for my friend Anita. I came very close to losing her, too."

Jan nodded. "Yes, Sunny told me a little about her before the pot-luck. It sounded like a harrowing experience. I'm glad she's safe now."

"She's come a long way," I said slowly. "But that's just it. She had a shock when we got here. She saw someone who may have been involved in the murder back east. That's why I may be less than neutral in this investigation."

Jan looked worried. "What do you mean?"

"You have to keep this quiet," I said seriously. "I don't want to endanger Anita.

They all nodded.

"You see, Anita saw Brendon at the airport and is sure he was at the house the night of the murder in Kensington."

Jan drew in a sharp breath, and Mike held her hand tightly as I continued.

"Fortunately, Brendon didn't see her the day before yesterday, so he doesn't know she's here. He made conversation with Andy and me, but he doesn't know my full name, so hopefully he hasn't had cause to guess my identity. I think we're all safe for now, but you can see why I would be suspicious of him in this murder. He is much more likely to be violent than you are, Jan. If he *did* have anything to do with this, the sooner I can prove it, the sooner he gets put away and Anita can be safe."

"Oh, my dear," Jan said worriedly. "Please be careful. This could be dangerous for you, too."

"Believe me," I said, "I will be very careful, and I am determined to keep Anita safe." I looked at Jan. "I hope I can be successful in helping you for all our sakes. Ordinarily, I wouldn't have shared this, but I felt it was important to let you know why I'm so determined to clear this up."

Glancing at a small clock on a coffee table, I noticed that some time had passed and wondered why I hadn't heard from Andy. "Jan, do you have a phone I can use? I want to call Sunny and make sure everything is okay. It isn't like Andy to forget to call if he says he will."

"Oh!" Uta said, jumping up. "We turned the phones off. They'd been ringing all morning, mostly the press with endless questions." Uta plugged one back in, and I quickly dialled Sunny.

"Sunny's," he drawled.

"Hey, Sun, it's Abby calling. Have you heard from Andy?"

"Why sure, Abby. He's right here telling me about your run-in with Mrs. Armstrong. Hold on a sec."

Andy came on the line. "Hi there, Ab. How are things over there?"

"I'm getting a few ideas," I said quietly. "Nothing conclusive. I'm glad Jan has Mike's support," I said thoughtfully, "although he is a bit restless. Maybe it's just that he feels so helpless witnessing her pain. Anyway, Andy, how did you do?"

"Well, I dropped the old lady at her friend's place. I made sure she was well settled, and then I called a taxi to get over here to call you, only I couldn't get through. I was about to get Sunny to drive me back over there. Do you think that you'll be ready?"

"It's okay, thanks. I don't like to drive, but I can make my way back on my own. Otherwise, it's too much of a bother for you guys. Thanks for stepping into the breach like that. You diffused the situation nicely."

"I was happy to help," he said simply. "Oh, and Abby," he added, "Sunny said to tell you that Anita called. She said she'll be fine and will leave messages at the lodge and at Sunny's if there is a problem."

"That's a relief. Actually, Andy, do you mind hanging in there for now? Jan seems pretty worn out. I'll leave here soon and swing by Sunny's to meet up with you. Maybe we'll have time to check out the murder site, if we can get in there."

"Never a dull moment, Ab," he said lightly.

"I'll see you soon," I said and rang off.

Unplugging the phone, I turned back to the quiet threesome. Mike held Jan close, while Uta cleared her throat and started collecting the tea items. I was happy for something to do, and helped her carry stuff to the kitchen counter.

Mike came into the kitchen with the last two cups, and I asked, "Do you think she's going to be okay? Do you want Andy to come back to see her?"

"No, no," said Mike. "I'm sure that's not necessary. She's pretty strong and usually pretty gutsy." He smiled proudly. "You should have seen her in the meetings fighting Armstrong and his cronies. She can be fierce. Sometimes I even wonder if she overdoes it a little in Jon's memory, but in terms of passion and values, she's right on." He leaned towards me and lowered his voice a little. "We'll be okay if we can just get this murder charge out of the way and start rebuilding our lives. In a way, it's a relief that that man is dead. He was a torment to Jan."

"Well, on that note, I think I'll get going. One last question though, Mike. Is there anyone, anyone at all, who comes to mind when you think of who might be responsible for this killing? Someone else who fights for the cause, perhaps?"

He looked doubtful. "I don't want to put anyone else through the mill, so to speak," he said.

"No, that's not my idea," I said. "I'm not a cop. I'm not interested in prosecuting anyone. I'm just trying to get a better picture of the scene here. Murder is so often a passionate crime, and it seems like tempers are high on this logging issue. I'm not a seasoned investigator. I still have to ask a lot of questions and look around some more. I can't even guarantee success."

"Oh, well, if you put it that way, I can think of one person who could seem a little more than headstrong — a young fellow in our group, a bit of a maverick. Jan thinks he's great. Hold on a sec." He turned to the nearby phone table and opened one of those old metal phone pads with a metal clasp and a little arrow on the side indicating the letters. He quickly jotted on a scrap of paper and handed it to me.

I thanked Mike and shoved it into my jeans pocket. "I'll head out this way," I said, pointing at the back door. "Thank Jan for me, will you Mike? I'll be in touch soon. If anything else comes up, could you leave a message at the lodge or with Sunny? We'll check with him regularly."

"Will do, Abby. Thanks for offering to help." I shook hands with Mike, waved to Uta and made the trek back to the car.

Chapter 13

I DROVE SLOWLY, carefully and tensely back to Sunny's place. Fortunately, I did not encounter any logging trucks, and the couple of cars behind me were very patient until we reached pavement, at which point they quickly zoomed by. When I finally bumped my way down Sunny's drive, my two friends were sitting side by side on a little bench outside the bike shop holding steaming mugs in their hands.

"Well, you two seem to be having a lovely time out here," I said as I walked up to them.

They both smiled, and Sunny said, "Andy here helped me in the shop while he filled me in on your exciting day. Then we thought we'd just wait right here for you to give us a further update."

"There's not much to tell I'm afraid, Sunny. I'm still just gathering information. I don't think Jan did it, but that's not really news. But there are a few more things I'd like to work on today, so I'll forgo asking you for one of those cups of coffee and just take Andy away. That is," I said, turning to Andy, "if you can tear yourself away from the scent of bike grease, my friend."

"Sure thing, Abby," he said agreeably. "Sunny was just telling me he has another engagement for tonight. A Trails Committee meeting, isn't that what you said, Sunny?"

"That's right, Andy," Sunny said as we began walking to the car. "Some of the locals keep the trails in good shape on the island. We meet regularly to discuss fundraising for materials, new trails that we might try to build and which trails need repair. It will be good to meet tonight. It might keep my mind off Jan's problem, if we don't just spend the whole time gossipin'."

"Well, Sunny, try not to worry. I'm going to keep at it, but you never know, things might just unfold naturally and the police will probably lay off Jan." I patted my friend on his broad back and gave him a little hug.

"Thanks, Ab, for all yer tryin' to do. You two have a good time later," he said, winking as he waved us off.

"What did he mean by that?" I asked Andy as he drove. "What have you got up your sleeve?"

"Well," he said, "I thought it might be fun to try a different place for dinner. There isn't much choice here, but Sunny told me that the other local lodge is good. It has a passable sushi bar, he says, and great seafood."

"Sounds great, Andy! I haven't had much but tea and coffee today. I'll be famished by night. But you can't keep paying for all this luxury. Let's split the bill. I'm feeling guilty about all this. I'm not proving to be a great holiday companion."

He smiled. "I'm beginning to see that, Ab. But it's not like I haven't been warned. Let's just have fun for now and let the future take care of itself."

"You are a fine human being, Andy. It might not be me, but you're going to make someone very happy someday soon." I squeezed his hand.

He took his hand away gently. "Let's not go there just now, Ab."

Subdued, I nodded apologetically, and he changed the subject. "How about we see if Anita wants to come along. She might be tired of trail mix by now, and that way, we can keep an eye on her."

"Listen, Andy. I know I'm pushing it here, but can you do me yet another favour and drop me by the logging site before you go talk to Anita? That would give me enough time to poke around, see if anyone wants to answer any questions, without pressuring you to participate too much in my snooping."

"How about this instead?" he said, his good humour already restored. "We just stop here," he gestured to a little grocery store, one of the two on the island, "and call to leave a message at the camp office. I noticed when we dropped her off last time that there was a message board, and I suggested to Anita that she might want to check it every so often in case we need to get in touch with her. We even set up a code name so we wouldn't be bandying hers about."

"Boy, Andy," I said, marvelling at his presence of mind for the second time that day. "I suppose you know the number, too."

"Yep. Right here," he said, flipping a brochure from behind his visor. "I'll just be a sec," he said as he pulled up and jumped out of the car. We had already figured out that cellphone reception was poor on most of the island, so Andy dialled at the handy pay phone. I decided to check out the store for a little snack to tide me over to dinner. This time the ice cream cooler caught my eye. I bought two ice cream bars, nice, sedate vanilla with chocolate coating, and emerged into the still-blinding sunlight. Andy was already in the car and took the ice cream I offered.

"Okay, we're all set," he said as he unwrapped his confection. "Anita happened to be in the office buying shower tokens, so I talked to her directly. She'll meet us at the Beakpoint Lodge at 7:00, so we have two and a half hours to visit the site, get back to our place for a shower and get to the restaurant."

"I am in your debt, Sir!" I said, saluting. "Drive on!"

From the road it was pretty hard to tell where the site was. I had learned from Jan that there are few real rules in private logging, but the logging companies often leave a few rows of trees at the roadside to hide the scars of a clear-cut. Fortunately, we knew where the new logging road was from Mike's directions. An additional "clue" was a long line of yellow police tape strung across the road opening.

We stopped a little way down the road where a path led into the forest. My plan was to hike in from the side of the road and to feign tourist ignorance if questioned by anyone as we poked around. Andy agreed to come along to complete the picture and to keep me from getting carried away if I got caught up in the moment.

We found a well-used trail. Apparently, the local forests, public and even some private, are used pretty freely for hiking and biking on the island. It was cool and quiet in there after the rumble of the road. The forest floor was fairly open, consisting of pine needles, dead branches and tall ferns. Majestic firs rose around us. To me, an Easterner, the tremendous size of the trees was staggering. There was nothing like this around Toronto, and these, we had been told, were mostly second growth. Peregrine had been logged twice completely in some areas, early in its settled history.

The cathedral canopy of green above us allowed in only a bit of filtered light, and we trod quietly, muting any conversation. It was easy to see how some people became protective of the trees. Bright yellow tape was tied around the trunks of many that we passed. I wondered if this identified which trees were to come down. I already found myself, a newbie, grieving for their probable demise. After walking for about ten minutes or so, we emerged into a clearing of fresh stumps, which was obviously the site we were looking for.

The scent of cut wood and diesel fuel still lingered in the air as we walked along deep, wide tire tracks past formerly gracious trees, now just sticks piled in pyramids. One dormant logging truck half-filled with wood was parked near another truck with a kind of crane on it and big pincers on the end of a chain. A little farther off to one side of the clearing was a blue and white mobile-office trailer mounted on cinderblocks, and on the other side, on a slight incline, was evidence of the most recent cutting. A mini-bulldozer sat stationary at the edge of the cut, and more yellow police tape surrounded piles of brush lying beside a number of fallen trees.

It remained quiet in the clearing, but a light in the trailer and a red pickup truck parked in front of it suggested that someone might be around. We proceeded blithely to the most interesting spot before anyone could stop us. We held hands, which Andy had suggested would complete our disguise as dense tourists, oblivious to property in our deeply-in-love state.

We made it across the clearing without incident, and I looked around for anything out of the ordinary. To the side of the dozer were a few metal gas cans and some rags. I leaned over for a better look.

The rags were dry. The top one had a fresh tear. I was about to mention this to Andy, who was politely holding his tongue, when I was startled by a man's voice.

"What do you think you're doing here? This is private property!"

Caught in the act, I tried not to look as guilty as I felt. As I straightened up, the frayed cloth still in my hand, I turned towards the voice.

Think up a lie quick, I thought to myself as I looked at a burly, bearded man. I was grateful that it wasn't Brendon guarding the fort.

"Oh, excuse us," I gushed in my most un-Abby-like voice. "We were just walking through the forest, looking for mushrooms, when we came across this clearing. I'm so sorry if we're trespassing, but I thought I saw a special mushroom at one side of your pile here," I said, pointing down, "only it turned out to be this bit of fabric." I handed him the triangle of frayed golden cloth, marked with what looked like a black design.

"Well," said the man severely as he looked at the cloth and then let it drop back to the pile. He looked around. "Hey! Did you move a bike from here?" he asked suspiciously.

We shook our heads.

He looked hard at us again and then said, "Nah, probably not. Who would want it with that wrecked wheel? Well, anyway, you *are* tampering with evidence, *and* you're trespassing. An accident occurred here today. Didn't you see the police tape?"

"Oh dear, is that what that was?" I asked brightly, feigning complete stupidity, something I hate to do. "We saw so many coloured ribbons on the trees in the forest; I just thought this was more of the same stuff. What *happened* here?" I asked innocently.

He seemed to relax, even though he kept glancing around looking puzzled. Maybe he had bought the idea that we were harmless tourists.

"Well," he said, "someone died here last night." He looked at us admonishingly. "A logging site can be a dangerous place. You should be careful where you walk on the island."

"How terrible. What happened?"

The man scratched his head. "I don't rightly think I should tell you too much, as the police are investigating. It happened right here, so you could be messing with a crime scene." He looked down and continued almost absently. "I just got back, took over from the cop who was parked out front. I guess he left before you stumbled in here." He looked up. "You didn't see him on the road?"

"No," I said, acting confused. "We parked down the road a ways and came through the woods. The forest just looked so pretty."

He shrugged. "Maybe the cops took it," he muttered to himself, and then he cleared his throat. "Well, you'd better get going. This isn't a safe place to be wandering around. If you leave that way," he said, pointing to the logging road that led out of the site, "you'll find your way back to where you started by following the main road."

I wondered whether to push him a bit to see what else he could tell us, but Andy masterfully interceded, putting his arm around me and drawing me close.

"I'm sorry, Sir. She gets so involved in what she's doing that she forgets herself. We'll take your advice. We have to get to dinner soon, anyway. We're so sorry to intrude. Goodbye," he said, hustling me towards the road.

I turned my head briefly as we walked away, and called out cheerily, "Bye." The bearded man just stared in our direction.

I thought about what the man had said about a bike, and had an alarming thought

"Andy!" I grabbed his arm. "I just realized something. That bike the guy mentioned, it might be the one at Sunny's. It has a wrecked wheel!" I felt a sense of urgency. "It could be evidence! We have to let Sunny know — tell him not to repair it, to call the police!"

Andy didn't seem to share my concern. "Don't worry, Ab. Sunny was finishing for the day when we left, and he hadn't got to it yet. You can call him as soon as we get to the lodge." We rounded a corner. "Look, there's the car. We'll be home in no time. Besides, it's a stretch to say a bike is a murder weapon. The man was strangled by prayer flags."

I relaxed. "Okay, Andy, but I'll feel better once I've gotten in touch with Sunny."

When we got back to the lodge, I was able to make the call and Sunny reassured me about the bike. Surprisingly, Andy and I still found the time to indulge in some brief before-dinner foreplay, which might have gone further, but the events of the day caught up with me and I drifted off into a pleasant dream in the midst of Andy's attentive ministrations. It's a good thing he had a sense of humour because this could have been considered very insulting. The first I knew of my lapse in etiquette was when he nudged me awake twenty minutes later.

"Better get up, sleeping beauty, if you want to have a shower before we go."

I blinked awake, feeling suddenly alert. There must be something to this power nap business. "Oh, Andy, I'm so embarrassed. I blew it, didn't I?"

"No problem, Abby," he said, laughing. "You're just getting a sense of the routine in the hospital: Sleep anytime there's a lull. You can make up for it later."

"That sounds like a plan," I said. I had a delicious cat stretch, gave him a quick kiss, and then, before things went too far, I sloped off to enjoy a boiling shower. I'm not the kind to need a cold shower. For me, all cares are eased, and ideas are stimulated, as hot water tap-dances my brain into a calm but alert state. Knowing I didn't have time to go over the case, I just let it all fall away for ten glorious minutes. With the combination of nap and shower, I emerged refreshed and ravenous.

I dressed very quickly. Choosing what to wear is easy for me unless I'm dressing for disguise. I have one wrinkle-proof, all-purpose dress that I pack for emergencies. Luckily, I had it with me, and while this was not an emergency, I decided it would be the appropriate costume for the night. That and some cheap but cute Japanese slippers I had purchased in Kensington Market, and I was ready to go.

I have to say this for Andy — he never seemed to care about my style, which most of the time runs to punk. As a matter of fact, today he was downright complimentary, if unrealistic.

"You look good enough to eat, Abby. Let's just dine on each other."

"Nice try, Andy, but I need other sustenance. I'm starving."

CHAPTER 14

BEAKPOINT LODGE IS at the tip of the beak on the map of Peregrine Island. To reach it, we had to wend our way down a heavily treed road that all but took the sun away. These lodges seem to make getting there part of the ritual, I thought, as we emerged from the womb-like tunnel to late afternoon sun in a clearing on the edge of the water. The lodge was long and rambling, an earlier vintage than the one we were staying in. Two sides of the building were surrounded by a floating terrace, while the main structure itself rested solidly on a large rock outcrop. From the small parking lot, we could see a scattering of cabins snuggled into the side of a hill behind the lodge, along a quiet inlet running back the way we had driven in.

On the main building was a sign announcing the celebrated dining room with an arrow pointing to a door nearer the floating terrace. We entered one door and found ourselves in a panelled hall where the walls were adorned with huge salmon mounted onto plaques. On closer inspection, we saw that they were dated back to what presumably were the glory days of salmon fishing, before overfishing, stream devastation from logging, water pollution and climate change conspired to threaten the stocks. I had read in a brochure at our own lodge that sport fishing still takes place, but such large salmon are now a rarity.

At the end of the hall was a little reservation desk, and beyond that, a beautifully appointed dining room with white cloths, crystal goblets — the whole bit — along with exquisite floral arrangements, deep wood panelling and large picture windows. A young woman in a red floral-print dress greeted us brightly.

"Hi there," she said, smiling. "Can I help you?"

Andy smiled back, his doctor smile on half-burner. "Yes, thanks.

We have a reservation for Dr. Jaegar at 7:00. We're a little late, I'm afraid."

"No problem," she said. "We have your table ready. Your other party just phoned to say that her cab was late, but she'll be here soon." The hostess picked up some leather-bound menus. "We have a nice table for you by the window."

We followed her through the restaurant, past a table laden with mouth-watering desserts, including cakes, fruit, pies and squares. I was so busy rubbernecking the table as we walked by that I almost walked right into Andy when he stopped. I readjusted my head forwards and found myself at our table. It was all so perfect, until I looked out the window.

Across the channel was the stinking pulp mill we had smelled several times already. Gross, I thought. Here we sit in a beautiful spot, only to have *that* fill our view. I averted my eyes, determined to behave, and sat down, proud of myself for keeping my mouth shut.

"Someone will be by shortly to see if you would like anything while you're waiting," the young woman said before she left.

I settled down to read the menu but had not gotten far in my second-favourite investigation — what to eat — when Anita arrived.

"Hello, you," I heard Andy say, and when I looked up, he had his full-burner, melt-in-your-mouth smile on for Anita.

She slid in beside me.

"Anita, you look great," I said. "The island is agreeing with you."

She looked relaxed, suntanned and happy. The short time she had been away from the grime and pollution of the city was already doing her good. I was grateful that she hadn't let the shock of seeing Brendon spoil her vacation.

Anita nodded happily as she turned to me.

"Abby, I can't believe it. You've been here two days, and you're already all involved investigating a murder. Sunny told me about it when I phoned. Thanks for the warnings about Brendon, by the way," she said breezily. "I'm hoping he might not recognize me if I come across him out here. And this time I'll be prepared so I won't freeze up ... I hope. So, are you going to give me the lowdown?"

I felt a little uncomfortable — eager to discuss the case, but not wanting to bother Andy — so I put her off by saying gently, "Maybe later. Andy and I have made a deal to relax this evening, and besides, I don't know much yet."

"Well," Anita said, "if you need my help, let me know."

"Thanks, Anita, but I'm happy if you stay safe and enjoy yourself."

Just then another young waitress, this time in a blue floral dress, arrived at our table to inquire about drinks. I ordered my restaurant treat, a Brandy Alexander, while Andy and Anita decided to start right in with an organic Chardonnay. Andy ordered some mineral water as well, to keep us from floating too far on the alcohol, as he put it. Since he was driving, he said, he was the one who would have to go easy.

Discussion turned to what we would order, which required some serious negotiation since I wanted to try everything. Fortunately, my friends were of similar mind, so we agreed that we would happily sample each other's food. Appetizers were easy — we decided to have sushi first: California rolls, salmon rolls and freshwater eel. Then, because we were excited by all the variety, we ordered a sampling platter of roasted vegetables with a splash of balsamic vinaigrette. Our appetizers would be followed by a lime and avocado sorbet to cleanse the palate, so that we could tackle fresh hickory-smoked wild salmon fillet, Alaska king crabs, local prawns in garlic and a large Caesar salad. It was a good thing I was hungry.

Once the business of planning our meal was out of the way, we sat back and enjoyed each other's company. Anita regaled us with tales of the campground. She was evidently enjoying her "neighbours." On one side was a couple from Manitoba, and on the other, a family from Oregon. Anita, naturally, had made friends with the young children in the family and was having fun exploring with them.

She loves children, and her tales of their antics made for easy dinner talk and kept our minds off the murder, though I have to admit that I wasn't always listening. At one point, my mind wandered back to the logging site we had visited. I hoped the police would let me be there if they decided to look over the bike. I'd asked Sunny to ask when he called them.

When our food began to arrive, I shook my head clear and focused on being fully present. As for quality, we were not disappointed.

Everything was beautifully presented and delicious. Portions were generous, so there was lots to share, to my satisfaction. I helped Andy and Anita with the wine, which disappeared all too quickly.

"Well," I said, "you wouldn't suffer nutritionally living on this island, if you had the money."

"I'll drink to that," said Andy. "A man I met today said that in the old days, you could eat well even when you were poor. He said they could live on venison, salmon, mushrooms and berries."

"That sounds sort of romantic in a rustic way, Andy, but what I could really use right now is a cup of roasted, ground, foreign coffee berries." I was about to follow this suggestion with a comment on the overloaded dessert table with my name on it when the sedate calm of the dining room was disrupted by the arrival of a noisy group of young men.

A few were obviously more than a little drunk, their voices unnaturally loud and boisterous. We watched as the leader of the group pushed his way into the lounge area and motioned for his buddies to join him at the one free table. I was about to comment on how boorish he was and what an inappropriate place for them to be in their condition, when recognition dawned.

"Oh no, it's Brendon again! He doesn't seem to be in mourning, does he?"

"No," said Andy soberly.

"Unless he's drowning his sorrows in booze," Anita said quietly, shrinking against my shoulder.

The group didn't seem interested in us, anyway, but Anita's reaction belied her previous calm statement. I felt the tendrils of worry creeping over me again.

"Some of his friends seem to be a little strung out, too," Anita remarked.

My antennae perked up immediately. "What do you mean?"

"I meant to mention it earlier," she continued unhappily, "but I didn't want to spoil the mood. A few people at the campground are using. I'm pretty familiar with the signs, you know. It's the one thing I've been a little uncomfortable about. The last thing I need is to be surrounded by junkies."

She was right. Anita had fought hard to overcome her own addiction and was justifiably terrified of falling back. I felt terrible that even here, on an island far from downtown Toronto, she had to deal with it.

"Oh, Anita, I'm so sorry. I hope that the dealers don't come to the campground."

"I don't think so," she said, smiling weakly. "I mentioned what I noticed to the woman who runs the place, and she quietly told me that there is an active trade in heroin over there," she said, nodding her head at the town across the channel. "Partly because of the port, I guess."

Our attention was drawn to the group again. Brendon's voice rose in slurred indignation as a hefty bartender stood implacably in front of him.

"What do you mean, you won't serve us? Who do you think you are dealing with? I could have you all fired. Now bring my friends what they want," he said with a mixture of whine and menace. As the bartender stood his ground, an impeccably dressed, harried-looking man, probably the hotel manager, rushed up and spoke in a low voice to young Brendon Armstrong.

By now, everyone in the restaurant was watching the exchange, something that seemed to dawn on Brendon's nearest friend, who I recognized as the same person who had cooled him out on the bike trail the day before. He got up and helped the manager calm Brendon down. A few minutes later, Brendon shrugged and walked away with the manager, while the peacemaker beckoned the now silent but jumpy party to go along.

"Wow," I said after they left. "That was impressive. I wonder how they got him to go without a scene. He seemed pretty belligerent." The pretty red-print hostess arrived at that moment with a tray of small wine glasses.

"This late-harvest wine is a gift from the manager," she said sweetly, "by way of apology for the disturbance."

"Well, thanks," said Andy. "Can you tell us how peace was restored so quickly? That young man looked like he was going to be difficult."

"Well," she said, "Mr. Lapointe, the manager, offered them a private cabin to continue the party, with complimentary bar service. He will take him to our most remote cabin so as not to disturb the other guests. We have dealt with Mr. Armstrong before. He tends to settle down after a while. Mr. Lapointe will make sure that car keys are removed so that no one will leave before sleeping off their night's energy."

"Very diplomatic," I said. "Why not just throw him out?"

She was obviously a little embarrassed to explain to strangers that the little brute was spoiled but influential. "His family is well known. We make every effort to make all our guests comfortable. That's why Mr. Lapointe wanted us to offer you these drinks to leave you with a more pleasant memory of your dining experience."

What a job, I thought, to have to constantly please everyone. I would be a lousy waitress or hotel employee. They would have to keep me behind the scenes in the kitchen, but there I would just eat up the profits.

"Would you care for anything else?" she asked.

I looked at Anita. She was pretty agitated, so I decided that I would have to forgo the sweets. I shook my head sadly, so Andy answered her. "No thanks, just the bill when you have a chance." She nodded and left the table. We sipped the sweet, cold wine slowly, our party dampened by the events of the night. The Armstrong clan had a far-reaching influence on life on Peregrine Island.

Drinks done and bill paid, we soon left the celebrated Beakpoint Lodge, fully fed but not entirely happy. We took Anita home to her campground, and before we left her, she gave me a hug and told me not to worry.

"That's a tall order, Anita, but I'll do my best if you promise to keep yourself safe." We hugged again, and then Andy ferried me back to our little haven.

It was late for that place, but a little bar was still open, so we stopped in to share a quick coffee. It put me into temporary hyper drive, a helpful jolt of energy after a very long day.

I was determined to banish the Armstrong family from my brain for a short while at least, and what better way than to indulge in some friendly physical exercise. Much to our mutual relief, I was wide-eyed and frisky to the end, at which point I gave Andy one last lusty kiss and passed out into a very deep exhaustion and wine-induced sleep.

CHAPTER 15

SUNNY CALLED AT around 7:30 in the morning to tell me the police would be by at 9:00 to check over the bike, so Andy and I settled for a short, light breakfast in bed, read the paper and primed ourselves with coffee. The death of our friend Armstrong, a small player on the international logging scene, merited a grand total of twenty-five words far back in the section of the national paper labelled "Around Canada Today."

"I'll have to find the local papers and see what their take is on all this," I said absently to Andy. "Hey," I said, "I have an idea. After we're done at Sunny's, why don't we drop in on Mabel Armstrong and see how she's doing. I can go along as your friend and maybe sniff around surreptitiously. I need to find out more about that family if I can."

"I suppose I can do that," he said agreeably. "Her friend's place is near here. It might seem natural enough for a doctor to check how she's doing, although I'm sure she has her own medical care."

"I have another idea," I said brightly. "Let's go on our bikes. It'll be even better to drop in, as if we were on a ride, you know, still on holiday. Besides, it would be good to have a ride. We missed out yesterday."

The idea of the ride made Andy happy.

"Done," he said.

Energized, he hopped out of bed, almost knocking over my remaining hit of coffee, which rested on the blankets. "Let's get organized."

"Hold on, bud. I need a quick cleanup," I said. "You get the bikes ready. We'll ride them over to Sunny's. Give me five minutes, and I'll be with you."

I washed and brushed quickly, and dressed in my most conservative bike suit of black shorts and a black and blue shirt, both gifts from the surgeon before we left on the trip. I dispensed with my nose rings and most of my earrings, and wet my hair to subdue the green streaks on the side. I was by Andy's side in the parking lot in eight minutes.

"How do you like my disguise?" I asked.

"Perfect," he said, kissing my nose. "You look just like a doctor's paramour, and," he added, noting my glower, "a sleek lady detective."

He gave me a chaste kiss, and we hopped on our bikes, carefully avoiding the roughest of the gravel as we sped along. A police car was already parked on the road outside Sunny's. We dismounted and walked in to save our butts from the bumps.

"I hope they haven't started without us," I fretted, wanting to be in on the event and prove myself.

Sunny was sitting on his bench alongside a stereotypically clean-cut, chisel-jawed Mountie, maybe thirty-five to forty years old. Both men held cups of steaming coffee. They stood as we rounded the corner.

"Hey, there," I called out as Andy and I leaned our bikes against the shop wall.

I walked forward, arm outstretched, to shake the officer's hand.

"I'm Abby Faria. I'm pleased to meet you."

He nodded almost imperceptibly. "Hello, I'm George Faraday. I understand that you found a bike that you *think* might be connected to the Armstrong murder." He looked doubtful.

"Not exactly," I said.

He raised his eyebrows.

"I mean, I didn't find it. Brendon Armstrong brought it to Sunny."

"I did mention that to the dispatcher," Sunny intervened. "There must have been some miscommunication. I just said that Abby thought it might be evidence, and she didn't want me to work on it if it is connected to the murder."

Officer Faraday nodded and looked at me appraisingly.

"So, what makes you think this bike is evidence?"

"Well," I said carefully. "Jan Field asked me to help out, and I have some limited investigating experience, so I agreed. Yesterday, I had a very short chat with the watchman from the logging site. He was circumspect, but he did mention, inadvertently, that a bike was missing from the site. He thought the police might have taken it."

"I see," he said sternly. "You know it wasn't appropriate for you to go there. It's a closed investigation site. We could charge you with obstructing justice, not to mention the fact that you should know better."

I began to squirm, knowing he was right, but feeling rebellious.

Fortunately, he relented, smiling thinly, now that he had asserted his position. "But, as you're a friend of Sunny's, we'll move on for now, shall we? As it happens, we did not collect the bike from the site. What makes you think that this might be the one?"

Sunny piped up. "Brendon brought it over very early yesterday. He seemed anxious to have it fixed right away."

The cop just looked at me again, somewhat speculatively.

"And what do you have against the Armstrongs, Ms. Faria?"

Was the man psychic or was I that transparent? I decided to be very cool.

"Me? Nothing. I'm a stranger here. I just offered to help Ms. Field."

He didn't seem satisfied. "Perhaps she shared her feelings with you. We all know that there was no love lost between her and Jack Armstrong."

I felt defensive again. "That's true, but is that enough to accuse her of murder? Look," I said, "I'm just trying to help."

Silently I wondered, why the third degree? I decided that, as is often the case, the police didn't like people interfering in their investigations.

He didn't seem overly satisfied with my response, but finally he nodded.

"Well, let's get to it, then," he said to Sunny. "Where's this bike?"

Sunny brought out the bike and set it up on the repair stand. We all crowded around. It was muddy, though not unusually so for a mountain bike. But it had been relatively dry the day before, despite the storm. The mud was heavier on the mangled front end, as if it had been ground into something. And the mud was a medley of two tones — flat grey-brown and rusty red-brown. It was caked on and held some twigs, pine needles and other detritus.

Faraday pulled out a clear evidence bag, and taking one of Sunny's tools, flaked a fair amount of the stuff into the bag.

"We'll look at this later," he said, setting the bag aside.

We looked at the bend in the wheel next. Usually, wheels that have been tacoed are pretzel-like, but this one was unusual. It groaned in pain. It looked as if an axe had chopped at it, making a sharp, clear bend; sacrilege to such a quality rim. The tire was gashed and flat, and the rubber hung loosely.

"What do you say, guys?" I piped up. "Weird bike wound, don't you think?" They nodded their heads. "Looks like someone didn't like it and took an axe to it. Sunny, did Brendon look injured at all when he dropped it off? If this bike had been in an accident, wouldn't he have been hurt?"

"You'd think so," he said. "Seems strange that the rest of the thing isn't banged up."

"Well," I said, shaking my head sadly, "the wheel's a write-off, anyway. Have you got another to replace it?"

He nodded. "Yeah, but it's not quite as good. I'm sure Brendon will complain loudly. I'm not even sure why he came here to get it fixed. He usually deals with the big shop in town."

"Hmm," I said, looking at the officer, who was busy scribbling. "I guess he was in a hurry or maybe he's staying on the island or, if you have a suspicious mind like mine, you might wonder if he's hiding something. You're sure he didn't seem upset or subdued or in any way different?" I asked Sunny.

"Abby, I don't know the guy that well. He always seems the same to me. He certainly didn't seem remorseful, if that's what you mean."

We continued our examination of the bike. The forks had escaped serious damage, miraculously. The paint was scraped, but the metal was still straight. The handlebars were askew, but apart from some scratches and a lot of mud on one side, they were okay. In fact, other than the obvious write-off of a wheel, the bike still could sing again.

We were about to leave it when Andy said, "Hold on. What's this?" He was poking at something caught in the chain. Even Faraday showed interest. Sunny handed Andy pliers from his toolbox, and Andy gently worked a scrap of muddy, greasy cloth from between the chain and gears. The officer readily supplied another bag, and Andy dropped the fragment into it. We all looked at it together as I held up the bag.

"What do you think, Sunny?"

"Can't really tell, Abby. Just looks like a scrap to me."

We sat back for a minute. "Well, that's it for the bike." Sunny sighed.

"Maybe we should look at the first bag of mud more carefully," Faraday said.

Sunny spread open a newspaper, and Faraday dumped the bag. Taking a screwdriver and a pair of tweezers from Sunny's workbench, he poked apart the clump.

"Check that out," I said excitedly.

They all peered closer.

"See there?" I pointed. "Those flecks of red and turquoise look like paint chips or something. Maybe whatever hit the bike wheel got scraped and left this residue."

Faraday harrumphed and looked at his watch.

"Okay, that was helpful," he said somewhat grudgingly. "Well done. Now, if you could just let me dump that stuff back in the baggie for the lab, I'll be on my way. I have to get back to the station. And Sunny," he said apologetically, "I'll have to take the bike, too."

"I'm happy to get rid of it," Sun replied.

Faraday mused, "Everything is still very circumstantial, but perhaps the boys at the station will have a chat with Brendon Armstrong — see if he'll cough up anything. But this doesn't change anything for your friend Jan Field," he said severely, looking at me.

"At least he shared that much," I said as George Faraday walked away with his loot. "He's a bit taciturn, isn't he?"

"Oh, George is okay," Sunny said. "It's hard for those guys — the RCMP keeps moving them every few years. They never get a chance to get connected with a community, and eventually they lose interest in tryin'. He's probably a bit out of his depth with this one. We usually only have drunk drivers and pot plantations to cope with, but," he mused with a frown, "civilization is encroaching. Now, what do you think he meant about the bike not helping Jan?"

I had an inkling, but as I was still working on the details, I only shook my head.

We sat glumly for a few quiet minutes, and then Andy perked up.

"Okay, Ab. Are we still on for that ride? We have a couple of hours till lunch. I don't want to waste the day."

"Fair enough," I said as I stretched. "Besides, we get to mix business and pleasure." Sunny looked up questioningly, so I explained. "Andy and I are going to check up on Mabel Armstrong," I said with a wink, "to see how she's doing."

"Ah," he said, comprehending our purpose. "Well, have a great day, kids. I have a shop to run."

Chapter 16

IT WAS WARM and sunny, almost hot, but fortunately, the road remained shaded by the unending column of firs. We rode up and down and around, enough to make the route interesting and challenging. The first thing we learned to do was to pull aside for logging trucks and the larger pickups, and once, a barking dog emerged from a hidden drive and I practically broke my neck trying not to run it over. An inch closer and I would have had to risk foregoing island etiquette by batting it solidly in the jaw as I sped past, a courier survival trick reserved for annoying animals and cars that get too close. All in the interest of the recipient's own safety, of course, though I wasn't about to try it on a logging truck.

Andy slowed to a stop in front of a more substantial paved driveway with wrought-iron gates that stood open. A woman astride a riding lawn mower was working on a large expanse of manicured lawn, adorned with clusters of ferns, a large circular bed of flowers and two towering maple trees. The palatial home, with its commanding Greek columns and large outer staircase, seemed more fitting for a Southern estate in Georgia than for woodsy Peregrine. We rode in and left our bikes leaning against one of the trees. As Andy led the way up the stairs, I felt like I should be dressed like Scarlett O'Hara.

A sporty middle-aged woman in tennis clothes answered our meek knock. I wondered idly where the courts were. "Oh, hello," she said, before we could say anything. "You're the kind doctor who helped poor Mabel yesterday. Come in. Come in."

Inside, the place looked homey, more fitting to the woman's hospitable nature. She turned to me. "I'm Mabel's friend Angie Middleton. Would you like some iced tea?" she asked, not once enquiring as to the

nature of our visit or who I was. She led us through a hall, to the opposite side of the house. We entered a large, bright kitchen with a wall of
glass doors that opened onto a deck, which appeared to run the length
of the house. The view took my breath away. The property was perched
on a promontory that afforded a view south down the Strait of Georgia
and to both the east and west. Terraced lawns broke up the steep drop
where, sure enough, down below, I saw the tennis courts. Far down at
the bottom was a rocky beach, and then the glistening water.

Andy was doing well explaining that we had come to see how
Mrs. Armstrong was today, but all I could think to say was, "You
have a lovely home, Angie."

"How sweet of you, dear," she said prettily. "But I'm afraid you've
come all this way for nothing," she said to Andy. "Mabel left for
home with her son on the 9:00 ferry. She seemed a little rocky, what
with the shock and all, and she has a lot to sort out now, but I'm sure
she'll be all right. Her daughter seems to know the business pretty
well. She was always her daddy's protégé. I try to stay out of all this
controversy about logging, but really, you'd think people would be
happy that the Armstrongs keep the economy afloat."

Andy squeezed my hand tightly, physically warning away my
likely retort. I wondered silently if everyone on this island was so
loquacious.

Angie continued speaking. "I'm sure Mabel would love to see you
again. She seemed quite taken with your support yesterday. We could
use a friendly young doctor around here," she said, practically batting her eyelids.

Andy had that effect on women. Even I, with my critical nature,
was initially wooed by his good looks and bedside manner. If he
wasn't so ethical, he would be a good detective around vulnerable
women, I thought.

She turned to me. "If you like my house, you'll *love* Mabel's. They
have a home on the bluff there." She pointed at the south end of
Bellweather. "The view at night is marvellous. You almost feel like
you can reach out and touch the cruise ships as they go by. Here,"
she said, "I'll just write down their phone number and address in case
you decide to go over."

"As a matter of fact," Andy said, "we were thinking of taking a look at the town. I'm really a surgeon, and I thought I might visit the hospital." My eyes widened. Andy was usually such a bad liar. Angie didn't notice my reaction — she was too busy being delighted.

"Oh, how wonderful! Won't Mabel be thrilled!"

She poured iced tea from a handy glass pitcher set on the little table, as if it had been waiting for us. "I see that you rode over on your bikes. That's hot work," she said, handing us each a tall glass. "My son Alex is an active cyclist," she continued conversationally. "He spends a lot of time with Mabel's son. They have some sort of business venture together." My ears picked up at this. What was Brendon up to, aside from making a profession of being obnoxious?

At that moment, a voice called, "Mom! I'm all set. I have to be on the twelve o'clock, though, so we should start soon. He's —"

A familiar young man similarly attired in tennis gear had stepped onto the deck from the stairs to the side. "Oh, I'm sorry. I didn't know you had guests." His eyes narrowed when he turned his gaze to us. "Don't I know you?"

"We haven't met formally," said Andy, coming forward to shake his hand. "We just crossed your path on the trails two days ago, when we were riding." He didn't mention the altercation at Beakpoint the night before.

"Oh, yes," he said, shifting awkwardly.

"How nice. You've met," Angie said, smiling. "I was just saying to these nice people, dear, that you share their interest in riding."

"What are you doing here?" Not waiting for an answer, he turned to his mother. "How do you know these people? I thought they were just tourists. This is not a bike trail."

"Why, Alex," said his mother with mild reproof. "Dr. Jaegar is the fellow who brought Mabel here yesterday. She was up at the north end, distraught about Jack's death."

Alex's clearly suspicious mind made a natural connection that his mother's had not. "You mean when she was confronting that environmentalist Jan Field? I'm sure it was very nice of the doctor to bring her back here, but what was he doing there in the first place?" He turned back to Andy. "What's your connection with *those* people?"

I didn't like where this was going, so I decided it was time to intervene before his mother got thinking too hard about his question.

"Yes, well, we were just checking the trails out when we drove by all those cars up there. Mrs. Armstrong's ... um ... outburst was hard to just drive by, seeing as Andy's a doctor. So the long and the short of it is that Andy offered to help, and drove her car to your place." I put down the half-finished iced tea. "We don't want to keep you from your tennis game or impose any longer. Thank you so much for the drink, Mrs. Middleton. I'm glad to hear that Mrs. Armstrong is feeling a little better."

I put my arm through Andy's. He nodded in agreement. "It was nice to meet you formally," he said, shaking Alex's reluctant hand. Angie walked us to the door. "Thank you again for coming, and do check out the town. We need successful professionals here." She smiled, holding Andy's hand a little longer than necessary, and then we sidled away.

We gave a little wave to Angie, and I whispered to Andy before we rode off, "Give me a little kiss, bud, in case the anxious lad is watching. Maybe he'll buy the innocent tourist story."

"Happy to oblige," he said, pulling me closer. While I was astride my bike, he planted an overly convincing kiss on my lips. I obliged in turn, to add realism, of course.

CHAPTER 17

WE RODE HARD and fast, concentrating to avoid logging trucks on the main roads, and arrived back at the lodge in time for lunch. I have a different biological time clock from most women — it goes off at mealtimes, which makes it more frequently pressing but easier to heed than the kind that signals the need to produce offspring.

The mellow coastal air must have been affecting my personality, because I was unusually content to follow Andy's lead. Today he suggested lunch, and I agreed. We ordered the same thing, and I waited, fairly patiently for me, for him to suggest we take a little trip to Bellweather to check out a trail or two and *maybe* drop in on the suffering Mrs. Armstrong. Sure enough, about five minutes later, Andy came out with the suggestion.

"Great idea, Andy," I said. "Perhaps you should consider a change in career, though investigating isn't very lucrative." He smiled as he dug into his salmon pâté and garden salad. "How will we find out about the trails over there?" I asked.

"I saw an info booth near the ferry when we arrived," he replied. "We can check in there. We won't have time to go far into Bellweather or beyond, so we'll have to pick something easily accessible. Do you want to ride over on our bikes or in the car?"

"Let's stick to bikes. Cars make me nervous, and we already used our carbon quota for a very long time on the flight to B.C."

He nodded as he sniffed the air. "It looks like we're in luck. The wind is blowing from the south, so we'll be able to breathe over there."

"It's easy to forget about that mill when you can't see it or smell it," I said. "So," I continued, making a quick topic change, "what did you think about Alex? Did he believe a word we said?"

"Hard to say," Andy responded. "He's a lot less hot-headed than Brendon, but perhaps more dangerous. He seemed to have brains *and* a suspicious mind."

"Yes, I noticed that, too. His mother said the two guys were in business together. What kind, do you think?"

"I'm not sure, but drugs come to mind, of course, especially after what Anita said last night, and Sunny said something the other day about charges, didn't he?"

We finished our lunch with the required local coffee and berries, and then I reminded Andy, "It's 12:30. If we want to catch the 1:00 we'd better go now."

"You're right, I guess," he said. "I was just starting to feel nice and lazy. You're a tenacious and tough taskmaster, Abby."

"Hey! It was your idea," I reminded him with a grin.

The ride to the ferry was particularly fun because it was mostly downhill and we could really get up speed. I know that mountain bikers rave on about the challenge of the trails, the serenity of the forest and the healthy air, but for me, it's speed pure and simple that turns my crank. Andy told me that Sunny had mentioned a ride to the highest paved part of the island that was a pure scream going down. I had to try that before we left. Anyway, I was exhilarated and refreshed when, twenty minutes later, we came to a halt at the ferry dock.

The cars were just loading, so we had enough time to get some water at the little coffee stand by the dock. Fortunately, the mill's trusty plume of death was spewing northwards across the way, "misting" the inlets in that direction as far as the eye could see.

The ferry trip across was quite different from the first one only a few days before. Today it was passably calm, the breeze causing only a ripple on the ocean. We sat on the deck next to our bikes and watched the passage to the south. It was busy with sport fishing boats and pleasure craft scooting about, and a tug with a barge full of sawdust chugged along down the centre. It was idyllic but short, the brief ride ending with a bump as the ferry docked.

We collected a trail map for Bellweather and the surrounding area from the info booth, just a two-minute ride from the ferry.

Conveniently enough, there was a trail called The Ridge that came out near the Armstrong's. Their street appeared to be a continuation of the ridge that ran parallel to the coast, which explained the view that Angie had mentioned. The fact that it was a bit south of the majority of the town must have made it more valuable, as it was farther away from the hoi polloi and the driving stench of the mill.

The young woman in the info booth knew the area well. When we asked her about the trail, she said it was not difficult. "If you're looking for something more challenging," she volunteered, "there is a hot baby at the back of the town with lots of switchbacks, and a few rocks and logs to jump. It's my favourite for when I have a few hours free. There are loads of great trails at Andrews Park and up Mount Washington, but those take a little longer. You'll need sturdier bikes for most of the trails. You wouldn't want to hurt those machines," she said, referring to our roadies. "They'll be fine on the ridge trail, though." She did a good job of selling the area. "If you like," she went on, "I can give you the name of some good bike rental places."

"That's all right," I said. "We can get some from Sunny's over on Peregrine."

"Oh," she said, "you know Sunny! He's a great guy and a mean mechanic, and he's turning some of us on to the speed of the road. I'm dying to try his recumbent."

She was extremely effusive and a fount of information, well suited to her job. She was a bit too bubbly for me, but she seemed to be a knowledgeable rider. I was about to see if I could get her going about ecotourism when a couple pulled up in a car and emerged to ask for directions to a hotel, and I remembered she was at work. We nodded our thanks and left.

"Boy," I said, "she was way over the top in her enthusiasm. Maybe it has something to do with being a small town girl. It would seem fake in the city."

"I don't know," he replied quietly. "I thought she was cute and very informative — good at her job," he said as an afterthought. He shrugged. "Well, are you ready to hit the trail?"

"Lead on," I said, somewhat chastened. "I trust your excellent sense of direction." You'd think that being a courier in the big city, I would be good with direction, but I'm not really. I just know the city so well that its streets are etched in my brain. Andy was proving to be quicker at picking up the lay of the land, so I followed him.

We rode carefully through the town. Unfortunately, the drivers in big 4x4s and hot rods did not. Pedestrians and bikers had to be on their guard. It was lucky for us that most of the souped-up vehicles were loud enough to warn us that we were about to be wiped off the road. My first impulse was to label them as "speeding rednecks," but then I grudgingly realized it could just have been that they were less used to cyclists on the streets.

At any rate, it was a relief to get on to the trail. Even though the guide had said it was easy, there were a few tight switchbacks on the way up. Not a Sunday ride, but it was dry, free of other riders and not too rutted, so who was I to complain? When we reached the ridge, we came to a clearing in the trees to find the guide's claim was true — the view was spectacular. We could see the ferry chugging back to Peregrine Island, the afternoon light reflecting in the water around the outlying islands beyond, and a gentle pink tinged the tips of the mainland range and highlighted the occasional snowcap in the sharp southern mountains. All of this was set against a sparkling ocean and an intensely blue sky.

They must set up the view spots carefully, because again we were facing away from the mill, so that the ugly smoke puffing well to the north was invisible. We recovered our breath while silently looking over the ocean, but I quickly got impatient. I was both anxious and nervous at the thought of encountering the Armstrong family. I hoped we could avoid raising their suspicion and actually learn something useful.

"Come on, Andy," I called out. "I'll race you." I hopped back on my bike and plunged back onto the treed trail. It was relatively clear and clean on the ground, which allowed for greater speed. I raced far ahead of Andy, pumping up the adrenalin as I went. Occasionally, flashes of light between the trees hinted at other view spots, but I didn't stop.

It was a rush speeding through the treed tunnel. I didn't look back once, and after about thirty minutes of hard riding through the canopied forest, I rushed out into the blazing light of a well-cultivated, cherry tree–lined street. Nearly crashing into the metal barrier, which was intended to stop bikes from rushing onto the road, I came to an abrupt halt.

It wasn't long before Andy brought up the rear. He looked like he had enjoyed himself, too. I found myself admiring the sweat glistening on his well-tanned skin. Despite my ambivalent feelings towards commitment, the sight of that handsome, healthy man smilingly catching his breath was quite a turn-on. It was all I could do not to jump on him, but my mind remained on the business at hand, and some stern internal dialogue quelled my desire. It was kind of unsettling to have all these lusty feelings when I was so ambivalent about the loving side of things.

As I took a sip from my hydration pack, I gestured nonchalantly at the row of stately homes on the street in front of us. "Looks like the right neighbourhood. Shall the concerned doctor and his blushing girlfriend go find Mabel?"

CHAPTER 18

THE ARMSTRONG HOME was not overly attractive or even large, but it was definitely ostentatious. A black wrought-iron fence with spiky posts guarded the hundred-foot expanse at the front. A large gate opened onto a straight drive to yet another house with Greek columns. You'd think that a lumber baron might have a fancy wood house, but not this one. In contrast with the West Coast chalet style on either side, this home was all stone, plaster and iron. The well-manicured lawn held some very obedient flowerbeds with not a tree in sight. To our left was a parking area and an open garage, which held two of the Armstrong trucks, Mabel's BMW and four bicycles lined up in a row, Sunny's familiar Kuwahara rental among them.

"Looks like the gang's all here," I observed in an undertone to Andy. We did not have time to knock, because as we stepped up to the door, it was swung open with great energy, and there was Mabel. She was less of a mess than the day before, but this made her even more formidable. Her hair was a wild mop of brittle straw and her makeup was not as heavily applied, so up close, I could definitely see bruising around the eye.

She smiled garishly. "Welcome! Welcome! Angie called and said you might drop by. I'm so glad you have, so I can thank you properly for helping me yesterday. Won't you come in?" she said, stepping aside. It would all have been very gracious, except for the scent of alcohol and the fact that she was having trouble keeping her balance. We thanked her, and pretending nothing was amiss, stepped into the cool interior.

Mabel ushered us from the metal, glass and marble hallway to a sitting room with a well-stocked bar to our right, which probably made it her favourite room. The only evidence of life was drink stains on the glass-topped coffee table.

Mabel was in serious drinking trouble. The question was whether this was due to the stresses of her husband's death, or if it was a more long-term problem. Judging from her worn face, I suspected the latter. Anyway, she motioned us to sit in two uneasy-looking chairs. "Can I get you anything to drink? Juice, coffee, wine ..." She sounded hopeful.

We had agreed earlier that we would meet her on her own terms in order to make her comfortable, so I said, "A little wine sounds lovely."

I guess the advantage to being a rich drunk is that you can get soused on quality stuff. She walked carefully over to the bar and picked up an open bottle of a good Merlot, a little heavy for me in the afternoon, but I didn't intend to drink much.

Most of the wine made it into the glasses as she poured. Ignoring the telltale tremors, Andy got the ball rolling, and soon we were making small talk about how nice her house was, how we enjoyed the ridge ride, what a lovely town this was and so on. Finally, Mabel finished the ordeal of social grace, put the bottle down a little too heavily on the table and sat back with her glass in hand.

"Thank you, dear," she said to Andy. "We enjoy the town, too, although it's a little uncivilized for me. I would much rather have stayed in my hometown of Surrey, but Jack's business kept him on the coast, so that's where we stayed."

"Oh, yes," I said, as if remembering. "I'm sorry for your loss, Mrs. Armstrong."

"Thank you," she said absently. "It's the shock, you know. I can't quite get used to the idea that he's gone. It's as if he might walk in the door any minute," she said with a shudder, whether from grief or horror, I couldn't tell."

"Thank goodness I have my children," she said unsteadily. "My sweet Brendon and the ever-efficient Melissa. They are helping me get ready for the service and burial. I'm not sure I could do it without them. I told Melissa about your help yesterday. She's on the phone right now, something to do with the company, but I am sure she will come to meet you when she's done. I believe Brendon is resting. He is taking this so hard, poor boy. They didn't always see eye to eye, but he loved his father." She seemed to melt when she talked about her son. He sure hadn't looked like he was suffering the night before. If she was sincere, then he had certainly pulled the wool over her eyes.

"It must be a very hard time for all of you," said Andy sympathetically.

He reached out to pat her hand. She smiled weakly into his warm blue eyes. Once again, I found myself marvelling at how people just sucked up his kind doctor stuff.

Feeling a need to "wander," I piped up, "Oh, Mrs. Armstrong, I just remembered that I have to call the lodge to cancel our dinner reservations. We're running late, so we decided to eat in town. Perhaps you could recommend a good restaurant."

"Of course," she said. "You must go to the Seafood Gourmet. It's a lovely place by the ocean, with very good food."

"Please don't get up," I said. She looked relieved. "Just tell me where to find a phone. I'm sure I can find my way."

"There is a phone table by the staircase in the hall. You'll find a phone book there, too," she said.

"Melissa might be using her cell, but if not, just push any button that is not lit up, and you will have your own line."

I thanked her and made my escape, trusting that Andy would be able to handle the grieving widow. So far everything had been so easy. I could not shake the feeling that this was too easy, but I happily went off to run my little errand, content that things were so far going to plan.

I would start by doing what I said I was going to do. Then I would do a little exploring on the pretext of looking for the bathroom, if anyone caught me. I have to admit I was experiencing a little thrill of excitement as I began to contemplate illicit exploration.

The phone was on an old-fashioned small phone table tucked in behind the curve of the massive staircase. It was so eerily quiet that it was hard to believe there were living people in that mausoleum. Shaking the feeling that Jack Armstrong's ghost was watching me,

I sat down and looked through the phone book I had found on the little ledge below the tabletop.

The phone book served for all the communities around the east side of the north island, with white and yellow pages included in the same compact volume, a far cry from the two massive phone books I used for doorstops back in the city. The listing for the Seafood Gourmet was easy to find. I forgot to check for an unlit line, and when I picked up the phone, I realized too late that the line was in use.

"I don't care what you think!" I heard the familiar hard voice of Brendon yelling. "Now listen! We're too close to closing this deal. I just got those guys at the airport the other day, and now they're gone till things cool down. They said something about wanting to see how we do on our own, but I think they were freaked out when the police called me in to question me again." Brendon laughed bitterly. "Something about the bike. As if they could get anything out of me. I just stonewalled them; I've got lots of experience with that," he said self-importantly. "The old man was always getting in the way. Even now that he's dead, he's getting me in trouble."

Given the nature of Brendon's rant, I guessed that the listener was Alex. He said little. Mostly, he was trying to calm Brendon.

Brendon settled down, saying, "Listen, I've got to go. The old lady is probably already up to her eyeballs in booze. I have to check on her. She thinks I'm sleeping off my grief, but the only thing I'm grieving is the timing. Mel wants me to keep the old lady calm while she arranges the service for tomorrow. It's the least I can do for her." He laughed. "What a drag. I still have to shower and dress the part of the sad son. So find out when the stuff should be delivered. I'll get away and meet you at the launch tonight, ten o'clock."

It was reassuring to hear that his Eastern business partners had gone home. That lessened the risk to Anita, and I was reassured to hear that the police had, indeed, checked in with Brendon. One thing was clear: There was no love lost between him and his late father. In fact, it didn't sound like he held anyone in the family in very high regard at all, except maybe Melissa.

After the two clicks signalling that both parties had hung up, I hung up the line, too. I was dying to know where the launch was. It would be interesting to be in on his little meeting. I sat for a minute thinking about what I had just heard. Brendon had not outright incriminated himself, but he sure acted like he had something planned.

One of the lines was still lit up, probably the sister, Melissa. When that went out, I remembered what I was supposed to be doing and quickly made my own call, booking a table for 6:30. Then, since the phone offered no further inducements to linger, I got up to look around.

French doors to the left opened to a large, formal living room that appeared to offer nothing exciting. Severe and nondescriptly furnished, it led to a large dining room panelled in dark wood with an ornate, heavy dining table, matching chairs and sideboard. The table sat on a large red and orange carpet of geometric patterns. This covered most of the floor, revealing about three feet of gleaming wood at each side. The style extended to the wall light fixtures, which were covered in matching geometric patterns.

Interestingly, there was no artwork, not even paintings on velvet. The kitchen at the back was institutional looking, all grey gleaming metal with very clean granite counters. I wondered if someone cooked for the family. They sure would have stories to tell, I guessed. I chuckled to myself — maybe the butler did it. I realized reluctantly that it wouldn't do to fixate on Brendon. I would have to take my blinders off, no matter how much I disliked him.

I circled back to the hall. Two doors to the other side, behind the staircase, stood invitingly, as if waiting for me to open them. So far my luck had held. The bathroom still evaded me. I turned the handle of the more ornate door, which opened into an office or study. On one side was a small fireplace, flanked by two plush leather easy chairs and a coffee table. The other wall held a floor-to-ceiling bookshelf about half-filled with books, and ahead of me, in front of a stained-glass window, was a large paper-strewn desk. Pay dirt, I thought.

As my heartbeat quickened, I did a rapid check to see if anyone was watching me. No one seemed to be around, so I darted into the room and made my way over to the desk. As I looked down at a stack of files on the right side of the desk, I noticed that the top one had the words "Peregrine sites" written on the left corner of the file. Bingo.

I was about to open it when a woman's voice rang out, "What *are* you doing?" I turned around to see a young woman standing in the doorway. Of course, this was probably the daughter, Melissa.

"Oh, my goodness," I said, quickly walking towards her, away from the desk. "You scared me. You must be Melissa," I starting gushing. "I'm visiting your mother with my boyfriend and was just looking for the washroom. I guess I found the wrong room. There's no washroom in here, is there?" I said, peering around to see if there was an ensuite in some yet-unexplored corner.

"No," she replied icily. I hoped she was disgusted with my seeming simple-mindedness. She gestured into the hallway. "The bathroom is right here," she said, turning the handle of the other door. There in its sterile resplendence was the WC.

"Oh, thanks ever so much." I slipped in and closed the door.

There wasn't much she could do. You can't very well tell someone to come out of the washroom, or wait outside, unless you want to be rude. I waited for my guilty little heart to stop racing, thankful for the tranquility and privacy of the room. It was designed for guests, I presumed, adorned as it was with cutesy floral towels, little shell-shaped useless soaps and the requisite matching floral tissues.

Once my breathing returned to normal and all business was taken care of, I steeled myself for the exit. Fortunately, the hall was empty, but when I took a quick glance to the left, I saw her standing by one of the overstuffed chairs near the fireplace in the office. She stared back at me. She looked familiar, but I couldn't quite place her.

"Well, thanks again," I said lightly. "I'm sure I can find my way back." I scurried down the hall. Now that I had seen that file, I really wanted to have a chance to poke around that desk some more. How could I manufacture another opportunity? I asked myself. When I returned, Andy appeared to be listening attentively to Mrs. Armstrong. A second bottle stood on the table.

"It's all set, hon," I said brightly as I slipped into a seat. "Dinner at the Seafood Gourmet for 6:30. Is it far from here, Mrs. Armstrong? Will it take long on our bikes?" Before she could answer, Brendon appeared at the door.

Maybe he was cleverer than I thought. He was dressed in a dark suit, freshly showered and shaved. When he came in to stand beside his mother, she looked at him adoringly.

"Oh, Brendon, darling. Thank you for coming down. I know how devastated you are feeling. I want you to meet the nice doctor who helped me yesterday. He dropped by to see how we are. I was just telling Dr. Jaegar and his girlfriend how much you enjoy cycling. They are holidaying on Peregrine."

He moved forward to shake hands.

"We've met, mother," he said politely. "How has your trip been so far, Dr. Jaegar? It's strange, isn't it," he mused, "how we keep crossing paths."

Andy replied. "It is peculiar. Anyway, we've been having a marvellous time on the trails."

Brendon nodded. "Thank you for helping out with mother yesterday." He played his role well, placing his arm around his mother's shoulder and looking suitably innocent as he said, "I was just talking to Alex, and he mentioned you would be visiting. I assure you that mother is well taken care of here."

"That's right, dear," she said, patting Brendon's hand. "As long as I have you by my side, I know we will be fine."

How can this woman dote on her son like that? I wondered. And how can she be so blind to his true nature? I'd had enough of that stomach-turning performance. It was time to get out of there.

I was silently praying that Brendon still didn't connect me with the whole Kensington business. I had no idea what the police had shared, but one could usually count on them to be professional. They were good at asking questions while not giving information. Besides, even if Brendon didn't know me yet, our popping up all the time was evidently beginning to make even him suspicious.

"Yes, well," I said, getting up. "We really have to be going now if we want to get some more riding in before dinner. If you could just point us in the direction of the restaurant, we'll be heading off."

Andy rose as well, but we were not to escape quite yet. As we walked towards the door, Melissa appeared again.

Now I remembered where I'd seen her before. She was the meek young woman we had bumped into outside the grocery store; only today, she appeared quite composed.

"Oh, Melissa," Mrs. Armstrong said. "I'm so glad to see you. I wanted to introduce you to my guests. This is Dr. Andy Jaegar, the nice young doctor who helped me yesterday." She turned to us apologetically. "Melissa has been busy making the service and funeral arrangements. She is ever so efficient," she said with a little edge in her voice, forgetting she had told us this once already.

Andy stepped forward to shake the young woman's hand.

"I'm pleased to meet you, and I'm sorry to intrude at such a sad time."

"Thank you," she said, smiling a little. "The preparations for the funeral are all taken care of, mother. Marilyn left a light meal in the fridge for us, so we can eat something while I go over the details. Brendon, could you take mother to the kitchen?" she said. "I'll see Dr. Jaegar and his friend out."

Melissa walked us to our bicycles and then turned to us and said, very directly and tensely, "I'm not sure what you want. My mother is very vulnerable, and I think it would be best if you left us to deal with our problems on our own."

She seemed to think that was enough, for she turned as if to go back to the house, only, to my surprise, Andy had something to say, too.

"Your mother is quite sick, you know," he said sternly. "You should consider helping her get treatment."

That was all he said, but the effect was dramatic. With her back still turned, she visibly crumpled. After a second or two, she turned and faced us, the little mouse I had first seen. She looked frightened, and would not meet our eyes. "I know," she whispered. "I'll try to do something." And with that, she fled.

"That was quite a change," I said. "I don't think the mother is the only one who is sick in that household."

"No," Andy agreed quietly. "Pretty sensitive girl."

CHAPTER 19

WE WALKED OUR bikes up the drive and along the sidewalk. An old man was clipping the cedar hedge, which served as a fence between houses. He winked at us as we approached.

"You friends of that lot?" he asked, jerking his head at the Armstrong house.

"No, not really," I said, stopping.

He nodded. "Thought not. You don't look the type that usually shows up there."

"Oh, really?" I asked, my curiosity antennae perking up. "What do you mean?"

"You look too normal," he said, looking more at Andy than at me. "Strange lot there, and not just business types and fancy big parties. They got their share of rough-looking young 'uns, too. Mostly friends of that Brendon kid, they are, but I've seen the daughter on the back of a motorcycle once or twice." He was warming up for more, the old gossip, and I was happy to listen.

"That's what I mean," he said. "You look too normal, not business, not rough. And that family, whoo boy," he said. "Now I'm sorry for them and all that, the old man dyin' that way, but I'm not surprised. He and that boy would fight something awful.

"Not that the kid didn't deserve it, but there wasn't a lot of peace over there. Not natural, they weren't. The old lady would fawn all over the boy and then scream at the girl and the old guy. And the old man, he would always treat the girl real nice, open the door when he took her to work. He was priming her to take over the business, I understand." He trailed off into silence.

"Have you lived here long?" I prompted.

"Sure have," he said proudly. "Longer than them. Built my house meself. I would have double-insulated the walls if I had dreamed of neighbours like them. This used to be a right pretty little town, before the mill came in. I was the janitor at the local school. Bought this land before it became crazy." He paused for a second, before adding sadly, "I should sell it, now that the wife is gone, but I can't quite part with the memories." His face grew stern. "The goings on at that house next door surely didn't help my sweet Wilma. She had cancer and was restin' at home, and she would cringe at the yellin' and the shoutin' over there."

His tone changed to anger. "She must have rolled over in her grave the other night — the night the old guy died. He had such a row with the boy on the back patio. He was yelling, something about not going ahead or he would not be part of the family, how Brendon was trash, not worth his dad's efforts. Old Mrs. A was drunk as usual, wailing away at her hubby to leave the boy alone. Then he turned on her something awful. Couldn't see, but I sure could hear banging and yelling and crying. Eventually, the young lad took off in one of the trucks."

We continued to listen attentively as he went on.

"I heard the old lady whimpering, but it got pretty quiet. Then … well, I usually never hear the girl, but this time, she spoke up. She said, 'Dad, this time you've gone too far. You're not perfect, either.' I couldn't hear what he muttered back, but then he said he was late for a meeting and took off in another truck. It seemed like the party was over, so I went inside to get ready for bed. I was just about to shut down when I heard their iron gate clang again. When I looked out, I saw the girl riding away on one of her brother's souped-up bicycles. Went to bed, then. I tell you, I've known it for years — that family is trouble." He shook his head.

I spoke up. "Mr. ..."

"Williams," he said. "Carl Williams."

"Mr. Williams, have you told this to anybody?"

"Nobody to tell," he said simply, shrugging his shoulders. "Nobody around here takes the time to listen these days."

It was hard to believe that the old guy had not relayed this story to anyone, but perhaps the friends he had were tired of his stories. He must have been lonely or really bored if he would tell two strangers all these details.

"Didn't the police question you?"

"No," he said. "Don't hold much truck with police, anyway. Can't see how it relates. The man died over on Peregrine, probably an accident, although I see they've charged some environmental lady. Once the police have an idea in their heads, it's hard to change it, y'know?"

"Well, that certainly is an interesting story, Mr. Williams. I pulled out one of the business cards that Juaneva Martin had made for me when I started doing small investigations for her and scribbled the name of the lodge on the back. I handed it to him and said, "If you think of anything else, you can call me."

"Well, I'll be, working for a law firm," he said, whistling. "I'm glad I spoke to you. I knew you looked more normal."

I was glad my hair was combed and my nose rings were out for the day. We shook his hand and thanked him again before riding off. It was getting closer to dinnertime, and my stomach knew it.

We rode down to the beach trail and slowly worked our way farther southeast to the Seafood Gourmet. The restaurant sat nestled behind a row of trees on a bend in the coastal highway. I couldn't imagine ever tiring of the view, which gave us the full glory of the ocean and the mountains through windows that ran the length of the north side of the dining room. Mountainous islands dotted the water, fading into the mainland Sawtooth Range.

The regular ocean traffic passed by during our meal; small and large sport fishing boats, yachts and barges pulled by tugs. There were two gigantic cruise ships that looked like small cities on the water, all lit up as they glided silently by. While cruising doesn't really appeal to me, the territory these ships cover on the way to Alaska is supposed to be amazing: fjords, wildlife, mountains, coastal villages and magnificent trees. Perhaps it would work for me if I could ride a training cycle on the deck as we travelled along.

We didn't talk much through the dinner. Andy seemed a little wrapped up in his own thoughts for a change, and I was lost in thought about the case. I had nothing concrete but plenty to think about. From the sound of it, no one in that house had an alibi for the evening of the murder, and everyone could have had a motive. Why did the police continue to focus on Jan?

From what I could understand, Armstrong had been at continual loggerheads with his son, and Mabel was a bit of a punching bag while she protected her son. And Melissa? Well, she was certainly weird. What had prompted her to say that her father had gone too far? Now it looked like it could have been her on the injured bicycle that night. And obviously, she was the one most in tune with the lumber business. But I needed more information. I kept thinking about those files on the desk in the study. I really wanted to get into that house to nose around undisturbed, but I was pretty sure Andy wouldn't take to the idea.

He'd been pretty helpful so far, but I didn't want to push my luck. Melissa had certainly made it clear she didn't want us around. I was feeling frustrated and restricted by my sense of responsibility to Andy. I hated the feeling because it brought me back to the thought that I might be better off unfettered.

I needed to take another tack. I cast about for a fresh approach. The Armstrong family was dark and tempting, but did that necessarily mean one of them was a murderer? I was halfway through my halibut cheeks with walnut pesto when Andy snapped me out of it.

"Abby, you're drumming that spoon on the table so annoyingly that the whole restaurant's looking pissed off at you. Are you even tasting your food?"

"Huh? Oh." I took my hand away from the spoon guiltily. "Sorry, Andy. I'm mulling over this whole business."

"I can tell," he said dryly. "Do you want to bounce anything off me?"

"Thanks, but not right now. I'm stuck in a rut, I think. I need to look somewhere else."

"Well, what about that other guy Mike told you about — the one who could tell you more about the environmental side of this business?"

"Andy," I said, "you're a genius. I'd forgotten all about him. I'll call him tomorrow or maybe tonight after dinner and see if we can get together."

"Abby." He shook his head ruefully. "You're a bit of a bulldog with this stuff, aren't you? Once you get your teeth in, you don't let go."

"I guess that's true," I said. "Tell you what. I'll let go long enough to finish chewing on this dinner, although it's so tender, it practically melts in my mouth."

With renewed attention, I ate my meal and chatted amiably with Andy. It was true, the halibut was perfectly cooked and the pesto was not overpowering, just gently setting off the flavour. We drank a light Chardonnay, and I forgot about logging for a while. For dessert, we shared a delicately tart key lime pie and lingered awhile over coffee.

As the sun began to set, Andy said, "Abby, I just saw a fish jump! Look, you can still see the ripples over there." He pointed out at the ocean. I watched attentively for a minute and was rewarded as two more salmon leaped and twisted in the air, the setting sun glinting off their iridescent scales.

"I bet they're hungry," he said. "They're jumping to catch bugs." We watched as a few more jumped, each unpredictable leap immediate and magical, elusive as a shooting star.

"Well," Andy said, stretching after we had paid. "We'd better get going. Maybe we can catch the 9:30 ferry."

"Ah, yes," I said. "The ferry is the boss, and it will take a while to ride on a full stomach. Wobble on, Macduff."

The forty-five-minute ride was easy on the paved trail along the shore. We rode at a leisurely pace, carefully avoiding the people enjoying the unusually mild evening so late in the season. Kids kicked at the sides of their scooters, couples rollerbladed hand in hand and teens wove in and out on their skateboards. We even saw three adept unicyclists. I felt sorry for the pedestrians, who seemed rather beleaguered competing for the path with all these people on wheels. We caught the ferry with minutes to spare, and soon became part of the twinkling ocean lights.

"Are you ready for the ride uphill?" asked Andy. "It's been a long day …"

"I can handle it," I said, "but I have an idea. I noticed a little pub by the ferry. We could go for a nightcap and listen to some tunes. The lodge quiets down early but the pub probably stays lively longer."

"Sounds good," he grinned. "Let's check out the night life."

Chapter 20

I WAS TOO busy watching out for the traffic as we got off the ferry to pay much attention to the outside of the pub as we pulled up. The parking lot was pretty full, and the building reverberated with '60s rock music.

"Sounds upbeat, anyway," I said as we walked up a nautical-like gangplank to the similarly themed doors with two round portholes. When we opened the doors, the sound felt more like an assault.

I must be getting old, I thought to myself. I used to love punk clubs, where this would have been mellow. The hostess sashayed over and nodded, words being superfluous in the din. I pointed at a corner table away from the action, but with a good view of the band and dance floor. She nodded again and handed us two menus. We sat down to a loud rendition of "Little Deuce Coupe." I looked around at the people sitting close to the dance floor. A few were smoking, which was supposedly not allowed, and a bluish haze enveloped the stage.

The song ended and the band announced a break. A waiter came over to take our order, and we decided to share a half-litre of white wine and a plate of cheese and fruit. Neither was worth writing home about, but sufficed for a late evening snack and a chance to people watch. After twenty minutes or so, the lead singer got up to introduce the next set. He seemed to be a local fellow, because he had a little repartee going with the audience as he joked about his band's great talent. He had a certain low-key charm, and I found myself lulled into a comfortable state.

I jerked to attention when he said, "I want to extend a special thanks to the manager of the Boat Launch for taking a chance with our band, The Ironmongers. So sit back or get up and shake a leg while we take the hammer to the next tune."

As they began to play The Beatles' "Twist and Shout," my mental wheels gave a sudden spin. Perhaps Brendon's reference to a launch had not been a boat but the pub! Wondering if he was going to show up, I was glad we were far from the action in a relatively inconspicuous spot. And then, as if on cue, there was a commotion at the door as a group of partiers came in.

They were loud enough to draw the attention of most of the patrons. It seemed to be mostly the same well-oiled crowd from the night before, with Brendon at the lead and two young women draped over two guys at the rear. Someone got up from a table near the stage and waved them over. I held my breath. It was Alex. I hoped he hadn't recognized us when we had entered, but he might have, if he had been watching the door. I gave a mental shrug. Not much to be done about it either way at this point.

I wasn't going to hear much conversation in that noisy place, so I sat back to watch. Most of the group sat down, while Alex and Brendon went to the bar. They spoke briefly to the bartender and then talked earnestly to each other. Brendon was getting heated, but Alex just leaned over and put his hand on his shoulder as if to reassure him. Brendon seemed to relax, and they walked back to their crowd of friends.

My attention was diverted when one of the young women, in the shortest skirt imaginable, got up and pulled Alex to the dance floor. He danced pretty passively, but she really let loose. Long blonde hair flew in her face as she spun around and swung her hips loosely back and forth. She was tireless, dancing with a succession of gangly boys in black and then by herself through four songs. I was fascinated. She had a wild energy, completely unselfconscious. Andy pulled on my arm.

"Hate to say it, Abby, but I'm getting a little bored," he yelled in my ear. "Okay," I said. "Let's go." He went to get the bill, while I took a trip to the washroom. As I washed my hands, the blonde dancer came in, flushed and smiling. It was none other than our Melissa. The smile vanished and her hair became a veil. "Oh," she said curtly. "You."

"Hi," I said lightly. "I liked your dancing."

"Thanks," she said.

Despite my normally curious, button-pushing nature, I decided to stay on the side of caution and just wish her well.

"I hope the ceremony goes smoothly tomorrow, Melissa. This must be a difficult time for you."

"Um, thanks," she said meekly. The change was dramatic. From wild dancer to sad and meek, she was a regular Ping-Pong ball of emotions.

"That's okay. We're leaving now, as we have a bit of a ride back to the lodge on our bikes in the dark. Have fun tonight," I said hopefully as I left her to collect herself.

Now that I knew Melissa and Brendon were at the pub, I had an idea. It probably wasn't going to be popular, but I was getting used to that.

"Listen, Andy," I said as we walked to the bikes. "I need you to do something for me."

"What's that, hon?" he said, pulling me close, almost causing me to have second thoughts.

"Go back to the lodge without me."

He stiffened and then stepped away. "What? Why?"

"I can't tell you. You'll have to trust me."

"But Abby, it's so late. What can you do now?"

"I can't tell you that, either. I might not get back tonight. So don't worry." I looked at my watch — 10:50. "Go on, Andy. I'll be fine."

He wasn't happy, but agreed reluctantly. "Okay, but I don't like it, and as for not worrying, that's impossible. Look, Abby, I know you need to do things your way, and I've tried to go along with that, but I've just about had it."

"I know, and I completely understand. I didn't plan for the past two days to go this way, but maybe it's made everything clear faster. I promise I'll be back by eight in the morning, or at least I'll call. If I don't, then you can start worrying, even call the police if you like, but I'm sure I'll be fine."

"I don't like the sound of this, Abby," he said shortly, and he rode off without another word.

Feeling bad for upsetting Andy yet again, I almost reconsidered. But the opportunity was too good to be passed up. I had seven minutes to catch the waiting ferry. I chanced a few more minutes to peek into the window of the pub. Melissa was deep in conversation with Alex and Brendon. At least I knew where they were, and they seemed to be engrossed, so I grabbed my bike and sped down the hill to the dock and onto the ferry, just as the horn blasted its warning of departure. As the metal ramp was raised and secured, and the cool night air mixed with diesel fumes rushed over my skin, I inhaled and wondered silently if I was crazy.

No, I decided — not crazy. Maybe a little overtired, a little too turned on by a hint of risk and determined to solve puzzles, but surely I wasn't crazy.

With both Brendon and Melissa at least temporarily away from their home, and Lady Armstrong likely to be out cold, it seemed like a gift.

I was glad that I had my trusty all-weather tool kit with me, strapped to my bike. I had already attached my powerful bike light, but I took a moment to check whether I still had my little pen-light and my lock pick. It was pretty cool, because it passed for an ordinary Swiss army knife, so it wouldn't arouse suspicion unless someone saw it opened.

When I reached the other side of the channel, I decided to retrace our path to the restaurant and up the town streets from there. Although the other way was shorter, I didn't relish riding on a trail bordered by trees in the dark, my fear of the wild surging up in me again.

I rode hard and fast this time. Speed and adrenalin kept me warm, which was a good thing since I hadn't dressed for a late-night jaunt. After climbing the hill to the Armstrongs' street, I ditched the bike at the corner in a clump of trees. Remembering the next-door neighbour's penchant for looking out the window and listening to the comings and goings of others, I made the approach as quietly as possible.

'Fortunately, the iron gate was open. I skirted the floodlights and inched past the back of the garage. My cleats would have clicked loudly in the house so I decided I would go barefoot the rest of the way. I took off my bike shoes and left them behind the back corner of the garage. As I stuffed my socks in my pockets I knew I would just have to risk stepping on one of those huge B.C. banana slugs. I had seen one of the six-inch slimy things on Sunny's trail off in the shade. When I had asked him about it, he said they come out in the evening when it is cool and damp.

So far all was quiet. The thumping of my heart and my gulping swallows seemed to echo through the night as I continued to the side of the house. I decided to try the side door I had seen when I was checking out the kitchen earlier in the day. Near that door, the ground sloped away, and a deck, which jutted out above the hill, abutted the kitchen wall. Around the back on the deck would be the row of glass windows with sliding doors in the centre. If the side door didn't work, I would try those.

It was locked, so I continued on, hoping that since the siblings were expected back, no alarm system had been activated. Happily, the back sliding door was open, with only the screen closed. Trusting folk. No guard dog, either. As I pulled the screen back very slowly, I hoped it was only to me that the grating sounded like a roar.

I left the screen open and looked around. Dishes were piled in the sink, presumably for the person named Marilyn to clean up. In my excellent detective fashion, I guessed she worked days. Except for a light emanating from somewhere down the hall, all was quiet. I tiptoed over to the study, eager to get in and look around, but when I turned the knob, the door didn't budge.

Melissa must have locked the door. Why? She couldn't have imagined that I would be back. Was she keeping her mother or her brother out, or was she protecting something within?

I looked at the lock: Standard Yale, so with my penlight in my mouth, I got out my pick and began to work. I had just manoeuvred past two ridges when I heard, in disbelief, the sound of a truck pulling in to the garage. Was it Brendon and Melissa? How did they get back so fast? I had taken the last ferry for the night. In my self-absorbed smugness, I had forgotten that they could have taken their own boat, or perhaps the water taxi. Immediately killing my penlight, I retreated to the kitchen, looking frantically for a place to hide. I decided to get outside and risk hovering in the garden under the deck to see what would happen next.

Even though it was a warm night by coastal standards, the ground under my feet was sticky. As I squatted uncomfortably, the cold began to seep into my tense toes. I was trying to decide the next-best course of action when I heard voices coming from inside the house. At first they were indistinct, just audible enough for me to tell that two different people were speaking. As they moved nearer the kitchen, their voices became louder and clearer.

"There's nothing to worry about, Mel. D'you want another drink, or something to eat? There's probably something still in the fridge. Marilyn loaded it up for the guests tomorrow."

I didn't hear Melissa's response, but a few seconds later, the screen door slid open and footsteps sounded on the deck above my head. The moon was starting to rise, flooding the area with light. I hoped they would not notice me below. Brendon, with his customary charm, cursed loudly, "Bloody door's wide open! The old lady must have been bombed, as usual. Anyone could have come in."

"It would serve her right if someone broke into her precious wine cellar," Melissa said acidly. Ice tinkled in their glasses as they leaned on the railing of the deck, and Mel continued. "I don't know why, but that girlfriend of the doctor really gets on my nerves. She always acts like a nitwit, but her eyes are smart. By the way, Brendon, I really appreciate your help, but this drug stuff is going to get you in trouble."

"Oh, Mel, you're starting to sound like the old man. Stay out of my business and quit worrying."

"Okay, but please don't say I'm like that monster, Brendon. I just don't want to see you in trouble."

"I know, hon," he said, the sweetest thing I had ever heard from his foul mouth, and unexpected between sister and brother. Of course, I'm no authority on close sibling relations, but all I had seen so far in that family was dysfunction.

"Don't worry, Mel, I'll take care of everything. Nobody will bother you." This was interesting, too. So far, Melissa had seemed to be the organizer in the family. Everything was as clear as the mud oozing between my toes.

"Here," said Brendon, "take one of these. It'll help you sleep."

"I don't know, Bren. I don't like to play with that stuff," she said hesitantly.

"Come on. Think of it as medicine. I don't think you've slept for two days. You don't want to break down tomorrow, do you? Me, I can always sleep." He laughed.

That figures, I thought. Devoid of any conscience.

"Come on," he encouraged.

"It won't hurt, I guess."

She must have given in because I heard what sounded like ice falling into the bottom of her glass and him saying, "Good girl. Now let's get you to bed before you pass out right here."

"Don't forget to lock the door this time," she said as their steps sounded across the deck. The screen door closed, and then the sliding door shut with a resounding thump and a click. Fortress Armstrong was secure, I thought with a sinking heart. Now that the excitement of their conversation was over, I shivered as the damp enveloped me completely.

What now? It seemed a shame to pass up the opportunity to prowl when the family promised to be dead to the world. Yet there were two "what ifs" to overcome. What if I couldn't get in? And what if they weren't so dead? As I crouched awkwardly, I tossed a mental salad of the consequences associated with these possibilities.

Chapter 21

I KNEW RIGHT away that I wouldn't be able to resist trying to get in again, but it was diverting to play mental chicken with myself while my toes froze in the damp mud. When I finally uncramped my limbs, I decided to try the side door, away from the possible prying eyes of the lonely neighbour. The little tête-à-tête of the siblings may have roused the old guy, and while he was more likely to watch and enjoy than to call the cops, I didn't want to risk entertaining him. I knew he liked to talk and he wasn't overly discriminating, despite his good taste in choosing to tell all to me earlier.

So, with my trusty penlight and Swiss army lock picks, I worked on the side door, allowing the adrenalin to warm me up. I quietly appreciated the fact that the folks in Bellweather did not appear to share the paranoia of Torontonians, who were already competing with New Yorkers for number of locks on doors. I have one or two on my door back at home, but also know full well that if someone wants to get in, he or she will. So why bother?

Eventually, I made it past the only lock, and fortunately, the door was well oiled. Thinking that my feet might leave marks on the floor, I pulled on my socks and hoped for the best as I tiptoed across the now familiar kitchen. Determined to gain entry this time, I worked silently on the office door in the moonlight, which shone in through the uninterrupted wall of glass.

Time is tricky. Clock time is one thing, but mental time is another. In reality, it was only a few minutes between my entry into the house and my final breakthrough into the hallowed chamber, but for me it was an eternity. I don't remember relocking the door, but maybe I did through some natural reflex.

What was I looking for? Something to connect the dots, to provide insight into the family? Or was I trying to see if I could unearth something in that office that would reveal someone's motive to kill? Both, I realized.

Fortunately, the desk remained tidy. I kind of felt a kindling of affinity for Melissa or her father — whoever worked at the desk — because she or he was a piler like me. Instead of files neatly tucked away or papers spread all over, everything was in piles, with a little space in the centre to be used as a workspace. Feeling right at home, I scanned the piles of manila folders in front of me, hoping something would leap out. Something easy, like "murder" or "Janice Field" or "Peregrine cut block," but nothing so glaring appeared at first perusal. So I dug in for a more thorough examination.

This time, I gently lifted covers and shifted down to the bottoms of the piles of folders and papers. It was a bit of a shock when the name Field *did* spring out at me. I opened the folder with shaking hands to find yellowed newspaper clippings, not about Jan but about her son, Jon! There were short clippings about his accident, and my interest quickened when further below I found a document titled "From Monkey-Wrenching to Negotiating: An Overview of Ways to Stop Clear-Cutting" by Jonathan Field.

Could this be the missing essay that Mike had mentioned? The last thing in the file was a bundle of envelopes held together by an elastic band. Each just had the name Jon. No address, no stamps. If delivered, it had been done by hand. I opened the envelope at the top and withdrew a sheet of pretty, lilac paper, lined with a nice, careful script.

Dear Jon,
I know you said that you are not interested in a relationship right now, and that my being who I am makes it even more difficult, but I'm writing one last time to let you know I'm here if you change your mind. I don't care who my father is. I love you. I'm sorry you don't trust me. I would never do anything to hurt you. I know you think we don't really know each other, but we could

make it work. We really could. Anyway, I won't bother
you anymore. I wait silently.

—Mel

Whoa! I noticed the corner of a photo sticking out of the envelope
and extracted it. A young face, with short hair, smiled back sweetly,
a younger Melissa. So, the lovely Melissa had been pining for Jon
Field. Curiouser and curiouser. I wondered how the letters man-
aged to get into this office. Maybe they had never been delivered, or
maybe they had been returned. But how, and by whom? I shook my
head. I looked once more through the other files, but nothing glared
up at my uncertain eye.

I walked over to the two armchairs where I had seen Melissa
standing earlier in the day. On a low, round coffee table sat a vase of
dried flowers and a leather-bound datebook. The entries were written
in the same elegant script as the letter, so I assumed it was Melissa's.
I glanced idly through the appointments. One for Dr. Aeron Glasco
showed up regularly, once a week, at the same time. What kind of
doctor does one see so regularly? Well, she definitely was stressed
enough to see a psychiatrist, and strange enough to need one.

A creaking noise from somewhere in the house reminded me
that I was pushing my luck and should probably head out right
about now. I had just come to that stellar conclusion when the door
handle jiggled. My heart practically jumped out of my throat. The
handle jiggled again, followed by a loud wail in a distinctly Mabel-
like voice.

"Ohhhh … Jack, dear! Let me in! I know you're in there! Why do
you always lock me out? I need you, Jackie."

As I looked about frantically for a place to hide, she called out,
"Where is Melissa? You two are always plotting against me. Jack!
Melissa! Let me in!"

The door handle jiggled furiously. When I heard Brendon's voice
a few seconds later, I went cold. In relief, I realized they weren't going
to come in when he said tenderly, "Come on, Mother. There's no one
in there. It's time to go back to bed. Come on," he coaxed. "You're
getting worse, you know. We'll have to have you locked up soon."

"Brendon, my sweet boy. Is that you? Mother will take care of you. Yes, dear, it's time you went to bed."

I started to have some sympathy for the jerk when he said, "Some mother — you really take care of me," exasperation creeping into his tone. Then I remembered the black eye she'd taken in his defence, and my sympathy evaporated.

Their voices faded as they mounted the stairs. That was it for me. As soon as I was sure it was quiet, I exited the room as fast as stealth allowed and got out of that crazy house.

The cold night air slapped at me for my audaciousness. I crept through the shadows to my shoes, grabbed them and ran like a wraith, accompanied only by the distant barking of dogs. When I reached my hidden bicycle, I stuffed my wet socks into my backpack and quickly put on my shoes. I had ridden half-blind most of the way down the hill towards the ferry dock before I remembered that it was probably long past ferry time. Since it was too cold to stay out, I decided to check in to one of the hotels by the dock.

Tired, but wired, I buzzed my way through registering and finding my room. My mind was too full to deal with what I had learned, so I threw myself on the bed, fully dressed, and turned on the TV. An old black-and-white movie, newly colourized, was playing: *All About Eve* with Bette Davis, so delicious in her evilness. As the buzz faded, fatigue took over and I fell asleep.

Chapter 22

THE LONG MOURNFUL call of a foghorn rolled through my clouded brain. As consciousness dawned, I became aware of a headache, which made the banging sound near the window sound as if a full complement of taiko drummers were in my room. I squinted one eye open, but from the vantage point of my pillow, all I could see was a blanket of grey outside. The wind whistling through the screen of the open window explained the noise — the heavy weight on the corner of the curtain was banging. Head exploding, I stumbled out of bed, trying to pry open my other eye, and staggered to shut out the offending breeze.

The wind had fully blown the fog away by the time I woke again, this time to an equally offensive sound from the hall — a vacuum cleaner roaring annoyingly nearby. Momentarily disoriented, I wondered why anyone would vacuum in a hotel so early. I groaned, rolled over and looked at my watch on the bedside table. 10:00.

This time I felt entombed in the stuffy room, so I walked back to the window, reopened it and was hit by an aromatic breeze that triggered a memory full of emotion. Wafting in was the smell of the ocean, a pungent layering of salt, seaweed, diesel fumes and fish — not everyone's cup of tea, but for me, it was heaven, not because of where I was vacationing but because I was immediately transported back to my fragrant little apartment above a fish shop in Kensington Market.

Surrounded by this beauty and adventure, how could I possibly be missing my cozy but slightly grotty home in downtown Toronto? Could it be the thought of my ten lovely bikes? Or my friends in the fish shop? No. I shook my head, frowning slightly. I'm fond of my home, permeated as it is with a fishy bleach odour, but what I yearned for was my independence.

With a sinking feeling, I realized, once and for all, that even though Andy was charming, witty, incredibly good looking and very sexy, he was not the right man for me. I allowed what I knew to be the truth to permeate my conscious mind. My unconscious obviously knew it already. Why else was I so difficult with such a nice guy? Jarred from my thoughts by the hoot of the ferry, I realized I'd better get back to the island and face the music. We needed to find closure, if Andy hadn't discovered it on his own the night before. He had been pretty steamed.

The night's adventure must have worn me out more than I realized because I was definitely slow that morning. The icy grip of memory finally flooded from toes to forehead, and I momentarily froze in dismay. I had told Andy I would call before 8:00! Oh God, I thought, he's going to kill me. Or worse, he might have sent out the alarm. I rushed to the phone by the bed and called the lodge on Peregrine. I asked the woman at the desk to put me through to Andy's or rather, *our* room, but the phone just rang and rang. I hung up and dialled the main number again, this time asking to leave a message.

"This is pretty important," I said. "If you find him, just tell Dr. Jaegar that Abby is okay and I'll be back soon! Please check the restaurant and the exercise room, and failing that, could you leave a note on the door of our room?"

"Sure, Ms. Faria," the woman said. "Bye, now!" That wasn't very good, I thought. Where is he? Of course, I resented having to report in, but I owed the guy at least a little peace of mind. As an afterthought, I dialled Sunny's place, thinking Andy might have gone to him for advice. I'd rather Sunny than the police. The phone rang four times, and I was about to hang up when his familiar drawl came on the line.

"Howdy. Sunny's Bike Repair."

"Oh, Sunny! I'm so glad you're there. It's me, Abby."

"Abby!" He sounded immediately alert. "Where are you? Old Andy's here, all worried about you. He said you took off last night on some mission. I was pretty sure you'd be able to take care of yourself, but well, you did tell him you'd call by 8:00. Then, there is also the thought that with Brendon on the loose, you could have run into him. We were both getting a mite anxious, and thinkin' 'bout calling the police. Didn't quite know what to tell 'em, though."

"Oh, Sun, I'm okay. I'm so sorry to have worried you guys. Listen, I'm in Bellweather, at the Fern Hotel. I don't think I'll catch this ferry, so I'll be on the 12:30. Can you tell Andy I'm fine and I'll be there soon?"

"Hold on."

I could hear Sunny mumbling something, and then he was back. "He says he'll see you back at the hotel later. He wants to go for a ride to cool down this aft and to explore the island a little more. I like Andy, Ab. Seems sensible to me. In fact, I think I'll join him. Business is kinda slow today. We'll see you later. Oh, and Ab ..."

"Yes, Sunny?"

"I'm glad you're okay. Haven't changed much, have ya?" He hung up.

I sat with the phone in my hand for a minute, relieved to have avoided a missing person's report and content to have a few more hours to myself.

After toying briefly with the idea of crashing the Armstrong memorial service, I caught the 12:30 ferry, deciding to stick to my plan to get back to the lodge as soon as possible. I would have a little more time to myself, time to think, to make some notes, to shower ...

The breeze was still up; a little chop disturbed the ocean, but compared to my first crossing only four days ago, the roll was minimal. Even so, I gripped the rail and watched the water run behind the ship, small variations in the wake marking the ups and downs of the vessel. My equilibrium was restored upon entry into the pretty little harbour on Peregrine. After a leisurely ride uphill to the lodge, I locked the bike in the rack inside the storeroom set aside for that purpose. Apparently, even on this peaceful little isle, bike theft was on the radar.

The staff at the restaurant made me a quick sandwich and coffee, and I took them to my room, welcoming the time to take stock and see what I could come up with. It was a relief to breathe in the much-needed mental space, but stray thoughts about Andy interfered at regular intervals. My ambivalence about our relationship had to be evaluated but I wanted to use my time to think about the mystery. After a while, I made a little deal with myself — if I let myself focus just on the murder for now, I would think about how to say goodbye later.

So I focused. I filled out some note cards I had picked up in town, listing all my possible suspects, all the events to date, all my ideas. It was a good exercise for two reasons. I was able to slow down and take stock. And I remembered a few potential threads that I could follow up on. First, to round out my investigation, I still should speak to Sunny's friend, the eco-activist. I didn't really think that would go anywhere, as all my instincts screamed that the guilt seemed to belong in that twisted Armstrong family. But I had no proof. And that's what I needed — proof. Besides, I didn't want to let my belief in one person's guilt stop me from having an open mind. That's what I had complained the police were doing to Jan.

I turned my mind to the file I had seen in the office. Why were the essay and letters in the Armstrong house, and who had put the file there? How much did Melissa know about it? Maybe it wasn't her; maybe her father had retrieved the papers somehow. Was the fact that the documents were there enough proof that Jon's death had been more than misadventure?

I also remembered the bags of evidence from the wrecked bicycle inspection, and what I had seen at the logging site. I thought about the mud from the bike and the rag caught in the gear. Were these a connection to the logging site? By the Asian markings on the scrap of rag and the similar golden colouring, chances were it came from the string of Buddhist-style prayer flags in the woods, I realized. A definite link, then.

And the file clearly showed an earlier connection between the Armstrongs and the Fields. Would I have to place Janice on my list of suspects? Had she found out about the location of the essay or about Melissa's connection to her son? Was the desire for revenge behind her actions?

I thought about Officer Faraday's reaction to the bike evidence.

Perhaps the paint chips were a clue. Mike's truck was the same turquoise blue, but I hadn't seen any patches of flaking paint on it.

I was still mulling things over an hour or so later when Sunny and Andy walked in.

"Hi, guys," I said, looking up from my notes.

"What're you up to, Ab?" said Sunny, coming closer.

"Sunny, didn't you say Armstrong had prayer flags wrapped around his neck when they found him?"

"Um ... yeah. That's right. That's why they suspected that Janice or another protester had done the deed."

"Well, I remember the rag we took from the chain in the bike had Asian symbols on it, and I saw something similar when Andy and I wandered through the site. That puts the bike at the site that night, and adds more potential suspects than just Janice Field. It could have been Melissa, or Brendon.

"It's not exactly proof, Ab. Those flags seem pretty common around here," said Andy.

"You're right and I'm frustrated. I'm just going in circles. Everybody seems guilty, and I haven't really eliminated anyone yet. It's such a ragged chain of pseudo evidence and possible suspects. Anyway, give me a minute and I'll put this stuff away." As I picked up my scattered note cards, the guys sat quietly in the two chairs by the window, watching me.

"Hey, Sunny," I said. "Can you give me the number of your eco-activist friend? Mike Porter gave it to me, but I don't know where I put it. I should talk to him."

"Oh, you mean Nigel. Now, Abby, remember. I don't want you barking too hard up his tree. You have no evidence of his being involved, and he's a sensitive guy."

"Of course, Sunny. I just need a fresh perspective. Maybe he'll say something that will unlock the puzzle."

"Okay, Ab. Tell you what. I'll call Nigel myself, ask him to come over for lunch to my place tomorrow, and you and Andy can join us. But I'll only do that on two conditions."

"Sure, Sunny," I said.

"One, that you quit detectin' for today, go for a hike on the trails for an hour and then have dinner with Andy and me here." He winked. "Andy and I already concocted that one. Now you've given me a lever to get you to go. And two, you go for a road ride with Andy tomorrow morning before lunch. As an added incentive, you can ride my recumbent."

"Well," I said smilingly, "I don't take too kindly to pressure, as you both know, but with such an offer and both of you ganging up on me, I guess I will have to acquiesce gracefully." They smiled.

Then I had a thought. "Maybe we should check on Anita."

Andy shook his head. "It's okay, Ab. We dropped in on her when we were on our ride. She's having dinner with some people at the campground tonight. I told her we might drop by tomorrow morning sometime."

"Fabulous!" I exclaimed. "Okay, I give in. I'm yours for the night."

"All right," exclaimed Sunny, high-fiving Andy. "Let's go. The tide's out, so we can go explore the beach trail."

Andy had been pretty quiet through all this, but he looked calm. Feeling a little twinge of guilt for my night's absence, I made nice. As we left the building, I took his hand for a bit, but soon the going got too tough as we scrambled down the trail to the ocean.

Chapter 23

IT WAS ANOTHER sparkling afternoon. The breeze had died down and the turquoise water was relatively calm as little waves lapped at the shore. The smell of ocean was strong as the seaweed-encrusted rocks steamed in the sun. In this patch of paradise, it was easy to let go of my questions, at least for a while. I am cantankerous and ornery, but I'm not so stubborn as to ignore such beauty and the chance to frolic with friends.

We had fun, picking up interesting rocks and bits of driftwood. A wide array of junk lay at the high-tide line, bits of netting, Styrofoam, fraying rope and other detritus. We were flanked on one side by the towering firs on the hillside, while the rocky beach, the ocean and the faraway mountains held us in their embrace.

Scattered amongst the loaf-sized rocks that made up the beach were larger boulders sitting stolidly like hunched figures overlooking the scene, though the odd one lay flat like a rounded table. They were worn smooth with age. Some had mini pond-like depressions that held water, but the ones higher up were dry, lined with white salt lines and broken shells, a reminder of earlier high tides.

As we walked nearer to the trees, we could feel the moisture from the earth and the trees. At one point, there was water running from a creek in the hill out towards the ocean. Even this small movement of water carried the sandy soil away from the hill to the beach. The sand covered some of the rocks, providing a tiny sandy beach. It was easy to see that if all the trees were cut away from a hillside, the soil would quickly be washed away, leaving no purchase for any newly planted trees.

"Let's stop here for a bit," Sunny said, sitting on one of the giant logs strewn along the beach. I sat on an adjacent "table rock," idly running my hand in one of the little depressions on the rock. It felt smooth and warm to my touch. I looked up to catch Sunny watching me.

"Some folks say those dips in the rock come from an ancient Aboriginal tradition," he said.

"Really?" I asked. Andy looked interested, too.

"Yeah," said Sunny. "See how this little creek is runnin' out to the sea?"

We nodded.

"Well," he said, looking pleased to be able to tell us a story, "they say this might have been a salmon-spawning stream, and the Native people many years ago would beat these big stones repeatedly, ritually, to call the salmon back from the ocean. Over hundreds, maybe thousands of years, they wore these depressions into the rock.

"As a matter of fact, there's supposed to be a petroglyph or two along this beach somewhere, too, ancient little figures etched on the rock. I haven't seen 'em, but I've seen pictures, and two rocks from another spot on the island have been relocated to the local Native museum. You can see 'em there. There's a few people on the island who have reported having visions of these ancient traditions when they are near these special stones.

"You should go to the museum at the Native village. They have a great collection of masks, and lots of info on the old tradition of the potlatch. You can ride your bikes there and back. It's not too far from this lodge."

"We might do that," said Andy. "We have a little more than a week left."

"My God," I said. "Almost a week has passed already?" Andy looked at me wryly.

"Five days, actually, but who's counting? You've been mildly preoccupied."

The sun was far behind us, the shadows starting to stretch over the beach and the shoreline beginning creep back in. Under the pressure of having to rationalize my holiday behaviour, I turned to my favourite diversion. "Hey, guys," I said. "Let's head back for that dinner you promised me. I'm starting to feel a little peckish." With a final respectful pat to my beautiful stone seat, I arose and began to climb back to our trail.

"Whoa," Sunny said, laughing. "Don't go bounding away, rabbit. There's another route back." He grabbed my hand. "This way." He gestured ahead. It looked like dense forest to me, but I followed obligingly. It felt altogether too nice to be touched by Sunny. I added this latest item to my growing list of reasons to stop leading Andy on. I had thought that sparks between Sunny and me were long since dead in T.O.

Andy looked happy enough, though, so I guess he was not one of those mystical sensitives who picked up hidden vibes or read auras. Or maybe he was simply a step ahead of me and had let go already. My ambivalence was painfully transparent, but he didn't seem plagued with self-doubt. Frustrated with myself, I closed down the whole train of thought and decided just to enjoy the day. About fifty feet along, we came to an opening in the trees at beach level, where a trail appeared. This one was a little more difficult, but with the odd grab at a tree or a root, we levered ourselves up the hill.

"Believe it or not," puffed Sunny, "this is a bike trail that some of the guys like to use. They like a rough ride and a challenge. Of course, it's on reserve land, so they have to ask permission first. As far as I know, no one's ever said no, but there is the courtesy involved here."

"But Sunny, how can a bike go here?" I asked in wonderment. Curbs, stairs and cars I could handle, but trees, roots, rocks and a cliff were beyond my ken.

"I've only tried it once myself," he grunted. "Not my kettle of fish, but it's great for business — more than one classy full-suspension bike has been mangled here, not to mention the odd head or elbow." This conversation took place in bits and pieces as we groped our way upwards, stopping to catch our breath a few times. Ten minutes later, we reached the ridge, having encountered no bikes along the way, fortunately. We walked through a wooded trail and emerged at the south end of the lodge's manicured lawn.

"Well, now I have a serious appetite," I said. "The air's good tonight and it's still warm. How about we eat dinner on the patio and watch the ocean traffic?"

"Suits me," said Andy. We headed for the stairs to the restaurant's outdoor patio.

"Guys, go ahead and order some wine while I go get my jacket," I suggested when we reached a table. They nodded, and sat while I scurried off to our room.

Normally, I don't worry too much about how I look to others. I dress up because it suits me to, or because I am in disguise. But for some reason, it mattered to me that night. I washed my face and combed my spiky hair, doffed my sweaty shirt for a clean, dry one and tossed on my jean jacket, the one with little beads and shiny metal bits. That was it, but I felt fresh and excited and a little bit risqué at the prospect of a date with two guys, both of whom had been my lovers. What would my mother think of that!

The evening went smoothly. Having declared an uneasy truce with myself, I behaved in a relaxed, neutral way and enjoyed the heady atmosphere — a combination of the aforementioned clean air, handsome and charming men, good food, a glorious sunset, the mountain view and, of course, a generous amount of rich, delicious wine.

Eventually, the air cooled so much that even the alcohol could not hide the fact, so we returned to the lounge for liqueurs and decaf. When the evening drew to a close, Andy asked Sunny if we should call him a cab, to save him the ride home. Even though his drawl was exaggerated by his relaxed state, Sunny had not really drunk much. He wasn't like me; he didn't need help to be calm. He got up, his impressive height towering over my not-so-diminutive frame, and shook hands with Andy.

"Thanks, friend, but I'll be fine. It's a lovely night for a ride. Besides, the taxis on the island are a little scary, so I'll stick to my trusty recumbent. It'll get me home, safe and sound."

Mr. Honey Blue-eyes turned to me as he held my hand in his two paws. "Be good, Abby," he said, smiling.

I melted a lot, inwardly, and returned his smile briefly. "Yes, Sir," I said.

Andy smiled, too. "That's a tall order for our friend here," he said to Sunny.

"Mmm …" said Sunny, one eyebrow raised in an expression I recognized, with a little pang, from the old days.

Andy put his arm around my shoulder. I let it all be — you know, love the one you're with, as the song goes. "Ab, I'll just walk Sunny out. From the little bit you shared with us on the beach about your adventures last night, it sounds like you could use some rest."

"Suits me," I said. "Good night, Sunny."

I retreated gracefully and decided to use the few free minutes to have a shower. All in all, it had been a fruitful and exciting twenty-four hours. In fact, for a laid-back holiday, I had been awfully busy. In my mellow state, I decided to continue to leave the mystery in the back of my mind. Closing my eyes, I let the hot water fall over my tired frame. I was about to reach for the soap when I became aware of other warm, soapy hands doing the job for me.

Now, sometimes I like the solitary beating of the water drumming on my head, but tonight, Andy's exploring hands were welcome enough. He had helped me in the shower during my convalescence, and despite my recent wandering attentions, his ministrations were as sensitive and keenly attuned as always. In fact, just perfect. I responded in kind, and it wasn't long before it was a choice of scrabbling around in the hard-tiled bathroom or quickly retiring to the bedroom. We opted wordlessly, but not really silently, for the bed.

It was lovely and familiar with comfortable embraces and eventual rising passion. I don't know about Andy, but I forgot everything as we reached an almost simultaneous climax. As we lay snuggled in the radiating silence of ebbing heat, I realized that this was probably the last time with Andy. I allowed myself a few silent tears through my closed eyes.

I held him a little tighter, a gesture that was returned. I don't know if he knew what I was thinking, or if he saw my tears, but as I drifted slowly to sleep, he whispered, "It's okay, Abby, I know." And with that benediction, I passed out.

CHAPTER 24

ANDY, AS USUAL, slept soundly. I, however, awoke again to that acrid mill odour through our open window. This time, as I wrinkled my nose, I knew what to do. I hopped out of bed, closed the window, turned on the canned air and padded barefoot to the bathroom.

It was 7:00. We had agreed to go to Sunny's early for the promised bike ride. I was nervously looking forward to trying his recumbent, with its promised virtues of speed and reduced back and neck strain.

As I was drying off, Andy stumbled into the bathroom.

"It's freezing in our room, Abby," he said, a little bleary-eyed.

I gave him a quick kiss. "I know," I said, momentarily gracious. "The wind is blowing from the mill again, so I turned on the air. Didn't check the settings first. Sorry." While saying this, I had pulled on my cleanest riding gear and a nice, loose sweater. "Why don't you warm up in the bath or shower? I'll alter the settings in the air system and get some stuff from the restaurant. It's my turn to get us organized."

He smiled, pulled me close for a little nuzzle. "You smell good," he murmured into my neck. "You sure there's any hot water left?"

"Oh, sure," I said as I slapped his butt playfully. "Now, get a move on, handsome."

Andy was dressed and dapper in riding gear by the time I returned with a tray laden with coffee, juice, muffins, toast and yogurt with fresh berries. We retreated to bike magazines, foregoing conversation over the sound of the air system, and ate a peaceful, tasty breakfast. Finally, after cramming in one last piece of toast, I groaned. "I don't know if I will be able to ride to Sunny's after all that."

"No sweat, Abby," said Andy. "We'll drop the bikes on the car rack and start our ride from Sunny's place. Look," he said, "it's cleared up and a breeze is coming up from the south. We'll be able to breathe."

"It's funny," I said, "but I'd take the pollution of the city any day over this godawful stench. I wonder what's worse for us, really, this single mill or the combination of cars and industry in Toronto?" With that question left hanging, we went off to Sunny's for a ride and to try to find out a little more about the politics of logging on Peregrine Island.

Sunny met us with his usual deceptive, shambling diffidence. "Howdy, folks," he said, smiling broadly. "You ready to try a great ride, Abby? This should satisfy yer love of speed, once you get the hang of it."

"I'm game," I replied, but I still felt a bit anxious when he wheeled out the long, low-slung machine.

"What's this for?" I asked, pointing at a tall pole with a Canadian flag at the top. "Feeling patriotic, all of a sudden?"

"Not particularly," he said, "although this country sure is beautiful — it's worth bein' patriotic, if only they would keep it this way. That flag is so car drivers can see you, Ab. The bike is pretty low to the ground. They're not always lookin' for you way down there. Now climb aboard."

He quickly went through the technical details and finished with, "... and the beauty of it is that you don't stress yer back, yer legs work naturally and ya can really go. After you've left Andy in the dust, ya might want to take a break so he can catch up. If yer willin', ya can switch ... But I wouldn't get my hopes up, friend," he said to Andy. "I know Abby and speed — once she gets a taste of it, she'll be gone. You'll see, Ab. Andy might not be able to get you to stop for lunch."

"I thought you were coming," I said, trying to hide my disappointment.

"Nah, babe, I took a spin earlier, an' I need to assemble a new bike for a customer, nice full-suspension number. Besides, I got some things to set up for lunch. You kids go have fun," he said. So we went.

We agreed to do half the main loop of road and then take stock from there. If it was true that I could go so much faster, I would only have to wait at the halfway mark rather than slowing throughout. That way, we could both just relax at our own pace. I was a little nervous trying something new, but I gave Andy a wave and pushed off.

At first, I didn't like it. I felt wobbly. It was too low to the ground and I couldn't quite co-ordinate myself. Andy was soon ahead of me. Of course, I perversely cursed him under my breath as, true to our agreement, I was left to fend for myself. But then again, I was just as happy to be embarrassed all alone with what I hastily named the Demonic Machine.

But miraculously, it seemed, after about seven minutes of struggling along, something clicked and I began to feel a little more co-ordinated. I slowly let the tension seep from my shoulders and released the scowl a little from my face. It took a while for me to admit to myself that I was having fun and that it was easy, and if anyone had been asking, it would have taken even longer to admit it to them.

The first real spark of delight came when I realized I was catching up to Andy. At that point, the competitive urge flowed and I began to use the bike in earnest. Very quickly, I caught up and passed him on an uphill. That was the wondrous part. It went fast uphill, and I had the leisure to ring the bell and give a regal wave. I could have read a book if I didn't have to watch where I was going. Best of all, once I had the hang of it, I felt quite in control.

I like speed, but I like safe speed — I'm not completely nuts, or I would not have survived long as a courier. As a matter of fact, many couriers look nuts to outsiders as they jump curbs and weave in and out of traffic, but they are just very well practiced and have forgotten how scary they might appear to car drivers. Of course, it is true, some couriers are completely gonzo, but they are usually young novices, not seasoned veterans like me. They don't last more than a season or two.

I digress.

Not only were the uphills easy, the downhills were a thrill, and when I stopped at our agreed-upon meeting place, I wasn't even breathing very hard.

It took Andy another ten minutes to show up, so I entertained myself reading signs plastered on the windows outside the grocery store. On offer were several different yoga classes, and various types of bodywork were available — shiatsu, Swedish massage, lymph drainage, acupressure, acupuncture and ozone therapy. I noted that the local legion and the local kayak outfitter both offered a "moon-light serenade" session, whatever that meant.

All sorts of boats were for sale, accommodations offered, dogs and cats lost, dogs and cats found, free kittens. Basically, the windows and message boards gave the impression that the island was a busy place full of community and healers. How then, such acrimony to bring about a murder? Perhaps the new age community was pitting itself in one way or another against the older resource-based workers. Somehow, someone was going to have to bring about an understanding between the two groups so that they could work together to preserve the beauty of the island.

These musings were cut short by Andy's arrival. He didn't seem to mind having been left behind in the least. He looked relaxed and fit. "Hello, you speed demon," he said, leaning over to give me a brief hug.

We seemed to have taken a step back since the night before. What I understood to be Andy's quiet acknowledgement that we weren't going to work out long term was helping me relax and let things flow. "How'd you like Sunny's bike?"

"It's cool, Andy ... it almost feels like cheating, it's so easy. Do you want to take a turn?" I asked, not very sincerely. And he, being the healthy, gracious male he is, declined.

"Maybe later, Ab."

"Let's drop by the campsite to visit Anita, like you suggested last night," I said. "I feel like we're neglecting her."

"Sure," said Andy. "We've got lots of time, with you going so fast."

"Let's see if she wants to join us for dinner tonight. We can keep it simple, go to the local pizza place."

He nodded as I pushed off with another regal wave. "Don't wait for me," he called after me with a laugh.

The next part of the ride was grand, full of winding, undulating, downhill stretches. I quickly figured out that I had a choice to make: I could look at the view of the bay and the mountains beyond, or I could keep out of the ditch. I chose to stay on the road, and soon swung into the campsite.

It was about 11:30. Sunny had said we would have lunch around 1:00, so we had some time for a visit. I saw Anita sitting on a log in the shade on the beach below her campsite, so I stashed the bike on the beach side of the tent and walked down to see her.

"Oh, hi, Abby!" she said, still looking relaxed and happy. The tide was coming in, slowly covering the rocky beach. "Isn't it a beautiful day?" She smiled. "It's so lovely here. I'm having a great time and getting some studying done, too!" She looked around. "Where's Andy?"

"He'll be here shortly. We're on a ride around the main roads. I'm using Sunny's recumbent. It's a gas, if a little too laid-back for me. But who knows? He might convert me," I said brightly. "I dropped by to see if you would like to join us for pizza tonight?"

"Oh, Abby, you've done so much for me. I think it's my turn. I was hoping to serve you here."

"Well, thank you, I'd love that, but let's wait to check with Andy."

Anita nodded and then looked at me seriously. "How's it going anyway, Abby? You didn't seem too happy with Andy last time I saw you. I don't mean to pry, but ..."

"Yeah, I know, Anita. I just don't think this commitment thing works for me. I guess I act out instead of admitting it to myself, and I'm afraid I've been too taken up with the Armstrong murder. I've neglected him and have been enjoying myself selfishly. Anyway, Andy's quicker than I am, so I think he's figured it out."

"Too bad, Ab. I like Andy."

"Do I hear my name?" Andy had come up so quietly, we both started guiltily when he spoke. I wondered how much he'd heard, but he looked so open, I assumed he had just arrived.

"Hi, Andy," I said brightly. "Anita beat us to it. She wants us to come here for dinner."

"Sure," he said. "Why not? How about we bring dessert?"

"Great," said Anita happily. "It's lovely here in the evening. Come at 5:30 or 6:00. The sunsets are beautiful, and we can have a campfire on the beach if it gets cool."

"We'll be here with bells on," I said, giving Anita a one-armed hug as I sat beside her. Andy, the ever-amazing, pulled off his pack with a magic-show flourish.

"Look what I have here," he said, and proceeded to pull out a thermos, three paper coffee cups, creamers and sugar packets, a spoon and three croissants.

"Where'd you get all that?" I asked, eyes agog.

"Well, Abby, you don't think you're *that* fast, do you? While you were dozing at the beginning of our ride, I nipped over to the coffee place and filled up. I was back on the road in a jiff."

"And I thought I was so clever, catching up to you," I replied with a smile.

"Well, I'm impressed," said Anita. "Thanks, Andy."

We had a pleasant little coffee break as the sun glistened on the ocean. Listening to the happy chatter of a little group of children looking for crabs at the water's edge, I took in the view with satisfaction. All was calm. Several large, white yachts and a dozen or more small sailboats lay moored in the protected bay. The spit where we'd had our first beach dinner stretched off to the right. The soporific effect of the warm ocean air was only barely countered by the robust coffee. What a life! I could almost relax. But not quite. Not me. After a quiet interlude, Andy reminded me that we had to move on so we would be in time for lunch.

"Oh, yeah, Anita — we're going to meet Sunny's environmentalist friend, Nigel. Sunny said he might be able to give us more background on the logging strife on the island. I had to promise to be a good girl and not badger him."

"That will be hard for you, Abby," she said, smiling. "I hope Sunny knows what he's asking of you."

"Damn right," I said. "Okay, Andy, I'm ready. You sure you don't want to try the sedan-chair bike?" Safe question, I knew — he was out of hearing distance before I asked it.

So we cycled up and up and up to Sunny's hilltop abode. He was just out at the road, flipping his sign to "closed" as I arrived, far ahead of Andy. I got off to walk back with him to the shop.

As we approached the garage, I noticed a battered old turquoise pickup.

"Whose truck is that?" I asked with interest.

"Oh," Sunny replied, "that's Nigel's beater. He parks it where he usually moors his boat so he can get around on the island or in town. Lots of the folks who live on the outer islands keep a beater here for that purpose." He nodded at the truck. "It's handy if the vehicle appears rundown so it'll be less appealing to thieves."

"Does it work?" I asked.

"Usually, though sometimes they get vandalized." Sunny changed the subject.

"So, Ab, did you like my little Betsy?" he asked, referring to his recumbent. "Are you ready to commit?"

"Sunny, you know I'm lousy at commitment."

"So I've noticed," he drawled. "Poor Andy. He's a nice fella."

"He is, Sunny. I'm the problem, and I know it. However, I think Andy and I have reached an unspoken agreement, so I'll be nice."

"Glad to hear it. Andy said something to the same effect while we were hanging out yesterday."

"Thanks for trusting your bike to me, Sunny. It was a treat."

"Anytime, Ab. How about Andy? Did he give it a try?"

Leaving aside any feelings I had about Andy and Sunny discussing the relationship, I replied, "No, he said he'd try later. He seemed happy on his own bike."

And as if to confirm my statement, Andy arrived, smiling. "What's for lunch?" he asked. "I'm starving!"

Sunny laughed. "Now there's a man who knows what he wants. Come on in. Nigel's inside, helping set the table." We wandered back through the shop and into Sunny's inner sanctum. His kitchen was a sunny little room with large windows looking onto his garden. One set of windows looked into a small greenhouse. A rustic round wooden table was set, and a slender young man was just placing a small vase of sweet peas in the centre.

Sunny said, "Folks, meet Nigel."

Nigel had dark hair, a small, pointy "anarchist" goatee, glasses and piercing blue eyes, which belied his attempt at nonchalance when he said hello to us. He looked a little edgy, as if he couldn't stay still. All of this, of course, could lead someone as suspicious as I am to suspect guilt or, at least, a secret.

He came forward to shake hands, and we exchanged pleasantries. Then Sunny spoke again.

"Abby, I've explained to Nigel what's going on."

Nigel nodded.

"Yeah, and I'm willing to help if I can, but Jan and Mike know more about the logging on Peregrine than I do. I'm a member of our local Sierra Club, but focus mostly on the issues affecting the island I live on."

Smiling, I said, "I appreciate your coming to meet us, Nigel. Maybe over lunch you can tell us a little about your place." I was trying to think of a way to help him relax. He was so anxious-looking that I thought he might calm down if he could talk about something neutral.

Nigel nodded, and after he had helped Sunny bring everything to the table, he sat down.

During lunch, I was torn. I wanted to concentrate on Nigel's description of his little homestead, but I was distracted by the meal Sunny had prepared. You wouldn't think a big, ambling aw-shucks kind of guy like Sunny could create a luscious floral salad, a cold salmon fillet accompanied by a smooth Béarnaise sauce with a perfect amount of tarragon, along with fresh-baked bread and a bowl of local huckleberries, blueberries and raspberries. I didn't know where to start; it all clamoured for my attention.

Sunny proved to be a superb host, plying us with a crisp organic Riesling and sparkling mineral water, and producing a fresh steaming pot of the delicious locally roasted coffee at meal's end. My mouth was too full to prompt the reticent Nigel into conversation, but fortunately, Andy was better behaved, and he's the one with the bedside manner anyway, so he helped Nigel stay relaxed.

I should have paid better attention, as it turned out, but this is what did filter through to my gastronomic, endorphin-filled brain. Nigel's home was located on nearby Homestead Island, accessible only by private boat. He'd been there for five years. He owned twelve acres, some of which lay in a somewhat protected harbour with a nearby sandy beach.

He had been slowly fixing up the hundred-year-old homestead located on his property. He had a small, fenced-in area of chickens and goats, an old but still producing orchard with apple, cherry, plum and berry bushes, and a vegetable garden. It sounded idyllic, until he started describing the daily struggle to keep the eagles from his chickens, the wolves from his goats and the birds from the fruit.

"My dog, Charlie, usually lets me know about any freeloaders," he said, "but he's getting a bit old now and is a little cautious since his run-in with a cougar." That stopped me with my fork halfway to my mouth.

"A cougar? You're kidding, right?"

He shook his head with a grin, obviously pleased at the effect his cougar talk had had on me. "They're not always on the island, and if they are, they usually stay away from people. But they roam a large territory, and we're part of a chain of islands that the big cats can swim between." He paused and leaned back, adding with a sly smile, "The bears will do that, too. Anyway, one day a big old fella wandered down my driveway."

I interrupted again, confused. "What would you need a driveway for? I thought you could only get to your place by boat."

"Well, that's true, if you're coming from another island, but we have roads, so to speak. On the island, you can use the roads to ride a bike on and the few locals will sometimes visit each other in their cars. And of course the animals use the roads to get around when they're feeling lazy.

"Anyway, Charlie got wind of the old cat and ran out to investigate. This cougar was pretty tired out, I guess, because he didn't run or fight until Charlie was practically on top of him. Then he just stood his ground and growled. I heard them, grabbed my rifle, and ran out to investigate. By then, the cat had taken a swipe or two at Charlie, who kept on barking though he was bleeding around the face.

"I yelled and shot my gun into the air, and fortunately that spooked the cat. He ran off, and Charlie came back to me, whining. I patched him up as well as I could, but he's been a little less forward since then. Never saw that cat again, but I've heard he's still around.

Usually, he's spotted just lolling about, has never done anyone any harm that I've heard of."

"Are they logging on your island, too?"

"Sure," he said. "Mostly private outfits, like that Armstrong company." He practically spat out the words. "You know, I don't mind some good woodlot activity, or horse logging on a small, sustainable operation, but the larger companies just keep trying to push the envelope." He frowned.

Then Nigel brightened, and actually smiled, instantly transfigured. "But you know," he said, "our group is starting to have some successes. Some companies are starting to leave salmon spawning streams alone, and when public pressure is strong enough, we can get them to back off the watersheds. We've figured out that working through the government is too slow, and usually they'll just back the business guys. So now we're focusing our efforts on the public and the companies that receive the goods — pulp, paper, or lumber.

"Our most successful project was when we went to Japan and explained forest practices and logging of old growth. We actually got them to stop buying from the worst offending logging companies and mills. It's slow, but we're starting to succeed. I'm afraid that Peregrine hasn't been a success yet. The people in the community don't seem to be able to stop fighting amongst themselves long enough to go after the logging. It's too late for most of Armstrong's land at the south end, so now we're going to focus on those burn piles."

"The what?" I said.

"You know, all those piles of wood and debris left behind after the loggers have been through. There are 180 or so of them. They're usually burned during the rainy season. Sunny and some others are going to try to get the company to chip them, leave them as mulch and for birds' homes and stuff. Have to wait, I guess, until the hubbub from Armstrong's death settles down. We don't know who will be in charge. Melissa Armstrong has been taking a keen interest in the business over the last couple of years."

As he started to speak specifically about Armstrong lumber, he became more tense and hunched over, his language terse. I was about to ask a few more questions when I caught Sunny's warning frown, so I figured this was not the time. Instead, I sat back reluctantly and looked out the window at Sunny's flower and vegetable garden.

"That was an absolutely delicious lunch, Sun," I said agreeably. He and Nigel both visibly relaxed as I changed the subject.

CHAPTER 25

THE REST OF the time in Sunny's clean little kitchen was spent in small talk. I remained enveloped in that pleasant tiredness from good wine, lovely food and conversation. At about 2:30, Andy nudged me as he said, "Well, Sunny, that was a grand meal, but we shouldn't impose any longer. I'm sure you have work to do."

"Well," said Sunny, stretching, "I do have a coupla tune-ups to get done."

"Can I help?" I asked, relishing the idea of getting down and dirty with bikes.

Surprisingly, Andy agreed. "That's a great idea, Abby. You and Sun can talk derailleurs, while Nigel and I clean up these dishes. It won't take us long in here. Then we can get the stuff for Anita's party tonight and still have downtime at the lodge."

"Well," said Sunny, with a grin. "How can I refuse such an offer?"

I was as good as gold and just as happy discussing the new inner hubs, the speed of the recumbent, carbon fibre, and old wrecks — the island specialty. This conversation took place at a safe personal distance. Sunny was working at his bike stand, while I was sitting on a sturdy three-legged stool, truing a wheel. I was grooving in my element when the two other men walked in, announcing that all was shipshape in the kitchen.

"Okay, Andy. I'm just about done this wheel. You should have seen what a wobble it had — hard to believe the bike was still moving." I gave it a spin on the stand. "There we go, all finished," I said.

I wiped my hands on one of Sunny's greasy rags before we made our formal farewells. Sunny and Nigel walked us to the car, and at my door, I proffered my hand to Nigel.

"Well, Nigel, it's been a pleasure to meet you. Thanks for agreeing to talk with us." I was surprised when he palmed a small wad of paper into my hand as he shook it. His eyes warned me not to say anything while the few words he offered matched mine, more or less.

He added, kindly, "I hope you can help Jan. I'm sure she's done nothing but fight for the trees." I nodded, mind whirring as I slipped the paper into my pocket.

I was itching to find a time to look at the paper privately. I'm not quite sure why I didn't just read it in front of Andy, but I waited through buying some fruit and cookies and a nice wine for the dinner, and a relatively silent drive back to the lodge.

In an attempt at conversation, Andy said, "Nice fellow, that Nigel."

I said, "Yes, but didn't he seem pretty anxious whenever we wanted to talk about the Armstrong case?"

"You think so, Ab? I got the impression he's just a bit of a recluse. Probably not used to talking to strangers, I bet."

"Hmm," I mumbled, not so sure that was the case. But maybe Andy was right. I was too suspicious, looking for a murderer under any rock I could turn over.

Andy yawned. "I'm looking forward to a nice, decadent nap this afternoon. What about you?"

"Maybe I'll shower first," I lied. "I'm still up from that ride. Or perhaps I'll walk along the beach for a bit."

"Suit yourself," he said. When we arrived at the lodge, Andy was true to his word and quickly fell asleep, as only an emergency room doctor can.

As Andy slept, I went to the little porch off our room, fished the scrap of paper out of my pocket and sat in a moulded plastic lawn chair. Although it was lovely and peaceful out, a bit of a breeze had come up, fortunately from the south, so I could still breathe. A few clouds scudded across the sky. The note fluttered in my hand as I read it.

Since you're so curious about Armstrong's death, meet me at the boat launch at Yardarm Bay at 4:30. Come alone. Tell no one.

To me, this was kind of exciting, smelling of cloak-and-dagger stuff from the movies. If I had acted sensibly and had shared this note with someone, things might have turned out differently. But I acted just like they would in the movies, too. I thought I could handle everything myself. Besides, Nigel seemed harmless enough — a little neurotic, but hardly a murderer.

Deciding not to be completely foolhardy, I wrote a brief note to Andy, something to the effect that Nigel had wanted to meet me at the bay, and that I would meet Andy for dinner at the campsite. I looked at my watch — 4:00. If I left right away, I would be able to get there on my bike.

I changed to my worn jeans and threw a sweater in my backpack, in case it got cold on the beach later. Helmet in hand, I closed the door very quietly. On my way out, I stopped at the front desk and asked the bored-looking young woman to knock at our room door at 5:00 and make sure Andy was up in time to go out. I gave her my note to pass on to him.

"We're having dinner at the campground tonight," I smiled, trying to liven her up. Instead, she looked doubtful. She glanced at the large windows to the south, which gave a view of the ocean.

"I hope the weather holds out, Ms. Faria," she said. "Looks like a southeasterly is blowing in."

"Oh?" I said as I followed her gaze. There had, indeed, been a quick change; the breeze was now a hearty wind, but the sky didn't look too threatening. "Well, I guess we'll just have to hope for the best," I said. "We can always change our plans if things get bad."

"Sure," she said, brightening, as if my plans really mattered to her. "We have a prime rib special here tonight."

"Hmm," I said, not bothering to explain my aversion to red meat. I was running out of time. "Gotta go," I said.

"Bye, Ms. Faria," she said. "I'll give your note to Dr. Jaegar at 5:00."

"Bye, now," I said lightly.

True, it was windy, but this was an island, wasn't it? Bound to be windy at times. It wasn't cold, though, so the ride to the bay at the other end of the bird's beak was quite pleasurable. I coasted downhill half the way and pedalled uphill like hell for the second half. It was my second good workout for the day, a nice break from flattish Toronto. As I cycled past the campground, I noticed the once-glassy bay was looking a little choppy. I hope it's protected at the campsite, I thought.

But once I got to Yardarm Bay, the cluster of boats was only bobbing lightly, and the harbour was pretty calm compared to the ocean I had passed on the way. As I rode down the last hill, I spied a wide ramp with a dock and small store nearby. I guessed this was the boat launch Nigel had referred to. It was exactly 4:25 when I wheeled down to look for a place to lock my bike.

I found a tree thin enough to put my Kryptonite lock around, but just as I was bending over, a voice behind me said, "Don't do that."

"What?" I said, straightening. "Oh, Nigel, you scared me. Why not lock it here?"

"Oh, sorry," he muttered. "I only meant you can bring your bike over to my boat. It will be safer there while we talk. Even though this is a small community, there are still folks around who might fancy a bike like yours. And as you may have noticed, some people here have no qualms about cutting trees."

"You're right," I said. "Shame to waste a tree. I should have thought of that. It happens in Toronto, too."

Nigel led me to a remote dock where a nicely painted wooden boat with a small cabin was moored. I'm not expert on boats, landlubber that I am, but this little baby looked worn but loved.

"Nice boat, Nigel," I said politely.

"She keeps me connected," he said. "Would you like some tea?" he asked as he hefted my bike onto the deck.

"Sure," I said, hoping to keep him happy and willing to talk, although about what, I had no clue. He waved me to a little table inside the cabin. "I don't have a lot of time, though. I have a dinner date at the campsite for 5:30."

He glanced out the window as he stooped to enter behind me. "Don't know about that," he said matter-of-factly.

"What do you mean?" I said, half rising.

"The weather's turning. There might be quite a blow."

"That's what the woman at the lodge said. It doesn't look too bad right now."

He shrugged, and turned around as a kettle on his galley stove shrilled. He poured the boiling water into a surprisingly dainty-looking teapot and said, "If you live out here long enough, you get a feel for the weather."

He turned, teapot on a tray with matching teacups and a plate of cookies. As he set it down, I observed, "With weather as wild as you say, I'm surprised such a tea set would survive on a boat."

"Yeah." He looked sheepish. "I'm just partial to it. It belonged to my old English aunt and reminds me of visiting her when I was a kid. She used to make me tea like this," he said, "weak, milky and sweet. Only now, I add some herbs and spices. Try it."

Dutifully, I took a sip of the sickly sweet, herbal mixture. There was a hint of a flavour I recognized but couldn't quite name. "You're a man of contrast," I said, "living out in the wild, yet with cultured tastes."

"I suppose," he said. "I just became tired of people and all the waste everywhere."

"I'm with you on the waste," I agreed. "Now, Nigel, I'm sure that you didn't ask me here for tea. You said you had something to tell me about this murder business."

The boat rocked a little as I drained my cup. I carefully passed it his way before I dropped it. I was feeling a little queasy. Couldn't be seasick at dock, could I?

Nigel looked concerned. "You look a little green," he said solicitously. "Maybe some more tea will help." He poured me another cup. "Here," he said. "Why don't you sit on my window bench. You might be more comfortable." I nodded and sat falteringly on a cushioned bench in the little alcove.

"Yes, the Armstrongs," he said. "It's a shame that Jan got caught up in that business. We've been fighting the logging for quite a while. But Armstrong was such a bastard that he never budged an inch. He just seemed to laugh in our faces."

I was distracted by my queasiness, having trouble holding on to the thread of the conversation, but it didn't seem to be anything I didn't know already. "I'm sorry, Nigel," I said. "I can't seem to stay up. Perhaps I need some fresh air." I gave him the cup and tried to stand. He came forward, concern still on his face. "I'm not usually so pitiful," I said.

"No problem," he replied, with a half smile, "but I don't think you'll make it outside right now. Why don't you just lie down for a moment?"

"Don't seem... to have a... choice," I said slowly, as I lay down. The room was spinning. What is wrong with me? I wondered. I don't get sick.

As the cabin continued to swing about wildly, Nigel, looking like a concerned host, took a damp cloth and placed it over my brow. "Perhaps I should call the lodge," he said, "to let them know you aren't well."

Just then, the boat rocked again and a female voice called, "Nigel, are you here?" A moment later, Melissa Armstrong popped her head into the cabin. We looked at each other in mutual horror.

"Nigel!" she cried. "No! ... What are you doing?" I could have asked the same if my mouth worked. This was getting way too strange. I realized that this wasn't seasickness; it was more like I'd been drugged. What was going on? Nigel's voice sounded far away as I listened in disbelief.

"Don't worry, love," he said. "She's been asking a lot of questions. Alex and Brendon suggested I take her somewhere we could straighten things out a bit."

"No!" said Melissa. "Don't get involved with them, Nigel!"

I tried to get up on my elbow to make some scintillating, brilliant comment. Instead, my head swam, and I fell back. Despite fighting it, my eyes slowly closed while I thought: If Nigel knows Melissa and Brendon, then I'm in real trouble.

Chapter 26

I CAME TO, briefly, sometime later. My muscles ached and I felt frozen. As I blinked my eyes open, I thought I was still really dizzy, until I realized the boat was moving. The sky was grey through the window as the motor droned and the boat dipped wildly. I was no longer on the cozy bench, and I was terribly stiff. I could feel the ache in my bad arm, the one I had injured when trying to help Anita out of a fix back in Kensington. The rest of me didn't feel any better, either — I was still nauseous from the tea and from the motion of the sea. Nigel was steering from the front of the cabin, and Melissa wasn't visible. Of course, my vision was limited, but it felt like she was gone.

As the little boat pitched yet again to one side, I rolled a bit and slid to a corner, banging my shoulder some more. I suddenly remembered my bike. Did he put it somewhere safe, or did it meet its end in the salty waters? That made me wonder about my own fate. Was I going the route of my bike? Had Nigel, by any chance, really called the lodge? It didn't seem likely, given my present circumstance. I really started to worry when I considered that somehow Brendon and Alex were mixed into the scenario.

Questions continued to swim around in my queasy brain. How had Melissa become connected to Nigel? Did she have some kind of kinky attraction to the enemy? And what was Nigel up to? Why would *he* have anything to do with her? Was he just pretending to care about the logging, or was he misguided by love? Could he be some kind of infiltrator for the logging industry, or was he simply caught up in Brendon's slimy drug business?

Bobbing up and down on the floor of a boat had sapped much of the spunk out of me. I couldn't think of any snappy jokes to entertain myself with as I was kept in suspense about my fate. For once, with little other choice, I decided to be sensible and to stay quiet and see what happened next.

Maybe we would just capsize, mystery unsolved — me, Nigel, his precious boat and my bicycle — all down into the murky depths, never to be heard from again. On that macabre note, I passed out again, and when I next became conscious, it was quiet and I was warm and dry. I was not at the bottom of the sea, and I was not in the boat, but I still felt stiff and sore.

Taking in my surroundings, I looked around while the wind howled outside the little room I was in. Along one wall were rows of books sitting on rustic shelving, and against another wall was a comfy-looking double bed. In a corner were a small desk and chair. And I lay, plunk on the floor, near the wall opposite the shelves. I licked my lips and craned my neck. Above me was a window, rattling from the force of the wind.

There was an open door in the wall opposite the foot of the bed. From there, warmth and the sweet scent of marijuana smoke emanated. That might explain the connection between Nigel and the boys. The light in my room came from a lamp placed on top of the desk. When I groaned involuntarily, my new "friend," Nigel, entered the room.

"Hi," he said, as if initiating a friendly conversation. "How are you feeling?"

I grimaced. "Not terribly comfortable, I'm afraid."

"I'm sorry about that," he said. "I couldn't have you running off before we got here."

"Where are we, exactly?" I asked.

"This is my cabin," he said proudly.

This Nigel is some strange guy, I thought. Now he's so civil, no menace in his voice or manner. He helped me limp over to the bed, where at least I could sit a little more comfortably. Still woozy, I wondered if I had the strength to overpower Nigel.

"What am I doing here, Nigel? There are other ways to invite me to your place."

"Ah, yes," he said sadly. "I'm sorry. This whole affair is very unfortunate. That man Armstrong deserved to die."

"I seem to have heard that sentiment before, but are you telling me you had something to do with it? Can anyone truly play God with the lives of others?"

"Pah," he spat out. "He played God, the way he abused his family and destroyed the great old trees." He continued talking. "Of course I didn't have anything to do with it. I'm sorry for dragging you out here, Abby. I kind of owe Brendon. I help them when they harvest their weed in return for a cut. When they heard you were having lunch with me, they kind of forced me to help them. Brendon can be pretty rough, you know." He looked at me pleadingly. "I had to bring you here, Abby."

"That's ridiculous. What are you planning to do with me? You can't keep me here forever, however pleasant the surroundings. You'll have to let me go eventually."

"I'm not going to do anything. We're waiting for Brendon and Alex. They wanted to ask you some questions and asked me to get you out of the way while they complete some deal they're working on."

"Kidnapping *is* a crime, Nigel, and did you *have* to drug me?" I asked snappishly. "I have a whopping headache."

"Oh," he said sheepishly. "I must have overdone it. I put a few of Mel's sleeping pills in your tea, just to slow you down."

"Well, it worked," I said. "I'm feeling slow all right."

"I don't know if they'll get through for a while, though" he said. "It's a bit wild out there. I don't suppose you want some tea?" he asked, his civil self again. "I'm just warming some up on the stove for the boys when they arrive. They'll need it if they make it over tonight."

"No, thanks," I said. "I have had enough of your kind of tea. How about a nice double espresso?"

He shrugged.

"Come to think of it," I said, "I could use a trip to the little girls' room."

"Huh?" he said, puzzled for a moment at my uncharacteristic use of this euphemism for the washroom. When his light bulb finally went on, he said, "Oh, yeah, of course. I don't suppose you can run anywhere in this weather."

I didn't bother to tell him that I am a bit more than a little nature phobic. "I promise I'll be a good girl," I said, getting up from the bed.

In the privacy of the washroom, I pondered my plight. Nigel was harmless compared to Brendon and Alex. How could I deal with him before the other two arrived? I looked around, thinking a baseball bat would come in handy, but no such luck. I looked hopefully in his quaint bathroom cupboard, not really expecting anything, but right there was a big bottle of sleeping pills with Melissa's name on the label. Those two must be cozier than I guessed, I thought to myself.

This gave me an idea that appealed to me for its potential irony as well as its effectiveness. Maybe, I thought, just maybe I could play Nigel's trick back on him. It was a long shot, but it was better than doing nothing. I pondered the dose. We were about the same size, and they had been strong enough to do a quick job on me, but I had no idea how many he'd fed me. Finally, I decided to just give him the lot.

I screwed up my courage and nonchalantly walked out of the washroom, straight to Nigel's wood stove, where a large brown Betty of tea sat, next to a steaming kettle. I called over my shoulder to Nigel. "You know, Nigel, I guess it's safe to take you up on that tea after all. Can I just pour for myself or would you like some, too?" I asked.

"Huh? Sure," he said. "It's good of you to be reasonable."

So I took two mugs from the dish rack and filled them with tea. I dropped three pills in Nigel's and tried his trick of adding lots of milk and sugar.

Then I said in my best tea-serving voice, "Should I top up the pot?"

"Sure, why not?" He said.

So I lifted the lid, dropped the remaining five pills in and pretended to fill the pot, carefully replacing the lid. Then I said a silent prayer for sweet dreams. There was enough for two cups left, and I didn't want to dilute the drug too much. While I handed him his tea, I tried a little psychology.

"Nigel," I said. "Why don't you give it up? You haven't really done anything you'll be sorry for yet, and I left a note for Andy saying I was meeting you, so at some point, you'll be caught up with anyway."

He shook his head. "I can't go back now; it's too stormy. Besides, Andy dropped by around 6:00 before I left and asked if you were there. I told him you'd left a long while back. So he won't be looking here."

Poor Andy, I thought to myself. He must be beside himself.

Taking a gulp of tea, Nigel went on, "I don't like Brendon much but he's calling the shots."

He was way too matter of fact about the situation. I politely sipped more, thinking I might as well keep him talking. I sat on the bed docilely while he sat in a chair opposite me, smoking and drinking his tea.

"What do you think those two drugged-out cowboys are going to do with me?"

"I don't know," he said. "I don't want to know. They had some fear that you were a narc. I let them know different, of course, but Brendon doesn't think much. He's the enforcer. Alex will figure out something effective. Maybe they'll just try to scare you, but I have this feeling you don't scare easy."

I decided to be straightforward. "Listen, Nigel. Brendon is more than a hothead. He has a history back in Toronto. He could be a killer. You can't leave me with him."

He put his elbow on his knees, hands to his chin, and stifled a yawn. "Where are those two?"

"They don't strike me as the most dependable individuals."

"Hmm ..." he responded, blinking his eyes.

Pressing a little, I said, "Nigel? Would you like some more tea? Might help you wake up."

"Huh?" he said, starting to look decidedly dreamy.

"Finish this," I said, handing him his cup. He obediently took the last two gulps. I quickly walked to his stove and refilled his cup. He took the cup a little unsteadily. It was kind of fun turning the tables on him so easily. It gave me back some of my much-needed confidence.

"Thanks," he slurred. I wondered if he was going to figure out what I had done. It seemed a little too obvious and too ironic. Nigel slurped about half the cup before setting it down at the desk, spilling some of the liquid as it almost tipped over. He leaned his elbow onto the desk and slumped, head on arm. His eyes were closed, but I waited for his breathing to become regular before I made my move.

I had no idea when the other two would arrive, but I thought my best chance, despite my fear of the outdoors, was to get out of there fast. I grabbed a raincoat off a peg by the door and, not forgetting my stomach, shoved some trail mix from Nigel's cupboard into the pocket. I turned the handle of the door. The wind whipped it wide open, slamming it into the wall. No longer a sleeping dog, Charlie raised his head and barked lightly.

"Damn!" I cried out, my voice mostly lost in the wind.

Once I tugged the door closed, my attention was immediately drawn down the hill towards a large motorboat trying to dock at the pier. The boat's bright spotlight lit up the area, where it looked like wild waves were making the task difficult. That must be Brendon and his friend, I thought grimly as I scurried under cover of the trees to the side of the house.

With a half-formed notion in my head of stealing the boat, I watched as they finally moored, disembarked and headed up to the cottage. As soon as they were both in, I dashed down to the water. The rain made the hillside treacherous, but I reached the water's edge with only one slip. Staring at the boat, I realized I had no idea how to negotiate it in calm waters, let alone in a storm, so I had no real choice but to walk away along the rocky edge. There was no sign of Nigel's sandy beach, probably due to the rough water; just rocks with pounding waves as far as I could see through the murk.

Smiling grimly, I wondered how much time I had. I imagined the chaos in Nigel's cabin as they tried to find out from him what had happened. Venturing a backward glance, I saw, sure enough, that they were at the door yelling, and then I heard barking. Maybe I should have drugged the dog, too, I thought, wondering if they'd be able to use him to find me. But surely he wasn't trained for that. And

Nigel had said he was getting pretty old. He wouldn't be up to sniffing out errant bicycle couriers in the dark through driving storms. Nevertheless, I moved faster when I saw the play of a flashlight beam through the haze. I figured that my only chance was to put as much distance as possible between us, and to hope help would come before they did.

As I stumbled along, getting wet and cold, I noticed the ledge was giving way to a beach in a more protected nook. A small dinghy had been pulled up onto a grassy verge near the far side of the inlet. It looked a bit more manageable than the big boat down at the dock. Desperate, I thought I might try to row further along. The dog, if it followed me, might lose my trail to the water.

Luck was with me. The dinghy had oars attached and seemed seaworthy as far as I could tell. I pushed it into the water and hopped aboard. At first, it seemed easy as I rowed out around the inlet, but as soon as I hit the wind and bigger waves, I knew I was in trouble. The one good thing, I thought as I vainly tried to keep away from the next rocky beach, was that the wind seemed to be blowing me away from the cabin.

Despite this, I knew I would have to abandon ship when waves began to surge over the little vessel. Hoping to hit a bit of beach where I could actually land, I ploughed on. It would be a colossal drag to be dashed against rocks after escaping some unknown doom at the hands of one confused, smitten environmentalist and two vicious drug-dealing spoiled brats.

I scored my usual portion of half-luck yet again. I gored the boat on rock, but I was close enough to shore to get there on my own. The rowboat continued to be inundated by massive waves as it wallowed on the rock, so I decamped into cold water. But after a second or two, it seemed quite balmy compared to the wind on my wet skin. After floundering a couple of times and swallowing a pitcher full of salty water, my feet found purchase and I finally straggled to land, congratulating myself on yet another narrow escape. Wondering how many of the proverbial nine lives I had left, I slogged towards dark bushes that waved alluringly in the wind.

It was a mistake to think about cats. Up until now, I had been too busy running and surviving to think about my surroundings. Now the memory of Nigel's tale of the cougar crept into my mind. Oh shit, I thought.

As I started the trudge up the hill in the shadowy, wet night, I cursed myself for ever leaving the comforting concrete of the city. Then the thought occurred to me that maybe all the big cats are hiding out, too, on such a miserable night. I held on to that hope as I worked my way inland through a mixture of grass, bushes, small fir trees and willowy plants. After a couple of nasty stumbles, I held my hands in front of me to avoid braining myself on anything too big or too hard. I made slow progress, tripping occasionally. Finally, my foot caught on something and I tripped again, this time twisting my ankle painfully.

All of a sudden, I just didn't care anymore. Overwhelmed by fatigue and pain, I lay down and curled up in the lee of one of the small firs, shaking and shivering under the wet raincoat I had stolen from Nigel. Was this hypothermia? I wondered. Would I die here in August under Christmas trees? I remember feeling sorry before drifting off. Sorry mostly for dragging my friends Andy and Sunny through my shenanigans. As I lapsed into unconsciousness, oddly lulled by the rain, I wondered if I would do things any differently if I had a second chance.

CHAPTER 27

I DREAMT I was in a sauna, or maybe a steam bath. It wasn't very comfortable, but it was warm. Opening my eyes, I was momentarily confused by the yellow glow around me, until memory flooded in and I realized it was light reflecting off my steamy, yellow raincoat cover. With aching muscles, I pushed away the slicker to allow the warm sun to penetrate and dry my soggy clothes. It was late morning, judging by the angle of the sun.

I luxuriated for a while in being alive and reasonably well, if a little sore and exhausted. Only able to muster up a small turn of the head at a time, I took in my surroundings. I was on a slight incline in a clearing. Since large trees loomed to my left and right, I surmised that I might be in a formerly logged area that had been reforested, hence the 'Christmas trees.' With a jolt of recognition, I realized that the little bushes popping up here and there were what looked like very healthy marijuana plants. It was strange, but on second thought, not entirely surprising. Maybe this was one of Brendon and Alex's plantations. If they legalized the stuff, B.C. would have a great source of taxation, I thought randomly.

When I finally tried to stand, I had a painful reminder of the twisted ankle from the night before. Sprained? Broken? I didn't know, but it hurt like hell to put weight on it. Hopping through the woods on one foot would be impossible, and crawling would take too long. So I tried again to walk. Fortunately, in that land of trees, I soon found a suitable stick for a crutch.

Down the incline was the wide ocean dotted by islands — and the wrecked dinghy, so I decided to go up the hill to try to find a friendlier Homesteader. The effort of walking took all other thoughts out of my mind. That way, I did not think about big cats. As I poked along, looking more carefully, I verified that those were indeed very healthy marijuana plants. Some of my acquaintances in Kensington Market would have been very excited, but I had no desire to harvest any. I'd had enough drugs in the last twenty-four hours. It was all I could do to trudge on.

Fortunately, dumb luck prevailed; there on the other side of a ditch full of water was a green bicycle leaning against another Christmas tree. Next to that was a rutted road filled with cavernous potholes and strewn with branches, but it was a road, which I thought most likely signified a route to some sort of civilization.

Very clumsily, I forded the water-filled ditch and edged the bike up to the road. The machine was a little large for me, but after a few tries, I developed a lopsided one-footed pedalling system and began the painful process of negotiating my way around the potholes and small bits of branches and twigs. Occasionally, I had to dismount to clamber over larger branches and two whole trees that had fallen, presumably in the storm. The sun was climbing higher, and with its warmth, the effort of pedalling and my fatigue, I was sweating profusely. I became thankful for stretches of shade provided by tunnels of forest.

During the less painful moments, I set myself to thinking. I knew that if a cougar or the boys didn't get me, I would eventually be okay. But what next? Andy was probably worried, or thoroughly pissed off, or both. I hoped he had taken Anita in again or she would be a drowned rat. Between the two of them and Sunny, they must have figured out that something weird had happened. They'd be out looking, but would they think to look here? I mused and pedalled and climbed and began to feel very hungry, very thirsty and very sorry for myself. Happily, as I emerged from another sweep of forest, I suddenly encountered Eden.

In front of me was a tidy orchard laden with ripening fruit, except where a few branches had broken in the storm. Below, on one side of the road, were more fruit trees, and down by the sparkling ocean lay a protected inlet where a couple of motorboats were moored. To my right, perched farther up the hill, past more fruit trees, was a rustic wooden farmhouse complete with a wraparound porch and solar panels. The idyllic little scene was set to a soundtrack of the contented bleating of goats, a number of which were grazing peacefully about the trees.

"Thank God," I thought. "I sure hope someone is home."

Climbing through a break in the wooden fence, I limped my way up the hill. I picked an overhanging apple, which tasted better than any in the world. As I munched and headed for the house, I felt like a mixture of Eve and Gretel, and I wasn't sure whether I was in heaven or about to meet the witch in her gingerbread house.

As I neared the house, I spied a group of four people on one side of the porch moving slowly in unison. I knew what they were doing. I had walked the streets near Kensington Market long enough to be familiar with Tai Chi. On the other side were three people sitting in lotus position, eyes closed, hands on knees, quietly meditating. After all I'd just been through, this was just plain surreal. It was not really surprising, I suppose, but I had seen so much lately — loggers, socialites, pot plants on the hillside, and now I had stumbled on a retreat of some kind. My mother would love it here, I thought inconsequentially.

I figured my bedraggled state would look quite daunting to these people while they were in their hallowed one, so I stood there inconspicuously for a while, chewing my apple as quietly as I could. Above, two eagles wheeled silently in the sky. Paradise regained, I thought, but my mental meandering was cut off by a voice in front of me.

"Peace, sister." I looked up at the porch to see a beautiful grey-haired woman in flowing yellow robes. "Why do you have Brendon Armstrong's bike?"

I looked at her questioningly, and then at the bike. "Oh, this? I found it by the road and ... sort of borrowed it. I didn't know whose it was." Hard to believe this apparition would know of Brendon and his earthbound doings. I became a little more wary. Better not give myself away.

She gave a small nod and said, "Would you like to come in? You look a little the worse for wear."

"Yes," I said gratefully. "I'm sorry to disturb you."

I quietly laid the bike down. The meditators and Tai Chi people continued doing their thing, either oblivious to or ignoring the interruption. I wouldn't fit here, I thought. I'd never be able to sit still long enough.

"I'm sorry," I said, "but could you help me? I seem to have hurt my ankle."

"Of course," she replied, drifting down to my level. Still somewhat delirious, I imagined she had a yellow halo, too. The diaphanous robes draped a body of steel, however. She seemed to not notice my weight as I leaned on her for support, and her grip was firm as she guided me into a cool and airy living room. After she made sure I was seated comfortably on a gaily patterned couch, she told me she'd be back soon and left the room.

I didn't notice much, other than a large fireplace and very simple furnishings. A stone Buddha squatted happily on the hearth. The Good Witch Glinda, as I had dubbed her, floated back with a glass of something.

"Here," she said, "drink this. It will make you feel better."

I looked at her suspiciously. "It's not tea, is it?" I asked.

"No, dear," she said. "It's my special herbal infusion, guaranteed to bring you energy and peace."

In other words, it was tea. I sipped it politely at first, but it was wonderful — a mix of lemon, mint and some woodsy flowers I didn't recognize. I drank thirstily, and immediately felt somewhat revived.

"That was fantastic," I said.

"Good." She looked pleased. "The others won't be in for a while. We can talk a bit before I find a place for you to get cleaned up. You look, pardon my expression, like hell."

"I'm sure I do," I replied. "Who is this Brendon Armstrong you mentioned?" I asked, feigning ignorance but trying to get the lay of the land.

"Oh, he is one of the less savoury characters whose family owns land on this island," she said. "He's an unhappy lad who makes a lot of trouble. He has some drug plantations growing on land his father, may he rest in peace, clear-cut a while back. I believe that Brendon uses that bike to check on his plants."

I relaxed. So she didn't like Brendon, either. "Oh," I said, "I saw some of those plants and wondered who was responsible for them." My stomach growled very loudly. "I'm sorry," I said. "I haven't eaten anything for a while, besides a wonderful apple I took from your tree down there."

My angel of mercy instantly levitated. "Of course! You need something to eat. I'll be right back." She returned quickly with a large slab of bread slathered with what looked like pâté. "Homemade bread," she said, "and homemade vegetable spread."

"You're very generous, especially considering I'm a complete stranger," I said with my mouth full, trying to be polite and not wolf down the food.

"Not at all," she said. "On an island like this, we learn to help each other out when we face the elements."

"I've noticed that," I said, "on Peregrine. I'm afraid I had a bit of an adventure last night. I was out on the ocean in a little rowboat when the storm blew up. I got swept over here and capsized on some rocks close to shore in the dark. I slept on the hill in a clearing with little trees in it."

"My goodness," she said, her eyebrows raised. "That must have been a terrifying experience; it's a miracle you didn't drown. I imagine you landed at one of the Armstrong clear-cuts. I guess that's where you found the bike."

I nodded.

"You are very lucky to have survived," she continued. "The ocean was wild last night. The power lines went down with some tree-fall. Fortunately, we have solar and wind power here, so we don't have to rely on the grid. It's too unpredictable out here."

She stood. "Luckily, we don't have a full house right now, so I have a little room with a sink where you can wash up and rest. I'm sure I can find some dry clothes for you." Imagining myself bedecked in her angelic outfit, I smiled.

"That would be wonderful, but I don't want to impose any more than I have."

"Nonsense," she said. "You're in no shape to go anywhere right now. We can ferry you back to Peregrine later."

I nodded. "Um, my name is Abby, by the way."

"Oh, how thoughtless of me. I'm Morningstar — Leyah Morningstar."

We shook hands and I asked, "Is there any way to get in touch with someone on Peregrine?"

"Why, yes, dear. We have a cellphone, and we're lucky to have reception at this spot on the island. I don't like to use it much. You know, radiation." She went to a drawer and pulled out a cellphone.

"I agree with you there," I said. "But I think I should phone my friend Sunny. He works on bikes over on Peregrine."

A wide smile lit up her already radiant face. "I know Sunny. He fixes our guests' bikes and joins us on wilderness walks. He is a good friend. And a lovely man," she added.

I nodded. "We're old friends."

"Well, dear, go right ahead and give him a call. He must be worried."

"Maybe," I said. I thought angry might be more likely, but held my tongue. "I don't have my phone book with me. Do you have his number?" I suddenly realized my backpack and ID were missing, probably dumped in the ocean somewhere, along with my bike.

"Certainly," she said, walking to a bulletin board and pulling off a business card. "Here you are."

I dialled the number but got only the answering machine with his familiar "Hi, y'all!" and an outline of his services and directions to the premises. When it finally ended, I left a short, cryptic message.

"Hi, Sunny. It's Abby. I'm okay and I'm very, very sorry. I'm at Leyah Morningstar's retreat on Homestead Island. Can you let the others know I'm okay? I'll talk to you soon."

As I handed the phone back to my hostess, she said, "If he calls while you are resting, I will talk to him, dear."

"Thanks," I said. "And I know this is a lot to ask, but if anyone else comes by looking for me, please don't tell them I'm here."

She raised an eyebrow. "Is there a problem?"

"No, no problem. I just need some rest before I face the world again."

She nodded and placed a motherly hand on my arm. "I'll show you your little room."

"Is this some kind of resort?" I asked as we walked to the back of the house. "You have so many guests."

"Well, in a way," she said. "Most of the year, it is our home, but we hold five or six retreats in the summer, when we offer yoga, Tai Chi, meditation, and healthy food."

"Sounds wonderful," I said politely. "Such a lovely setting."

"Yes," she replied, "although last night's storm was a bit of a shock for our guests. It was a bit unseasonable, but with global climate change, anything is possible. Here we are," she said as she opened a door at the end of the hall.

It was a small pleasant room, more like a large, narrow closet, with pale yellow walls. A small bed filled half the space, its head just below a window overlooking a vegetable garden. A very small triangular sink sat in the opposite corner, while a tiny wardrobe and some hooks took up the other wall.

"It's all we have free, I'm afraid," she said apologetically.

"Oh, no," I protested. "It's perfect. Thank you again."

She smiled and said, "I'll check on you in a few hours. There's a toilet just down the hall. Don't worry about how much water you use. We have a gravity-fed artesian well, so we never run out, and there's a good septic system." She gave me a brief hug, murmuring, "Peace be with you," and was gone.

I made a quick trip to the bathroom, and once back in the little room, I hardly had the energy to undress and wash. But she was right, even that little procedure made me feel better. I felt safe in this stranger's house, and once I slid between the clean sheets, my eyes were closed before my head hit the pillow.

Chapter 28

AWAKENING SOMETIME LATER in the day, I felt a warm breeze issuing from the window near my head, the diaphanous curtains wafting by my face. Before testing my foot, I took a few moments to enjoy the comfort and peace so kindly bestowed on me after my ordeal. It was still sore, but not excruciating, probably a light sprain at the worst.

I sat up and spotted a pair of jaunty crimson sweatpants and a sweatshirt at the foot of the bed. There was no need to emulate the angelic Morningstar after all. While I dressed, I noticed that the shadows were lengthening over the vegetable garden. It was late afternoon, I guessed, as I gingerly limped to the sink to wash my face. Sitting on the bed for a few minutes, I gathered my strength to face the world. I knew I couldn't impose on Morningstar much longer. Besides, my friends were probably anxious to see me, and there was a murder that truly needed to be solved.

The sunflowers in the garden waved their bright faces at the sun slowly disappearing around the front of the building. Then I noticed some movement on the path between the cabbage bed and a trellis of some kind of beans. Perhaps a deer had got into their garden. I had learned that the voracious deer were a problem in island gardens, so I was about to go and warn my host when the animal emerged and stopped me in my tracks.

It was not a deer but a dog, an unmistakable dog — Nigel's old Charlie. He limped up the path, a dark patch matting his coat near one forepaw. My heart began to race. If the dog was near, Nigel might not be far off, which meant, perhaps, that the two more dangerous young men might be around as well. I didn't believe they would cause any trouble in this peaceful place amidst so many people, but one couldn't be too sure.

I went to my door and opened it a crack. The hall was clear, but muted voices wafted from somewhere up front. Wrapped in reflexive fear, I tiptoe-limped down to the front hall. Peering around the stairway and looking into the front room, I saw Morningstar and Nigel seated with their backs to me, talking quietly on the couch facing the front window. I couldn't hear a word, but I recognized his distinctive voice. Morningstar was patting Nigel on the shoulder in what appeared to be a consoling manner. I turned and worked my way back to the little room, shutting the door quietly and letting panic consume me.

What was I going to do now? Was Nigel alone? It was unlikely that Morningstar could be involved in his crazy plot to get rid of me, but I was in panic mode, overwhelmed by the impulse to try to get away. Perhaps I could get on to one of the boats and drive to Peregrine. It was calm enough.

I gave in to my first impulse. I had no fear of the dog. He had not bothered me when I was in Nigel's cabin. It was the human animals inside the house I was not sure of. So I decided to climb out the back window and skirt my way around and down to the water. In retrospect, this seemed like a crazy plan, but at the time, I thought it quite sane.

With a little difficulty, I climbed from the window without hurting my ankle too much. The dog approached, panting a little. We limped towards each other, and while I patted his head, I glanced at his matted paw. It looked like a mix of mud and blood. "Poor pup," I whispered. "How did you get hurt?" He just licked my hand and whimpered. I shushed him and whispered to him to stay, and began circling the garden. He followed, of course, and as I neared the corner of the house, I turned once again and told him, "Stay!" in as authoritative a whisper as I could. He sat down, looking pitiful. Satisfied, I turned around again and walked right into Sunny's arms.

"Whoa, girl. Where are you going?" he asked. I felt a strange mix of fear, relief and excitement as he held on to me. In a flood of irrational paranoia, I thought, not Sunny, too … But I remained mute, too weak to struggle, and resigned myself to fate.

"What are you doing, Abby?" he asked as he held me at arm's length. "You're supposed to be snoozing in Leyah's house, and here you are running around in the garden. Come on, girl, you're shaking. You don't look so good. I think we should go in and have a chat." He started walking me towards the front.

"No, Sunny! Nigel's in there," I said, pulling back.

"Yeah … So?" he puzzled. "What's going on, Abby? You disappear in the night, giving everyone a fright, and then I hear from you today that you're here. Then Nigel calls me, too, asking for help." He looked at me suspiciously. "Abby, you didn't have anything to do with Nigel's trouble last night, did you? He's looking pretty rough. Won't say nothing, either."

I stared at him, nonplussed. "Nigel's trouble?" I blurted out. "He's the one who caused the trouble. He tried to kill me!" Sunny stared at me.

"Nigel? He couldn't hurt a fly. He's a pacifist."

"Some pacifist," I said grumpily.

"What happened to Nigel?" Sunny asked sharply. "Old Charlie's injured, and Nigel's all bruised and bloody, looks like he's been beaten. And his boat is sunk at its dock."

I felt stunned, but slowly regained my common sense. "I don't know! But you're right, Sunny. It is time to go in and have a chat. Maybe Nigel can help us put a few more pieces of this puzzle together. Besides, I think I do have to sit down."

Drained of adrenalin, my fatigue, aches and pains were getting the better of me. Fortunately, Sunny was hale, and now that he had lectured me for deeds done and not done, he became solicitous. He helped me limp to the front door and enter slightly more decorously than I had left. The dog came along.

As Morningstar and Nigel looked up, Sunny said, "Look what I found out back. Seems she thought she had to get away without saying good-bye. Where you thought you were goin', Abby, I can't imagine," he said, smiling.

I hate being patronized or made a fool of, so needless to say, I didn't smile back. I did offer my profuse apologies to Morningstar, however. "I'm sorry, Morningstar, after you treated me so kindly. I believe I owe you an explanation."

She rose graciously and glided over, looking concerned and shaking her head. "Not at all, dear," she said, leading me towards a chair next to the couch Nigel was resting on. "Nigel has been explaining some of what went on last night. You two need to talk to each other."

As I came to the seat, I looked at Nigel, who stared blankly out the window. He *was* a sight. His left hand was bandaged, his face bloodied, and he had a cut on his cheek. One blue-black eye was mostly shut with swelling. I began to have a little more compassion for him, but remembered wryly that he had been setting me up for perhaps a similar fate.

He finally turned to look at me with his one good eye. He looked embarrassed, if that was possible through all the pulpy flesh. "I'm sorry," he said. "I was wrong."

"Okay, Nigel," I replied, "but this can't go on. Are Brendon and Alex responsible for this?" I asked, gesturing to his wounds. He nodded almost imperceptibly.

"I think you're right, Morningstar. Can Nigel and I speak together privately for a few minutes?" I looked at Nigel. He nodded.

Morningstar nodded, too, and took Sunny by the hand. "Come with me, dear. I'm afraid, with all this excitement, I'm behind on dinner. Perhaps you can help me." She turned to me, saying, "The guests are all in their rooms doing silent meditation for another half-hour, so you won't be disturbed. Perhaps we can all have dinner together before you return to Peregrine."

Sunny looked hesitant, but went along with Morningstar. I waited until they had left the room.

CHAPTER 29

LOOKING AT NIGEL helped me feel like I finally had the upper hand, and I decided it was time to use it. "I guess the boys weren't too forgiving last night," I said. "I'm sorry you were hurt, but I can't say I'm sorry I left you there. My fate would probably have been much worse."

He nodded, looking appropriately miserable.

"You know, Nigel," I continued, "what you did was illegal. I could have you charged with assault, kidnapping, conspiracy, and all sorts of other stuff."

Charlie's two eyes and Nigel's one good one gazed at me liquidly. My heart melted a little more. "Anyway, I'm not interested in charging you. Looks like you've already paid enough."

He mumbled something through swollen lips.

"What?" I asked. It was hard to understand him well. His usual, eloquent speech was garbled, as if he had a mouthful of marbles. He straightened a little, cleared his throat and said a little more loudly and clearly, "I was wrong to think that getting you out of the way would help." He looked at me defiantly and then continued, his voice gaining strength as it filled with emotion.

"After you took off, they tried to follow you; they even tried to send Charlie out to search, but he wouldn't leave me, and I was too groggy to be any use. They must have been high on something, because they were very agitated. The weather was too rough to put out to sea again, so they decided to let you go and figured that if you took the dinghy, you would probably drown.

"They took their fury out on me, or rather, Alex watched while Brendon vented his frustrations. While he was punching and kicking me, he kept telling me I was stupid, that it was all a stupid mistake.

I wasn't sure that he was telling the truth. Charlie was frantic, and he was jumping at Brendon, trying to protect me.

"That's when Alex got involved. I didn't see what he did, but I heard a whack and Charlie started whimpering. Then Alex hauled Brendon off me and Charlie crawled over. I was angry about the dog but still so stunned that I couldn't do anything. I kept coming in and out of consciousness. They slammed the bedroom door and left us there. I passed out again, so I have no idea when they left. When I came to, Charlie was still whining and licking my face. It was quiet and the storm had passed."

He went on. "It took me a while to get up and clean up. Poor old dog was injured; they must have hit his paw with something hard. I guess I deserved my own beating, having called them there in the first place. I just didn't know what to do."

"What do you think Brendon meant, talking about a stupid mistake?" I asked. "Was he talking about the murder?"

"I don't know. Maybe Brendon did it, but I was so sure it was Melissa. I thought she'd finally snapped. You see, her father had abused her when she was young. She was messed up for years, but she didn't know why because she had repressed the memory of the abuse. Then, when we got together, she started to have flashbacks, you know, of what her father had done to her. She's been seeing a psychiatrist and told me that she'd had fantasies of killing the old man. I thought she had just, well, finally dealt with him."

He was silent for a second and then started to speak again.

"Besides, I ..." he trailed off.

"What Nigel? You what?"

"No," he shook his head. "That's all that I know."

I was frustrated. I was sure he was about to tell me something significant.

Some of what Nigel had said made sense. It explained the repeated appointments with a doctor in her datebook and that scene I had witnessed with Mabel Armstrong outside the dead man's office the night I was in their house. Had that been one of his places with his daughter? It truly made me sick and gave me a bit of sympathy for the multi-faceted Melissa. I had read of sexual abuse cases where young children had learned to split off in order to cope, to be somewhere else or someone else, to divorce themselves from what was happening.

While I was mulling this all over, Nigel seemed lost in his own thoughts. He brought me back when he said aloud, "I just wanted to help her."

"That reminds me, Nigel. Why should you care? How did you, the quintessential reclusive environmentalist, get involved with Melissa, a messed-up logging baron's daughter? She seems quite involved in her father's business. One would think you wouldn't have had the time of day for her."

"Well," he said. "I didn't like her at first. I hated her, in fact. I didn't know her, of course, but I hated everything she stood for. Then I met her when the local Sierra Club was given an opportunity to meet with Armstrong, to explain our issues and to see if there was any room for negotiation. Well, he couldn't have been more unpleasant. He actually laughed at us."

"I know," I said. "I heard about that from Jan."

"Well, Mel was there, too. She was silent during the meeting but followed us out when we left, and she came up to me as I walked to the ferry. She apologized for her father and asked if I could explain more about the islands to her. Seems that she knew about the environmental issues well enough, but all she had ever heard about Peregrine and Homestead was that we were a bunch of dope-smoking hippies who were trying to take away loggers' jobs."

"That's a joke," I said, "given her brother's predilection for using and selling drugs and, possibly, killing people."

"That's what I thought," he said, "although I do smoke, too. Anyway, I thought maybe I could get to her dad through her, so I agreed to meet again to talk. We had to be pretty secretive about it, seeing as he would have had a fit if he knew she was 'consorting with the enemy,' and my friends would have had a fair deal of difficulty understanding it, too."

He continued. "As I got to know her, I realized she was a pretty troubled person. She was lonely and confused, but bright, too. And, well, I found her interesting. Things just got more and more complicated as we got involved. As I have made patently obvious, I'm not exactly a picture of adjustment, but she was, well, more than troubled."

He blushed a little. "When we became intimate, she started to freeze. Finally, she told me she was having flashbacks to her dad using her. It freaked her out, and me, too. It almost destroyed our relationship, such as it was. I broke it off for a while, but she begged me to reconsider. So I told her that if she got help, perhaps we could continue."

"Dr. Glasco," I said.

He nodded, and then looked up. "How do you know about that?"

"She had regular appointments with a doctor — makes sense it was a shrink. What other doctor would you see weekly?"

"Yes, well, she's been going for a while. It seemed to help, but it confused her even more, too. Then her father was murdered, and I guess I jumped to conclusions. I figured she did it, you know, crashed. I just figured I had to help her, which is why, with Brendon's added pressure, I agreed to get you to the boat. I know I was stupid. Frankly, I can't believe I could have been that stupid.

"They didn't know about my connection with Melissa. They just wanted to get you out of the way for a while because they thought you were getting too nosey just when they had a big shipment of narcotics coming in. At least, that's what they said when they told me to try to get you to my place.

"It was coincidence that Melissa appeared on my boat when you were there yesterday. Now it appears I may have been wrong about her part in it all, and I almost had you hurt, maybe killed, for nothing," he said dully.

"I'm using up my nine lives," I said. "And I've been in harm's way more than once. So, Nigel, what do you say? We try to work together to figure this out, and see if we can help Melissa, too?"

His unswollen eye brightened a little. "I'm game as long as Mel doesn't get hurt," he said. "What do you suggest?"

"I'm not sure yet," I said. "We could start by requesting a little conference with your love. Will you come back to Peregrine with us? We can give her a call."

"Okay," he agreed. "It's the least I can do."

Chapter 30

CONVENIENTLY, WE FINISHED our conversation just as the house began to stir. Morningstar and Sunny emerged from the kitchen noisily, possibly to alert us to their presence.

"It's such a lovely evening," Morningstar said as she wafted in carrying a large vase of flowers. "We've decided to eat outside on the porch." She was followed by Sunny, who ambled along carrying a tray loaded with cutlery, napkins and glasses.

I got up creakily to offer my help.

"No, no, don't trouble yourself," said Morningstar. "Just come out to join us. We'll eat buffet style. Sunny and I will collect your food."

"That's right," said Sunny, smiling. "I hope you two have patched things up, because I don't like my good friends quarrelin'."

"We're cool, Sunny," I said as I sat down in a plastic garden chair at a long, wooden table that was quickly being transformed to a beautiful *Better Homes and Gardens* table for best picnics ever.

The conversation turned to a more sociable surface gloss as we were introduced to the other guests — a teacher couple from Calgary, three bankers from Seattle and a few Vancouverites. With that broad a mix of beatific souls, it was wisest to stay mellow. Sunny gave me a plate laden with a variety of delicious vegetarian morsels, and uncharacteristically, I spent some time inhaling my food before eating it. All I can remember is that it was definitely edible and that Morningstar was a skilful hostess who kept us on our best behaviour.

The setting sun danced on the softly undulating waves while voices drifted over from boats far out on the water. I watched a pair of eagles wheeling lazily overhead as the shadows lengthened over the little haven of tranquility. Fed, tired and safe, I felt the deepest peace I had in a long time. Perhaps I could get used to this, I thought.

After we finished off a plate of fruit and some exotic lavender shortbread cookies, Sunny announced that we should get going before it was dark. He had borrowed a sleek little motorboat, which wouldn't have been much use in the storm but was fine for that evening. The guests drifted off for their meditation or whatever, and Morningstar walked beside Nigel and me as we limped to the boat. Sunny stayed behind briefly to phone a friend to pick us up at the harbour dock.

"It was a pleasure to meet you, Morningstar," I said. "You've been my saviour. I thought I'd walked into paradise when I first came across your place."

She looked pleased. "As I mentioned before, we learn to help each other on the islands. I hope you can visit again under different circumstances. Perhaps you will even come to one of our retreats."

"You never know," I said. "Perhaps I'll come with my mother. This is her kind of place."

Morningstar turned to Nigel on her other side, his trusty mutt limping along beside him. "Now, Nigel dear, you take care of yourself. Don't get into any more trouble," she said. He nodded, studying his feet. She put her arm around him. "It will all work out, my dear. You'll see."

When Sunny arrived, Morningstar gave him a hug and said, "Now I must return to my guests." She put her hands in prayer position in front of her, bowed slightly and said, "Namaste. Peace." She turned, her robes billowing behind as she floated up the hill.

Sunny helped us into the boat. I felt a little unnerved about going out on the water again, but told myself not to be silly. Besides, my thoughts were already turning towards my return to Andy. He had been far from my mind for a while, but now the fact that I would have to face him filled me with anxiety. I felt awful about the way he must have worried.

Sunny had already told me that he had let Andy and Anita know that I was okay. Would Andy be angry, and would that make me defensive? Could I be apologetic? Would I welcome any doctoring ministrations? These questions left me uncharacteristically quiet.

The ride was quick as we sped across the channel between the two islands; the breeze created was deliciously cool, and the salt spray was vivifying. The coastal mountains in the distance were tinged with pink as the light of the setting sun bounced off their glacier-encrusted peaks. When we reached the harbour, Sunny slowed and manoeuvred into the boat's home berth. After he had tied her up, he helped me out. Nigel and Charlie followed.

"Thanks for coming to get me, Sunny, and please thank your friend for the use of the boat, too, will you?"

"Sure, Ab," he said, absently, not his usual cuddly self.

Was he mad at me, too? I was tired enough to be wise and leave it for the time being. "Nigel will stay with me tonight," Sunny said, "and tomorrow we'll have a little conference when you're ready."

"Sounds good," I said as we walked over to a decrepit-looking Volvo station wagon. As we approached, an aged, wizened man got out of the driver's seat with surprising agility.

"Abby, Nigel, this is Albert. He's a neighbour of mine who's agreed to chauffeur us around, right, Albert?"

Albert grinned a gummy smile, only a few teeth still apparent. I wondered about his ability to drive, but I was frankly too tired and apprehensive of what awaited me at the lodge for that additional twinge of worry to amount to much. I'd survived a drugging, a wild boat ride, a near-date with two young hooligans and a nighttime wilderness trek, so what difference would a little ride in an antique car with an antique driver make?

As I climbed into the back seat of the well-preserved vehicle, the springs creaked. Nigel climbed in beside me, and Charlie stood in the back, his head on Nigel's shoulder. Sunny sat up front, and once we started off, kept up some lively chatter with old Albert. I had to hand it to Sunny; he was a sociable, easygoing soul. I closed my eyes and let my mind drift. As I mused, snatches of their conversation caught my ear — mention of the storm, trees down, power out, nobody hurt, some damage, hydro service mostly back.

"There's some good come of it, though — ain't no dry wells anymore," Albert said. I heard it, but didn't really think much about it as we sped along. They dropped me off first, in front of the warm, beckoning lights of the lodge. The night was still, no ill wind to befoul my return, or so I thought.

Sunny helped me out of the car. "I'll just make sure you get in safe and sound, Ab," he said gently.

"It's okay, Sun. I can do this by myself," I replied half-heartedly.

"Sure thing," he said as he settled himself into an easy chair in the lounge. "Ah'll just wait here to make sure."

"Suit yourself," I said. I left the lounge area and limped down the hall to our room, girding my loins, so to speak, for a confrontation with Andy. I was primed, apologetic, sore, tired and defiant, all wrapped in a tight little ball. But there was no answer to my knock. Perhaps he's out for a walk, or sleeping, I thought as I wandered back, past Sunny and over to the front desk, where a businesslike male clerk presided this time. He looked up pleasantly as I approached.

"Excuse me," I said. "My name's Abby Faria. I just got back from Homestead Island and my friend, Andy Jaegar, is not answering our room door. Do you have a key I can use to get in? Room 114."

He smiled. "Ah, Ms. Faria. Dr. Jaegar said you would be returning this evening." I relaxed a little. "He asked me to give you this." He handed me a sealed envelope and a plastic card, which is the hotel equivalent of a key. "If you need anything else, the desk will be open until 10:00. Have a pleasant evening."

"Thanks," I said. "Sunny, Andy's out," I called across the lobby. "I'm just going to wait in the room for him. You don't have to hang around."

I gave him a quick wave, took the envelope and padded back to our room, relieved to have momentarily avoided confrontation. It all seemed a little formal, but I assumed that the letter would explain his absence. He obviously wasn't pining for my return.

My blithe self-centredness was knocked off kilter by the appearance of "our" room. It was very tidy, but something didn't feel right, and I looked around warily. Some of my stuff was draped over a chair. I began to clue in when I looked in the bathroom. Andy's stuff was gone — no toothbrush, no toiletries case.

Retracing my steps, I looked in the closet. His clothes were gone, and then I noticed that his books were gone from the bed. So there we were. Andy had taken off. I sat on the edge of the bed and opened the envelope. Inside was a letter in Andy's doctor scrawl.

Dear Abby —

I'm glad you are okay. Sunny let me know, and I passed the word on to Anita. She stayed at the lodge last night because of the storm. She's all right, too, but we were all very worried about you.

By now you will have noticed that I've left. I'm sorry, Abby, but I think we both were realizing that things weren't going to work out. You are never really on holiday, are you? Don't get me wrong. You are wonderful, up front and intelligent, but I don't think relationships are your strong point. I don't know if you will ever let down your guard enough to really let someone in. Anyway, I'm off to enjoy the rest of my holiday. You remember Sally, the tour guide in town? She's agreed to give me a quick tour of Andrews Park on the island. She seems to know the good trails.

Thanks for trying, Abby. I'll call down in a few days to see how it's going. By then, I'm sure you will have Jan off the hook and the mystery all sewn up. Don't change too much. You're pretty special. Take care of yourself.
— Andy

Well, I couldn't blame him, could I? I was too tired to know whether I felt jealous, confused or relieved, and I decided I had no choice but to sleep on it. Just then, there was a light knocking at the door. I'd forgotten about Sunny. Opening the door, I blushed.

"You knew, didn't you, Sun?"

"Yeah, Ab. Andy asked me to make sure you're okay. He's not a bad guy. He just couldn't handle your energy anymore."

I bowed my head. "I know. I blew it. Thanks for caring, Sunny. I just need a little time. I'll talk to you tomorrow. Besides, you've got people waiting in the car. Andy didn't deserve my antics. I've been a jerk."

On tiptoe, I gave Sun a quick hug. "Good night, my friend, I'll be fine."

He nodded gently, and I closed the door.

Although less cozy when half full, the bed was still pretty inviting. I slowly doffed the loaned clothing and pulled on a cleanish T-shirt. Hardly able to muster the energy to brush my teeth and limp back to bed, I hugged the other pillow and fell into a deep, dreamless sleep.

CHAPTER 31

I PROBABLY SHOULD have slept longer, but the demands of my aches and pains and my empty stomach got the best of me. Even so, it was past noon by the time I pried my eyes open. Once I regained my bearings, happy to be in a dry and warm, albeit emptier, bed, I decided to start with the obvious: a hot shower and food. I let the water pour down, the heat penetrating every pore. As usual, that did the trick and my brain started to work, the synapses clicking into place.

Andy was gone, another good guy relegated to the Abby waste heap. And what of the murder? Having gone through such annoyances as near-drowning, drugging, exposure and injury, I was not in a hurry to quit, but most of the nests I had prodded in the past week seemed to be buzzing with the wrong hornets. Bad Brendon and Alex were likely only protecting their own territory, and Nigel had been trying to protect the unfortunate Melissa.

There was the interesting attraction Melissa had for young male radical environmentalists. I tried to sort out what stones I had left unturned. By this time, the water was turning cool, which was a surprise. I didn't realize the hotel could run out of hot water so early in the day. I turned off the tap, shaking my head at my most wasteful vice, and dried myself hurriedly. My stomach was calling.

I didn't have to wait long to stuff my face. The remnants of a buffet lunch were still laid out in the restaurant. Apparently, a large tour group had just finished their lunch, and the tired servers were determined that any other guests would partake of the prearranged meal. It suited me fine. I enjoyed the fresh vegetables, a morsel of sockeye salmon, some squishy focaccia, fruit for dessert and two cups of coffee. That got me revved for the next step on my journey.

I was still limping a little too much to ride to Sunny's, and besides, my bike was missing in action; I'd have to ask Nigel about that. So I went to the desk to ask them to call me a cab. Another guest, a young man, clean, tanned and slim, was paying his bill and looked up. He said, "I'm just leaving for the ferry, but I have some time. Perhaps I can give you a lift if you're not going far."

"That's very kind of you," I said. "I don't want to take you out of your way. Once you get to the main road, I'm going about five minutes in the other direction to Sunny's bike shop."

"I know that place. I rented a bike from him earlier this week. I'd be happy to drop you there." I thanked him, and we began to walk to his waiting car. As I limped along, he looked at me and asked dubiously, "I don't mean to be rude, but will you be able to ride a bike with that bad ankle?"

I grimaced. "Oh, no, Sunny's an old friend of mine. I'm just dropping in. I guess it'll be a day or two before I'm riding again." I didn't bother to tell him I'd misplaced my new bike and that I was just recovering from another previous injury. We crossed the parking lot to his car, which was topped by a snazzy one-person kayak. As we got in the car, I asked politely, "Have you had a nice holiday?"

He smiled. "Well, it was a mix of business and pleasure. I'm thinking of expanding my ecotourism business to this island, so I thought I'd check out the resources and the competition." He began to drive out to the main road.

Too wrapped up in myself, I hadn't noticed the devastation the night before. It was startling — whole trees lay at the side of the road, and small branches were spread all over.

"Whoa! What a mess!" I exclaimed. He nodded while I continued, curious about his assessment of the eco-business potential. "What do you think? Does the island have possibilities?"

"Well, there's some nice coastline for kayaking and the lodges are cool, but there are a few established businesses here already, and as you can see, the logging isn't doing us any favours," he said, frowning as the controversial clear-cut hove into view.

I stared.

What had once been a hidden clear-cut protected by a "buffer" of trees near the road was now wide open. A few matchstick trees remained, but most had been blown down. No wonder the storm had done so much damage here. With no protection from the wind, the little cosmetic buffer had been wiped out right onto the hydro wires on the side of the road. I was stunned into silence by the sadness and ugliness of it all.

My chatty chauffeur continued as he turned into Sunny's drive. "Sometimes I think that, between the follies of man and the force of nature, we don't have much hope, do we?"

Sunny walked out of his shop, much as he did the first time I had arrived, smiling and wiping his hands on a rag. As my new friend and I got out of the car, I thanked him for the ride. "No problem," he said.

"Howdy, Fred," said Sunny. "I see you've met my pal, Abby." He put a friendly arm around my shoulders. "How'd she lasso you into coming this way?"

"Nah, Sunny. I offered. I'm leaving the island today, and she was just heading your way, so I offered a ride."

"Mighty kind of you, Fred, and you don't even live here, yet. Yer good island material. Have you made any decisions yet?"

Fred shook his head. "I'm going to mull it over, Sunny. But thanks for all your info. You were a great help."

"Glad to be of service," said Sunny, shaking Fred's hand. "We need all the eco-business we can get, especially with people who understand the issues."

Fred nodded and turned to go. "I'll probably be seeing you in the future, man. Take it easy."

"Sure thing," said Sunny. We waved as the young man bumped away over the drive.

Then Sunny looked at me. "You all right?" he asked.

I nodded. "I feel like a heel. I hope Andy has more fun now. At least he doesn't have a broken heart."

"No," said Sunny, "or he's hidin' it real well. You don't either, Ms. Faria, do you? Always did have that stubborn streak of independence," he said, smiling as we turned towards his shop.

"Where's Nigel?" I asked.

"He got restless this morning and called Melissa. He went to visit her in town. They'll be over soon, I think. He left old Charlie here, though," he said as we stepped over the sleeping dog. "Poor old thing. He's been moanin' fer Nigel ever since."

We sat down at Sunny's kitchen table. "Well, maybe we can get some answers when Melissa shows up," I said. "Have you called Jan, Sunny? I just realized she must be anxious up there."

"Nah. Phones up there are still down."

"Is this normal, then, Sunny, this kind of storm?" I asked. "If so, it's surprising there are any trees left on this island."

"Well, Ab, we get blows, more often in the winter, but not so wild and not from the west so much. Usually southeast, but it's all the clear-cuttin' that causes so much tree fall. There's nothin' to stop the wind. The measly buffers they leave up to hide the devastation from the people just fall down like toothpicks. The storms might be gettin' worse and less predictable because of climate change. The patterns, currents and stuff have gone all wonky."

"It's all pretty sobering, isn't it, Sunny — murder, storms, abduction, clear-cutting, drugs. Maybe I'm safer in the city!"

"Ah, Abby, the island's just a microcosm. People are people all over."

"I guess," I said. "One thing for sure, Sunny, is that here I feel slower, like my brain and I are swimming in molasses. Is it just the ocean air, the lack of pollution, except when I smell that mill, or what? I thought negative ions were supposed to aid one's health."

"Yeah," he said, "but they're relaxin', too. You just need to let go, girl."

"Moi?" I said, doubtfully. "You might be right. I sure haven't done much to help so far, except stir things up."

"Well, Ab, you've always been a good shit disturber."

"I suppose," I said, "and I've got the wounds to prove it. Let's change the subject, Sunny," I said. "All this introspection is making me crazy."

"All right," he said, standing up. "You can help me make lunch. What do you fancy?"

"You know what I'd like," I said, joining him companionably at the counter, peering into his fridge, "and I can do it all by myself."

He grinned. "I know — a Faria special. I remember those. Okay, I'm game."

A Faria special is about all I have time or room for in my cozy apartment in Toronto. I mix whatever really healthy things I can find with some fruit and yogurt in a blender. In Sunny's fridge, I found some wheat germ, flax oil, blueberries, spirulina ginseng, vitamin C powder, and yogurt. I blended it all with some water and a banana. Sunny provided two large glasses, which we filled to the brim. We returned to the kitchen table, clinked glasses and drank demurely. It might not have been quite up to Morningstar's gourmet standards, but passable and undeniably just what I needed.

We had lovely purple milk moustaches at the end, which provided a necessary measure of levity. After wiping his away, Sunny said, "Ahh … that reminds me of the old days. Now you sit, Ab. Rest that leg, while I wash up."

"Sunny, you sure are happy here," I said as he worked away, humming.

"Yeah, Ab. This place is perfect for me. I definitely don't need the city anymore. I think I overloaded on gonzo-couriering back then. What about you? You ever consider lettin' that life go?"

"Maybe someday," I said. "But I don't think I'm ready yet. Besides, I have just made a start on that new gig, working with the lawyer I told you about. I'm learning how to be a real live investigator."

Sunny finished cleaning up and came back to where I was sitting. "It might be a bit presumptuous, Ab, given the timing and all." He took my hand. "But we could hang out a bit together. We had a pretty good time, once." He smiled. My stomach flip-flopped as I returned his smile.

"I have to admit, I've thought about that, too, Sunny, but I think I need some time. It would be too quick a hop from one man to another, even for me. Give me a few minutes — I mean days. Ok?"

He laughed, but my hand still tingled.

"Besides, you know I'm due to go back to T.O. soon."

Before we went any further down that road, I changed the subject.

"Sun, have you talked with Anita since I got back?"

"Yeah, Ab. She'll be coming up here later. Cindy, the woman who runs the camp, said she'd drop her up here on her way to the reserve office around 4:30 or so."

"Is she okay?" I asked. "With the storm and all?"

"Sure," said Sunny. "Everything will have dried up by now, but she was very worried about you, near frantic, in fact. It was hard on her, Ab."

"I know. She didn't need that after all she's been through. She's become a good friend, and I'll try to make it up to her."

CHAPTER 32

THE DOG STARTED whining at the door as soon as he heard the truck in the drive.

"That must be Nigel and Melissa," Sunny said, standing to let the dog out to greet them.

Today Melissa was sweet and diffident, almost dreamy, when she came in with Nigel, his arm around her waist. She looked exhausted, though. As she stooped to pat the old dog, he rubbed against her.

"Come in, come in," said Sunny. "I'm glad to see the two of you together. Sort of a nice symbol of peace."

"We had a talk," said Nigel, "and realized that we both want to work things out. We don't know for sure what will happen. Mel has lots of work to do still and a business to run, now that her father is gone."

She looked up and smiled. "Nigel and I are going to look into ways to work together, to try to change Armstrong lumber. We will have to work with the shareholders, though."

"That sounds promising," I said dryly, trying my best to feel glad for them. It all seemed too pat. I suppose I was still a little miffed about the treatment I had received recently. "Aren't we all forgetting one small thing?" I asked. They looked at me blankly. "There is still this nagging little question of who did away with your father, and where your brother and Alex have disappeared to."

"Oh," said Melissa, smile fading, eyes perhaps a little over bright. "I think I have the answers for you, but you might not like them."

"Try me," I challenged.

Sunny intervened. "Why don't we all sit down at the table here? It'll be more comfortable than standin'." He took me firmly by the arm, and I allowed myself to be steered to the nearest chair. As Sunny sat beside me, Melissa and Nigel took the chairs opposite us at the table.

"I owe you this much at the very least, after what my brother orchestrated," Melissa said evenly. "I'll start with him and Alex."

I nodded.

"When the storm abated a bit, they left Nigel's place in their boat and made it back to Peregrine to wait for the weather to settle down further. Then they headed for our place in Bellweather. When they reached the house, I was at the Bellweather office and my mother was at home nursing her usual hangover.

"I was more than worried. I wanted to know where they had been because I knew that they had had a hand in Nigel's plans for you. I'd spent a sleepless night wondering what had happened and had gone to the office partly to keep my mind off things.

"Well, Brendon and Alex relayed some version of the story to my mother. She's not as dense as she looks; the drinking has just become a way to avoid seeing what is distasteful to her. I guess she figured that Brendon was in worse trouble than ever, so she took it upon herself to help him get out of town."

"What?" I said.

"Yes, well, she paid for his airline ticket to go see some distant friend in Amsterdam."

"He should be happy there," Sunny said, "until he gets in some dealer's face."

"But Melissa, I hate to say it. He might have murdered your father."

She nodded, her eyes welling up so quickly that I almost softened. "I know," she said. "But I'm not sure if it was him. I was at the office assessing the damage from the storm when, late this morning, I received a call from the police. My mother was at the station, saying she wanted to confess. Apparently, she'd waited until Brendon was gone."

"Oh, come on," I said. "Your mother? She barely seems conscious, from what I've seen."

Melissa nodded. "But it sort of made sense when I talked to her later. First I called our family lawyer and headed to the station to see what was going on. When I got to the station, it was in an uproar. Apparently, the officers didn't want to hear her statement without one of us, or the lawyer, there.

"Anyway, my mother was beside herself, screaming with anger. She said that she wanted to talk then and there. She wanted them to listen. I called our doctor and led her into the chief's office to get her away from curious eyes.

"A short time later, there we were, my mother, our lawyer, the doctor and me. First, the doctor gave her a mild sedative to calm her down. That worked too well, because then we could not get her to communicate. I wanted to take her home, but the police said they had to hold her on suspicion until she made her statement. I guess I couldn't blame them after the big stink she had made, but I wasn't happy. I didn't like the idea of my mother being treated like a common criminal. Our lawyer agreed to stay with her until she felt ready to talk, and they let her rest in the chief's office."

Melissa stopped her narrative and looked at Nigel. "I honestly didn't know what was going on. I know that my family is a mess."

I decided to shake her up a little bit. "Are you serious, Melissa?" I asked. "What about Jon? Weren't you the least bit suspicious about his death?"

"What?" She stared at me. "How do you know about Jon?" Her eyes brimmed with tears. "Jon had an accident, a terrible accident."

Sunny gave me a warning look, so I backed down. "I wonder," was all I said. "We can come back to that later. Why don't you go on?" I was still having trouble buying the story about her mom being the murderer.

She looked miserable, and Nigel gave me a withering glance, reaching to hold Melissa's hand. She withdrew her hand and went on.

"After a while, my mother surfaced. It took her a while to figure out where she was, but once she remembered, she seemed to take possession of her wits and went on. I believe that what my mother told the police is true because I was there for the beginning of it all, back at the house.

"Mother told the police that Brendon and our father had had

an argument that night. Brendon wanted to borrow money, which he said he owed to his friend. Dad had correctly surmised that he needed it for some drug deal. He said there was no way and that he'd heard talk about Brendon trying to get in with organized crime. Usually, Mother would bail Brendon out, but he needed more and more money, and she didn't have any left just then.

"Well, my father and Brendon had a terrific fight. He pushed Brendon over a few times and told him he was good for nothing, a drug addict, a momma's boy, and he wouldn't get a thing from him. As usual, Mother defended Brendon, and my father turned on her. He hit her in the face with such force that she fell over the coffee table. I'd had enough, and I told him so."

All this jived with the story old man Williams had told us, so I believed Melissa. But I found it hard to believe that her mother would air all this dirty laundry in her statement.

"Hold on, Melissa," I said. "Is this what your mother told the police?"

She looked up from her tumble of thoughts.

"Huh? Oh, no, I'm sorry. I got caught up in remembering that night. Mother just told the police that Brendon and my father had a huge fight, that my father became violent, and that when she tried to stop him, he hit her. She told them that Brendon left the house in one of the company trucks. She said that my father left for an appointment a while later, and that after I checked that her eye was okay, I left on a bike."

I sat back to hear the rest of her story.

"When we had left, she said that Brendon phoned home to apologize. He told Mother that he was at the bar on Peregrine and wanted her to meet him there. He wanted to tell her something. Mother said she didn't feel up to driving, so she called a taxi and went down to the docks."

Melissa looked up and explained. "Mom often took cabs since she was stopped for drunk driving twice."

She shrugged and continued.

"Mother said Brendon met her and told her that he wanted to go with her to the logging camp to speak to our father again. She agreed, but said to us she had been nervous about confronting my father again that night. She knew he had a meeting with a few of the crew in preparation for the next day's work, but she didn't even know if he'd still be at the site."

Melissa stopped for a moment. Nigel gave her an encouraging smile, and she went on.

"As it turned out, he was still there, Mother reported. I know Mother was telling the truth, because I was at the meeting, too."

I raised my eyebrows in surprise but didn't stop Melissa's story.

"We had just finished the meeting, and everyone had left. Either my father or I was going to stay until the watchman returned for his shift. He was a local man, and he had to go home for a short while that evening."

Melissa stopped again and looked at me. "What I'm going to tell you next is not quite what my mother reported."

She took a deep breath.

"I was alone with my father for a while at the site. I was just going over the details for the truck loads that were to go to the mill the next day when Daddy, I mean my father, started to say how lucky he was to have such a special little girl. I'm not sure what else he said, because I sort of lapsed into a kind of trance. I could hear his voice, and feel his hands on me, but it was as if I were watching from a distance."

Melissa faltered and then, taking a breath, stuck out her chin and continued.

"This hadn't happened for a long time, and it threw me back. I don't know how long it went on, but not very long because I began to hear myself saying no, and some inner voice telling me I was okay, that I was strong and that he was wrong. I snapped back and began yelling at my father, something I'd never done before as long as I could remember.

"I know I was near hysterical. I think I told him he was gross, that he was sick and that he should never touch me again. He looked mad and hurt, and said something like, 'Melissa, sweety girl.' But I didn't care. I ran out of the trailer and down the logging road. In my state, I forgot the bike near the old 'dozer.

"Just as I was running out, Brendon was pulling into the drive, and he almost hit me. I jumped out of the way, just kept on going and started running down the main road. I didn't see Mother in the truck, but she says she was there.

"Brendon has always known what was going on. He had tried to protect me but couldn't stand up to our father. I don't know what my father thought about that night, but I sure felt different. I had said no. I was just angry, but I knew I was getting better." She smiled wanly, and Nigel squeezed her hand.

"I walked for a long time. In fact, I walked to Alex's house. His mom is used to us sleeping over there when we're on the island. I went to sleep with no difficulty. I felt freer than I had for a long time."

Melissa looked at me directly and clear-eyed, as if to defy me to put a hole in her breakthrough on the night of her father's death. I nodded sympathetically. "You've been through a lot, Melissa."

She nodded too, sticking her chin out again bravely. After she had composed herself, she said, "I'm sorry. I'd better get back to my mother's story."

"If you're ready," I said gently.

She took a deep breath and continued. "Well, Mother told the police that when she and Brendon pulled in, they almost ran into me and Brendon crunched the bike when he parked near the bulldozer. She said that Brendon was in such a hurry, he went straight to the office. They found my father sitting on a chair at the table, with his head on his arms. When he raised his head and saw them, he was silent."

Melissa's eyes filled with tears.

"Mother said that his silence was almost more frightening than his anger. Brendon plunged right in, though, begging for money. He had a big deal that would get him his money back, he said. Then, apparently, Dad laughed and said if he wanted money, he'd have to work for it. He could work at the site the next day, but first he had to show him how well he could drive the bulldozer. Brendon thought he would humour my father, so he said okay.

"Apparently, my father took them outside, taunting Brendon as before, telling him he was useless, incapable, clumsy. Mother said that he seemed delighted to be taunting Brendon. But she said he also said something strange as Brendon climbed into the cab of the big machine. He said Brendon was just as useless as that environmentalist Field, who couldn't handle the pressure, either."

Melissa stopped and looked at me. "Hold on a minute," she said, eyes widening. "I hadn't thought that this might refer to Jon, but now that you brought him up, it makes me wonder ... I didn't even think my father knew about me and Jon." Her eyes widened as she brought her hand to her mouth, the full implications obviously dawning on her. "Oh, my God!"

I nodded. "It's a possibility. Go on."

Gamely, she went back to her narration. "Mother told them that Brendon was familiar with the machine, but that my father's taunts were unnerving him. First, the machine stalled, then started, then he moved it in reverse instead of forwards, all to my father's amusement. Mother says she tried to stop him laughing at Brendon, but he just told her to shut up and look what a sissy she'd made of her son, and he pushed her away. Brendon got angry and jumped down from the machine to confront our father, who had wanted precisely that. They began to swing at each other. Brendon mostly dodged and landed ineffectual hits on our father.

"But the machine had been left running, and according to Mother, she climbed up into the cab and tried to turn it off. Instead, she swung the body around, moving the wrong lever. As the machine lurched around, Brendon ducked. But it hit the old man, and he fell right in the pile of flags. She panicked and tried again to turn off the machine, but it began to rumble forwards towards my dad, pulling the flag pile with it. Finally, Brendon jumped up and turned it off."

Melissa looked at us helplessly.

"Mother said Brendon helped her down, but she was scared of what my father would do next. She panicked, ran for the truck and told Brendon to get in and drive her home.

"The last ferry was just about to pull out, so they drove onto it and went back to Bellweather. Mother said that neither she nor Brendon talked about any of it. They never referred to the incident again. Maybe she hoped it was all a dream. In her usual state, I guess it could have seemed that way."

Melissa stopped a moment. "I found out about his death when I got to the site the next day. I didn't know what to think. I guess I hoped it was true about Jan, but I don't think I really believed it. I also wondered if Nigel could have been involved. He had reasons to hate my father. So I kept quiet and watched. I was pretty confused about my feelings in all this, too. I suppose, if you hadn't been prying into it all, it might have taken mother longer to act."

"Do you believe your mother's story, Melissa?"

"I want to." She looked miserable. "It could have been the way she said, but I don't know," she said helplessly. "I wasn't there. Brendon could have done it. She could be protecting him, I suppose. He hated my father, too. Mother says that Dad was alive when they left. She saw him moving."

"I don't know, Melissa. There are a few things that still bother me. Your father was strangled with the prayer flags. How did that happen?"

She put her hands over her face. "What a mess! What will happen now, do you think?"

My heart melted for her. "I don't know," I said gently. "I imagine the police will investigate further and see if any evidence supports or refutes your mom's statement. That may be difficult because it doesn't sound like they did a very good job collecting evidence or keeping the site clean. With a good lawyer and her mental health in question, if your mother is charged, it's likely that she will be treated lightly. After all, it sounds like an unfortunate accident."

"I'm prepared to stand by my mother," she said, "and I also have to continue to run my father's business, but with the softwood lumber tariffs and the slump in the U.S. housing market and the pressure of environmental interests, I'm hoping we can make an effort to develop some secondary industry. You know, use the lumber for cabinetry or furniture instead of selling the raw wood."

Nigel took her hand. "We discussed this on the way over," he said. "Mel has agreed to let me help her restructure the business if we can get support from the shareholders and the union."

"It will take a bit of work convincing the shareholders, but my father always maintained controlling interest, so I should be able to swing something."

"What about Brendon, Mel? Do you think he knows about your mother's confession? Do you think he'll come back?"

"I don't know. Probably no, to both questions. To be honest, I don't think he'll care."

"If they find evidence against him, or if they want to question him, they might ask you to try to get him back. Wasn't he supposed to stick around, anyway? I heard some talk of house arrest. They could even ask the Dutch authorities to extradite him."

"Brendon's last set of charges was dropped, so he was free to leave. We have a good lawyer, Abby. I'll talk to him," she said.

"And Mel, what about Janice Field?"

"I know," she said. "My family owes her an apology."

"I agree," I said.

Melissa rose. "I have to go back to help my mother, Abby. I'll call Janice Field as soon as I can to apologize personally."

Nigel had risen, too, clearly intending to stay by Melissa. She seemed to welcome his support. I hoped for their sakes that this new partnership would last, perhaps symbolic, as Sunny said, of a new peace in the woods. Maybe they would do better than me in the relationship department, too.

Nigel turned to Sunny. "Will you take care of Charlie for a while longer?"

"Sure," said Sunny. "Take your time, pal. Try not to let the town get you down, though. I know you're not used to it after all that time on your island paradise."

"I'll be fine," said Nigel, with a clear sense of purpose. He and Melissa headed back to the truck just as another pulled in.

CHAPTER 33

"NEVER A DULL moment, Sunny," I said agreeably.

"Nah, Ab, but it's just Cindy with Anita, I believe."

Anita jumped out of the car and ran to give me a painful hug. "Oh, Abby," she breathed, holding me tightly. "I was so worried about you. Are you okay?"

"Slightly the worse for wear," I replied as I limped back through the shop with her. "I'm on the road to recovery, but I'm not in a hurry to get on a boat in a storm again."

She smiled. "Oh, Ab. I'm so sorry about Andy."

I winced.

"I like him, Abby, but I could see it wasn't going to work. You're just not ready to settle down."

"Maybe sometime soon," I said. "I'm not sure I'm up to all these crime-solving antics much longer."

Sunny laughed. "Wait a day or two before ya say that, Ab. I think you'll change yer mind when yer more rested." They laughed.

I swatted at him.

"Look at you, Sun, your drawl gets more pronounced as you relax. But maybe you're right," I said ruefully.

We sat in the kitchen for a while, catching up and talking about Anita's plans for school. After a while, I had an inspiration. "Hey, you two, I have an idea. Why don't we see if the phone line is back on, and we'll call Jan and Mike and go out for dinner. I think it's time to celebrate. My treat. There's still a few bucks in my bank account, and I am supposed to be on holiday."

"I'll try to give them a call," said Sunny, "and break the news of

Mabel Armstrong's confession to them. Why don't you two go out to the garden and sit and chat till I'm done," he suggested.

"Good idea," I agreed.

It was a little surreal to find myself sitting in Sunny's peaceful, lush garden. The large trees surrounding the clearing swayed slightly in the gentle breeze. The warm air stirred, heavy with the drone of bees and wafting a mellow scent of flowers and herbs our way. Although the atmosphere was mellow, my mind still swam with the macabre events relayed by Melissa.

At least Brendon was out of the way, so I didn't have to worry about Anita's safety. The surroundings gave me a semblance of peace, but something was still nagging at me. The story didn't add up; the old man died of strangulation, not the blow from the machine.

"I'm not letting you out of my sight for a while," said Anita, rousing me from my thoughts. "I was worried to death about you out in that horrendous storm. It was lucky that Andy found a room at the hotel for me. He was worried, too, Ab, really worried. I think that's what finally did it for him, not knowing what was going on. He said it was thoughtless of you to go off without telling anybody."

"Well, I did leave a note," I said defensively. "I didn't think of Nigel as dangerous at the time." I shook my head. "I'm going to have to learn to always watch out for the quiet ones!"

Sunny stepped out from the open glass doors, smiling. "Well, I just finished speakin' to Mike. He and Jan are overwhelmed by all the news. I told them about your adventure, Ab, and about Mabel's confession, but I thought I'd save the details for when we see them. Anyway, they want all of us to come there for dinner tonight. They were expectin' some guests who put off their trip by a day because of the storm, so they have food that needs eating. They really want to thank you," he said. "Oh, and they said Melissa called, so they invited her and Nigel over, too."

"That's big news," I said.

Sunny nodded and went on. "Mike said enough debris has been cleared off to get through, and the power's back on up there. I'll take you two and the dog out in the bike van," he said, "if you can stand the mess." Sunny is very orderly, so I knew his idea of mess was not the same as mine.

"Are you up to it, Abby? You still look a little sore, and the road will be even bumpier after that downpour."

"I can manage," I said. "I wouldn't miss this for the world."

Maybe I could get some answers to my nagging questions over dinner.

"Hey, Sun?" I said, walking back with him to the phone. "Can you do me one little favour?"

I explained quietly what I wanted him to do. He nodded his agreement, though looking puzzled, and I walked back out to Anita.

Sunny came out with the dog a few minutes later and locked up the shop.

"It's all taken care of, Ab."

He turned to Anita. "D'you need anything at your campsite, Anita?" he asked.

"I've brought a sweater for when it gets cool in the evening, so I'm set," she replied, smiling back at him.

"So, let's go then," he said. "Mike suggested we come as soon as possible to enjoy the early evening on the farm. Perfect weather should be taken advantage of," he added firmly.

We piled into the van. The dog's droopy head suggested to me that he missed his master. Anita chattered with Sunny as we drove. At last, I was given more time to be quiet and think.

As Sunny's van rumbled over the new and old ruts in the road, I replayed Melissa's story in my head. As we neared the north end of the island and drove out of a dense canopy of trees, the light shone brilliantly, coinciding with a sudden flash of insight in my brain. Of course! Biting my lip, I ran through it all very carefully. If my hunch was accurate, it would explain everything. I knew I couldn't rest until the truth was told. I spent the rest of the ride figuring out just how I could get that to happen.

The pastoral scene of the farm seemed unchanged by the storm. The sheep grazed and chickens blocked the drive while Mike worked in the garden. As we pulled in, their young Lab bounded out to greet us, barking and wagging his tail. Charlie perked up with a loud bark back.

"Those two are old pals," said Sunny, laughing. "Better let Charlie out before he hurts himself. He needs a break, the ol' guy."

Anita opened the side door to the van, and Charlie hopped out to greet Jan and Mike's dog, Sam. After a quick sniff, they bounded off, Charlie looking like a young dog again, loping along.

"Sam'll wear him out soon enough," said Sunny.

Jan emerged from the house as we walked through the yard.

"Welcome, welcome. I'm so glad you're here," she said, hugging each one of us tightly. When she got to me, she said, "Oh, Abby, I'm so sorry. Sunny told me about your ordeal. I hope you're okay."

"Nothing that a good rest won't fix," I said, smiling.

She linked arms with me and said, "Come on, everyone, let's sit on the porch. It's a lovely evening."

We followed her to her west-facing verandah, which looked over the small duck-filled pond and a sheep pasture bordered by fir trees. In the distance, two of the firs leaned over against the arms of the other trees, but otherwise, there was no evidence of the storm of two nights before.

"It looks like your place wasn't damaged too much by the storm," I offered conversationally.

"Not that you would notice now," she said. "Just some damage in the garden and a few downed trees in the woods. But if we didn't have our generator, the stuff in the freezer would have all thawed."

Mike walked up as she finished. "Yes, our neighbours by the back weren't so lucky. Their little Laser sailboat blew onto shore and got a nasty crack. Some stuff in their freezer had to be moved to ours, and some was lost, and more than twenty trees were downed."

Jan nodded. "They're more in line with the clear-cut up the road, so they've little protection left from the wind. But everyone is all right, thank goodness. That's a mercy, anyhow."

We were interrupted by the dogs barking, announcing the arrival of the familiar Armstrong truck.

Jan brightened. "Melissa Armstrong called, and I convinced her and Nigel to come join us for dinner. You don't mind, do you?"

"Sunny told us," I said. "It's a bit strange, though. I'd have thought she'd want to be with her mother."

"I don't know about that. She sounded anxious to talk with me, and I feel sorry for her, finding out like that that her own mother may have killed her father. I didn't like the man, but there is no reason his daughter should suffer. Besides, if Nigel likes her, that is a good reason to get to know Melissa. He is a fine young man." She stood up. "I'll be right back," she said, and she went to greet the couple as they emerged from the truck. Charlie pressed against his owner, who played happily with his ears.

Mike left to join Jan, Melissa and Nigel as they walked towards us through the garden. Melissa looked a little tentative, but pretty clear-eyed. Jan was patting her hand, in consolation, I guessed.

Chapter 34

"HEY, YOU TWO," Sunny said as the couple approached. "What happened? I thought Melissa had to stay with her mom."

"We thought so, too," said Nigel, "but when we got back, there was a police officer watching the house and a nurse with Mel's mother. Mabel had been given some sedatives and was out for the night, but Melissa was restless."

Melissa nodded. "I wanted to talk to Jan, to make amends for how my family treated her."

Nigel continued. "She was worrying herself into a state, pacing around the house, so I suggested we call here. She did, and Jan, who we know is pretty soft with anyone in a tough spot," he smiled at her, "understood immediately and suggested we come over and stay in the cottage. She mentioned that you were coming and said we'd be one big happy family."

"So, now we *are* all here," said Jan. "How bloody marvellous. Mike will get some drinks, and we can start with some chips and my homemade salsa."

We settled and chatted on the verandah and, after a while, Jan said, "You were right, Abby, things worked themselves out. We truly appreciate your efforts to help. I feel so badly about what happened the night of the storm, but maybe that's what got things going."

Without waiting for a response, she turned her motherly face to Nigel. "It seems you paid a heavy price for your antics, what with the damage to your boat and the harm that befell you and Charlie. I think we need to learn to communicate better and stop hiding things from each other."

"That's true, Jan," I interjected, "but I'm not sure we know everything yet."

"What do you mean?" she asked.

"Well, some things are still bothering me." I plunged on. "For one thing, I've been wondering whether you noticed a bicycle lying around when you made that late-night visit to the logging site after the potluck."

Jan and Mike both shook their heads. "I don't think so," said Mike. "We didn't see any bikes. It was around 8:00 or so. But there were plenty of trucks. A bike might have been out of sight behind one of them."

"I was too busy being angry at Armstrong to notice whether there were any bikes around," Jan added.

I shrugged. "Just wondering. I'm trying to sort things out. Let's leave it for now."

"Don't let her kid you," Sunny said. "She's not leaving anything. When she gets like this, she's like a dog gnawing on a bone." Everyone laughed at my expense, so there was nothing I could do but take the heat and grin good-naturedly.

"Speaking of gnawing," Jan said, getting up, "dinner is pretty much ready. I'll just take Melissa into the kitchen with me to finish up. That way, we can have some time together — just the two of us."

Melissa seemed happy to comply.

"We won't be long," Jan said over her shoulder as the two walked away.

So the rest of us were left on the verandah to enjoy the chips and salsa, a pitcher of sangria and each other's company.

As the wine and the mellowing sun warmed me, anticipation began to compete with fatigue; the adventures of the last few days were catching up with me. As I half-listened to the others, my mind drifted, and I lazily watched a butterfly working industriously at the pollen in Jan's potted plants.

Jan's sparkling voice broke my reverie. "Well, folks, I think we're ready. The food's on the table. Help yourselves and find a place to eat, inside or out. Take your pick."

The quiet moment had passed. We did as instructed and surveyed the amazing spread — quiche with eggs from Jan's hens, fresh-baked salmon, salad picked from the garden moments before and some cheeses Sunny and I had brought along. "And that's not all," Jan said proudly. "After, we'll have some of Mike's deadly homemade dessert wine and fresh-picked blackberries."

I was beginning to accept as the norm such fresh and delicious cooking. This kind of fare in Toronto would cost many days of couriering, I thought ruefully.

We all opted to remain outside. Jan stayed near Melissa and Nigel, while Anita and I chatted about her beach adventures. She couldn't remain lazy on holiday, either; she'd collected a few camping children and had organized beach walks and games. I'm sure there were some very grateful parents down there.

Mike had been quietly sitting apart, lost in thought, when all of a sudden, he said, "Wait a minute. I just remembered. When we were leaving the logging site, I noticed someone on a bike turning into the site when I checked over my shoulder for oncoming cars."

Mel nodded, putting down her fork. "That was me. I saw you leave as I was riding up. I noticed you because your truck is the same colour as Nigel's, and at first, I thought it was him. I was worried because I didn't want him to run into my father. When I got closer, I realized it wasn't Nigel's truck." She smiled. "Yours is in much better shape."

"True," I said, "but it could be confusing in the dark. Hmm … that must have been sometime just after 8:00, right?"

She nodded as she took her plate off her lap and placed it on the ground. "Yes," she said sadly. "Everyone was still joking about Jan's behaviour with my father. I thought they were being pretty cruel in the things they said, but I didn't stop them."

She turned to face the couple beside her. "I'm sorry."

They acknowledged her apology with weak smiles as she continued.

"Then we got to work on the plans for the next day's logging. The meeting didn't last long, and my father and I were soon the only ones left at the site."

Mel looked at me. "Should I go on, Abby? The others haven't heard my story yet. This won't be the best time, but maybe they should," she said bravely. Nigel put a protective arm around her.

Jan nodded her agreement.

Looking around, I noticed that we had pretty well finished the main meal. The group looked intrigued, so I said, "Whatever you're comfortable with, Melissa. I'm just interested in getting a timeline of what happened."

Mel huddled into herself a little as she began to tell her story, a recap of what she'd told us at Sunny's. She held back a bit on the abuse from her dad but told enough that she had everyone's sympathy. She looked up at me. "It must have been around 9:30 when I left the site. I just ran away blindly after Brendon almost hit me with the truck. I was so pumped with adrenalin that I walked without thinking for quite a while, until I … well, I decided to go to the Middletons's for the night."

After a few seconds of silence as people digested Mel's story, Sunny piped up.

"That would match your mom's story. Brendon picked her up from the 9:00 ferry and, after waiting for her to disembark, wouldn't get to the site until around 9:30, just in time to almost run into you."

She nodded. "That's right."

Anita, Jan and Mike hadn't heard the full confession story, so I filled them in on Mabel's version of events. "All we have for that part of the night is her story, so it's possible that things could have happened differently from the way she told the police. We do know that your father was injured during that time, but even though your mother has taken responsibility for it, Melissa, she could be protecting Brendon. Anyway, they left him there around 10:00 in order to catch the 10:30 ferry."

"So that's it then, Abby," Sunny said abruptly.

I nodded. "That's true, so far, Sun. But there are still some missing pieces, and I'm hoping that Mel, Nigel and Mike can help us out with those."

"Whatever do you mean, Abby?" Jan asked curiously.

Mike sighed as he laid his hand on hers. "It's okay. Let's hear her out, Jan. I want this cleared up, once and for all." Nigel and Melissa nodded.

"Actually, Mike," I said, "aren't we all ready for dessert? Let's clean up a bit here and continue later."

"Good idea, Ab," Sunny said, stretching. "I think we already have a lot to digest."

There were nods of agreement all around, so we cleared up the dinner dishes while Mike made coffee. Conversation remained light, as if we all needed a break from the heavy stuff.

We started our dessert in silence, but eventually, all eyes were on me. I took one last bite of the marvellous fresh fruit and got ready to wade back in. Sunny gave my hand an encouraging squeeze as I cleared my throat.

"Okay," I said. "Let's backtrack a little first. This might be a bit tough, though. Remember your mother's description of events, Mel? She said your father goaded Brendon by saying he was a wimp just like that tree hugger Field."

She nodded.

"Well, when I first heard it, I thought he was referring to Jan, but what if he was referring to Jan's son, Jonathon?"

Jan gasped, and although Mel had skirted this idea already, she paled again.

I kept on going. "You knew, Melissa, that Jan had a special distaste for your father, not just because of his logging practices, but also because Jon died at one of his logging sites down island." Melissa shifted awkwardly in her seat, obviously realizing where this was going.

I went on. "But Jan probably doesn't know that you were friends with Jon at school."

Jan stiffened. "Is this true, Melissa? Why didn't you ever tell me?"

"Go on, Mel," I said quietly.

"I had nothing to do with Dad's business back then," she said imploringly. "It's true. I did have a crush on Jon when I hung out with his crowd for a bit. I even wrote him letters. But Jon made it quite clear he wasn't interested. When he died, I ... well, I never got closure." She looked at Jan. "Oh, Jan, I'm so, so sorry. I know you hated my dad so much, and now I'm wondering if he might have had something to do with Jon's death. It sounds sick, but it might even be that he was jealous of Jon."

"But Abby!" Sunny said. "What does all this have to do with Armstrong's murder?"

"You're right, Sunny. I will try to explain. The first thing I learned about murder investigations is to look for means, motive and opportunity, and that's how I've been trying to organize my thoughts about this murder. Jan's anger with Armstrong for both the logging and the loss of her son gave her a motive. But it also could have given Mel a motive if she knew about or suspected her father's involvement with Jon."

Leaning over to pick up a large envelope Nigel had given me earlier, I continued. "I came across some material in your father's office, which I asked Nigel to bring out here today."

Nigel interjected. "I showed her the stuff before we came, Abby. It was only fair."

"Of course," I said. "I understand."

Mel continued a little shakily. "I didn't even know he had this. It was his private office. I have one in the main office building downtown. I've been trying to deal with his home office, but it has been very difficult for me to spend any time in there. You see —" she faltered and Nigel took her hand. "That's where my father usually abused me. He called it our special place. The few times I went in there, all I could do was just stare at the desk. It upset me so much that I had to call my psychiatrist in crisis one day."

"That explains your phone book on the side table." I looked at everyone.

They shifted restlessly.

I pulled Jon's manuscript out of the envelope and handed it to Mike and Jan. "Does this look familiar?"

Mike looked at the title page and then said with amazement, "This is the paper I was searching for when Jan and I first met. Where did you find it?"

"I ... er ... came across it on Jack Armstrong's desk. It was in a folder with these letters."

I held up a few of the letters Melissa had penned to Jon long ago. She spoke up.

"Those are letters I wrote to Jon." She looked very sad and sighed. "If those were all together, my father must have taken them from Jon, either by stealing them from his place or by forcing him to hand them over. If Dad knew that I had professed to love Jon, he would have had a reason to want him dead. My father was very possessive. He thought of me as his special girl."

"My mind is reeling," Jan said heavily as she put aside her untouched dessert. "Are you suggesting that I did kill Armstrong, after all? Because I can assure you I had no opportunity. I have very poor night vision, so I can't drive at night, and I was completely incapacitated by the sleeping pills Mike had given me when we got home. The police had a hard time rousing me when they barged in at 2:00 in the morning."

"I know, Jan," I replied. "But Mike was able to drive and was quite upset by how you had been treated by Jack Armstrong. Isn't that right, Mike?"

"That's true," he said soberly.

"Do you want me to explain what I think happened?"

"No, Abby," he said. "I'll do it." He squeezed Jan's hand.

"When we got home that night, Jan was in a state. I did everything I could to help, but she finally decided to take a couple of sleeping pills and try to get some rest.

"Once Jan was down for the night, I tried to relax, but I couldn't. I decided to go for a drive to calm down. I don't know if I intended to go back there or whether I just found myself driving in that direction, but eventually, I was on the logging road that led to the site. I had no idea what I thought I could do, or if Armstrong would even be there."

I interrupted briefly. "Mike, do you know what time it was when you arrived back at the site?"

"Huh?" he asked, clearly lost in his own story. "Oh, I think it was somewhere between 10:15 and 10:30."

I nodded for him to continue, and sat back.

He looked at Jan briefly, and she gave him a weak smile of encouragement.

"When I got there, it seemed quiet," he continued. "The trailer lights were on, and one of the Armstrong trucks was parked in front. I didn't see anyone around so I went up to the trailer door and knocked, but there was no answer. I might have missed the old man, but he started muttering. I looked over towards the tractor, and there he was, sitting up against the machine. I think he made some comment about my returning to the scene of the crime. I didn't know what he meant and figured he was just commenting on the altercation earlier.

"Armstrong goaded me, saying 'the Field family, mother, son, husband — you're all troublemakers.' I didn't know he'd been injured. The way he was slurring while he talked made me think he might be drunk. He continued to insult me, and I'm sorry to say I lost it. I bent over and grabbed him by the lapels and shook him like a rag doll. I think I may have banged his head against the wheel of the big machine. He suddenly slumped in my arms."

Mike looked up and took a breath. "I honestly thought he had just passed out. I was sure he was breathing, but when I called out his name, there was no response. I tried to pull him up, even tapped his cheek a couple of times, but nothing. God help me, I panicked. I swear I didn't mean to kill him, but maybe I did finish him off. I don't know what possessed me to run and not say anything to anyone about it. I had hoped it was a bad dream. I couldn't have been there more than fifteen minutes." Jan was staring at him, her face white with shock.

"Oh, Jan!" he implored. "I'm so sorry for the hell I put you through. I am such a coward."

"But why didn't you just tell me? We could have worked out what to do. This is unbelievable!" she said, acutely distressed.

"I know," he said. "I was out of my mind with compassion for you with that awful man. I can't believe it brought me to this." Mike turned to me. "I guess that's why I was glad when Jan wanted you to help, Abby. I hoped you could ferret out the truth and save me having to take on admitting my guilt alone."

In the ensuing silence, Jan began weeping quietly, and Mike eyes welled, too.

Feeling like a heel once again, I said quietly, "Thank you, Mike. I'm sure you've felt guilty about this. I could tell something was bothering you ever since you met us at Sunny's after Jan was released. I thought there was something more, and then when I remembered the turquoise paint we found in Mel's bike, that led me to think it might have come from your truck. But now ..." I took a deep breath before continuing. "Now I'm not so sure you were the last to see Armstrong alive."

Jan looked up with a glimmer of hope in her eyes. "What are you talking about, Abby? After all that, are you saying Mike didn't kill Jack Armstrong?"

"I don't know for sure, Jan, but the police didn't say it was a blow to the head that killed him. Tell me, Mike. Did you see the prayer flags around Armstrong's neck when you were there?"

Mike looked at me for a few seconds before answering.

"The flags were on the ground, Abby, right by where I lay him down. It was hard to tell because of the dark, but, no, I don't think they were around his neck when I left him. What's this about Melissa's bike?" he asked hopefully.

At this, Sunny came to life. "I think I can answer that, Mike. I'm beginning to see where Abby is leading us. Armstrong strangled on prayer flags. You didn't see any on him at the time, so you may have helped him along, but you didn't actually strangle him. Isn't that right, Abby?"

"That's right, Sunny," I replied, smiling lightly. "Your turn. Tell us about the bike, too."

Nigel interjected. "Hold on a minute. Mel is shivering. Maybe we should go inside."

She was, indeed, shivering. The sun had set, and we were starting to swat at bugs. Jan stood up a little unsteadily. "Goodness, I've become so wrapped up in this sorry tale that I didn't notice the cold creeping in. Come on in to the living room, everyone." We followed Nigel and Mel in, while Jan directed Mike, "Break out the brandy, dear. I think we need it."

CHAPTER 35

AS IF GLAD to have a task, Mike quickly poured the golden liquid and passed the small glasses around while we settled in the living room. Nigel and Melissa sat on the couch with Jan while Mike sat in an easy chair to their right. Anita sat cross-legged on the rug with the dogs in front of the wood stove. Sunny and I sat facing the others on the two chairs in front of the large plate-glass window.

Brandy in hand, Jan spoke up. "Well, this hasn't been quite the evening I had planned, but," she said heavily, "now that we've come this far, we'd better see it through. You were going to explain about the bike, Sunny."

"I'll do my best," he said. "But I might have to hand the torch back to Ab soon. Well," he began, "Brendon came by my shop the mornin' after your dad's death, Mel. I think he might have been trying to help you clean up any loose ends in case you'd killed your dad. Did you ever speak to him about what happened that night?"

Mel lifted her head. "No. None of us talked about it at all. I think we each thought we were guilty or we were helping the other person. I was confused."

Sunny shook his head. "That's a shame. Maybe we would have got to this point sooner if people had had more heart-to-hearts. Anyway, when Abby figured out the bike might be evidence, we looked it over carefully with the police. We tried to figure out what had happened to it. The wheel had a nasty bend, and not one you would get by falling or hitting a tree, so we figured something ran over it, which you confirmed for us, Mel." Sunny looked at me as he faltered.

"I'm gettin' lost now, Ab. Maybe you should take over."

"Thanks, Sunny," I said.

Perhaps he'd figured out more but wanted me to have the pleasure of the final revelation.

"Well," I said, "while we poked around the bike, we found a piece of torn prayer flag caught in the chain. That helped us to place the bike at the scene that night. The last pieces of information from the bike were chips of red and turquoise paint in the mud stuck in the wheel.

"The red paint and the bent wheel probably came from the truck Brendon was driving, but I originally thought the turquoise was from your truck," I said to Jan and Mike. "So my assuming you went back was partly a lucky guess, Mike.

"I began to have doubts when I saw Nigel's truck. I realized that it was much more likely that the chips would come from his truck because it was practically shedding as he drove. What do you think?" I asked, looking towards Mel and Nigel.

A hard, cornered look came over Melissa's face as she shook her head, but before she could speak, I said gently, "The police have the paint sample. It's only a matter of having the labs check it."

"Okay, okay," Mel sighed.

She looked at us pleadingly as she said, faltering, "I think maybe I did it. I don't know anymore."

I said gently, "What happened that night, Mel? You went back, didn't you?"

She nodded and took a deep breath.

"After I'd walked for about half an hour, I had second thoughts about going straight to the Middletons's. My head had cleared, and I started to wonder what Mother and Brendon were doing at the site, especially after the hot scene at the house earlier that night. And ..." she hesitated for a minute and looked at Nigel questioningly.

"Go ahead, Mel. It's okay."

She went on. "And then I remembered that I *had* to go back. I'd promised Gary, our watchman, that I would watch the site, and I remembered that Nigel was coming to meet me. We'd planned to take advantage of the fact that there would be no one there for a couple of hours after the meeting and that we could meet. I didn't want him to show up when my family was there, or get there and wonder where I was.

"The watchman was scheduled to return around 11:00 or 11:30, so I knew I had to hurry. I was just coming to the junction where the road divides, one way to the ferry and one way towards the south end where the Middletons live, when I saw one of our trucks speed by. At the time, I thought it could be either Dad or Brendon. Now I realize it was likely Brendon heading for the 10:30 ferry. It must have been around 10:15 at the time.

"I reached the site just after 10:30. Like Mike, at first I thought there was no one there. Then I heard a groan and I followed the sound to the tractor where my father lay. I couldn't see him very well, but he knew me.

"He said, 'Is that you Melissa? You've come back. My little girl has come back. Help me up, Melissa.' I walked over, but I couldn't bring myself to touch him. Somehow he'd become entangled in the prayer flags. I didn't know what had happened, but I could tell that he was injured and confused. I was worried that Brendon had done something, but I just didn't know what to do. I was paralyzed," she said helplessly.

"I just watched him as he called out to me weakly. He struggled and pushed himself upright, still with those flags around him, and … and then," she whispered, "and then he fell to the other side, and the flags were caught on the machinery." She looked up imploringly. "It was so awful. I could hear him strangling, choking, but I couldn't move."

She stopped talking. Nigel took her hand, and looked around at us all.

"And then I drove in," he continued the story. "All I noticed at first was Mel standing there, looking down. When I got closer, I saw that it was her father on the ground she was looking at. I stopped the truck and rushed over to her. The old man looked dead, but I didn't want to wait and find out. I just assumed that Mel had finally snapped and that she'd done something to her father to end their misery.

"I couldn't get Mel to say anything. I think she was in shock, so I just walked her slowly to my truck. As we started to drive out, I saw her bike and heaved it onto the truck-bed. Then I got the hell out of there."

He continued. "Mel collected herself a bit as we drove. She made me take her to the Middletons's house, insisting she didn't want me involved. She was becoming more and more agitated as I argued, so I thought the best thing was to agree. She told me to go home and said she would call me in the morning.

"When I dropped Mel off, I saw that the bike wasn't in the truck anymore. It must have slid off, back at the site. I didn't return for it. I didn't want to risk running into the night watchman." Nigel looked at us with clear eyes. "It seems pretty silly now, but all I wanted then was to protect her," he said shamefacedly.

"I was still crazy with worry, so I went to the bar and called Brendon from there. I told him what I'd seen and that I thought maybe Mel had killed the old man."

Nigel laughed harshly at himself. "Boy, Brendon must have thought I was nuts. Anyway," he said. "Brendon told me not to worry about the bike. He'd take care of it. I don't know what he did, but somehow he snuck the thing away from the site after the watchman saw it. The ferry wasn't running, so I don't know if he took the family launch over or what."

Sunny mused. "He wasn't driving an Armstrong truck that morning."

Nigel looked at Jan sorrowfully.

"I felt badly, Jan, when I heard they had arrested you, but I was sure it wasn't going to stick. I was crazy with worry about Mel, so when Abby seemed to be getting too close, I called Brendon again. He was already bothered about you, Abby, because of his drug stuff, so he was only too happy to insist that I help him get you out of the way. I feel like an idiot."

"You already paid dearly for what you did, Nigel," I said. "I'm just glad we all survived."

Jan stood up unsteadily. "Whew, what a mess." She looked at me and said, "You have given us a lot to deal with, Abby, and I should be grateful, but right now I have a heavy heart. I think it's going to take a while to heal some of our wounds."

Mike stood, too, and Jan kindly put her hand in his as he said, "I know that I will be calling the police in the morning to admit my part in the mess. I am completely ashamed of myself."

Sunny stretched and reached over to give my arm a squeeze. "Wow, bulldog! Way to go. You certainly kept at it until you ferreted out every bit of information. But now I think we should let these folks work things out for themselves."

"You're right," I said. "Jan, I'm sorry. Let me know if I can help you and Mike in any way."

She simply gave me a flat smile, a brief hug and had the good grace to say, "Thank you, dear," instead of pointing out that I had 'helped' quite enough already.

A contemplative Anita joined us in our goodbyes to the two couples, who looked like they still needed to talk to each other.

With all the bits and pieces sorted out, I should have felt triumphant, but I was suddenly exhausted. Yawning as we got into the van, I simply said, "Home, James," and closed my eyes.

CHAPTER 36

WHEN I AWOKE, the sun was streaming through the window and I was fully clothed, lying in a small bed in a lovely room that I didn't recognize. From my vantage point, as I blinked my way to awareness, I could see tall firs gently waving. The giveaway was the one picture on the roughly panelled wall — a tasteful sepia poster of an old Tour de France bike race. I was obviously at Sunny's.

I smiled and relaxed. It couldn't be his room; must be a guest room. I must have been so unconscious that he decided not to return me to the lodge. As I sat up and stretched, I noticed a little note on the bedside table.

> Hi Sleepyhead,
> I had to get to work. Season's short here, you know. Take your time. The bathroom is just outside your room. A shake awaits you in the fridge. You'll find me in the shop.
> —Sunny
> P.S. Reminded me of old times, when we went carousing on Queen St. and I had to help you home. You're such a party animal.

I smiled. While it's not strictly true that I'm a partier, I did used to like checking out the scene with Sunny in the early punk days in Toronto.

My stomach told me it was late, so I remade the bed as quickly as my still-sore muscles would allow before checking out the shake in the fridge.

Sunny was my best pupil when it came to making breakfast drinks. The fridge held a jug full of healthy (and somewhat tasty) ingredients — fruit, yogurt and whatever else had stirred his fancy. This was true comfort food, after all the gourmet meals I had savoured in the last two weeks. It made me homesick for my apartment above the fish shop, replete with bikes, blender, bed and shower. For about two seconds, I hankered for the hot, dirty, dusty city, until Sunny walked in from the shop, a vision in his overalls, with bike grease under his fingernails. My stomach gave a little flutter, and I licked the saliva off my lips while I did a quick rethink on what qualified as home.

I guess it was inevitable that I would slip into intimacy with Sunny. That evening, we renewed our old friendship. He knew me so well, it was a bit disconcerting, as our hands explored what we discovered was still familiar territory. We talked, too. He told me little anecdotes about life on the island and described people in such a funny way that we laughed and laughed.

I realized I had needed that laughter. I had been serious and sardonic for too long, and it showed. And then there was the night. That long burning ember for Sunny that I had been fighting was allowed to spark, and soon my laughter turned to pure, unadulterated lust. We had a feverish grand time. At least I did. Sunny is too laid-back for fever. Perhaps that's what kept me there for a while — the sense that he was there but not in a hurry; not needing me, but liking me.

Of course, that's what scared me, too.

I moved out of the lodge and stayed with him for two more weeks. Anita hung out with us for a day or two and then went back to T.O., looking healthy and happy. I spent some of my time helping Sunny in the shop, which was my idea of heaven. We did some riding, and I watched the islanders clean up from the storm and get their lives back in order. We also visited with a few of Sunny's other friends.

I stayed out of the way after Melissa confessed. Mike told the police his part at the same time. The local media had a heyday with the whole affair, what with the revolving door of suspects and confessions, but only for a day or two. Nigel and Jan stayed with them through the whole thing, and the lawyer said that the charges would probably be reduced to involuntary manslaughter.

Mabel Armstrong was receiving treatment for her "health condition." That was the extent of the airing of that family's dirty laundry. Brendon didn't reappear during my time on the island, but I did hear that Nigel and Melissa were actually planning to go ahead with revamping Armstrong Lumber, if they could keep Melissa out of jail.

They came by once to tell us that Melissa's firm had hired Nigel as a consultant for better forestry practices, and the big news was that Armstrong Lumber was looking into donating the recently logged land where Armstrong had died, and what was left unlogged in that parcel, to the island in trust. They were going to set up a foundation to help teach young people on the island alternative practices, such as horse logging, and promote secondary industries, such as cabinet-making. They were just waiting for this idea to pass by the board of directors before making it public. It sounded too good to be true, and perhaps it was. But Mel and Nigel seemed so happy, I kept my mouth shut and my fingers crossed.

Much of the time, however, Sunny and I spent alone together. He fed me romantic, delicious meals from his garden and we went for walks on his trail and generally had a good time. He was attentive and responsive. I had a few twinges of guilt about hopping from Andy to Sunny so quickly, but most of the time, I was just happy and relaxed. Andy called once to say goodbye. He'd had a blast mountain biking with Sally, and she was going to visit him in T.O. when the tourist season ended, so I think he was fine. We parted amicably but firmly.

Eventually, three things brought me up short. One, my bank account was shrinking; two, I felt like I was losing my edge; and three, I began to miss my bikes.

Now that I'm back in Toronto, I have to confirm I'm still feeling a little divided. The fish store is a bit of a liability at the moment because I can't quite shake my memories of the coast with that fish smell around all the time. It's wonderful, however, to have my place and my own wheels and to be on familiar territory while treading emotional water. The local animals I can deal with easily. But I keep remembering my last night with Sunny.

He was very cool about it, which made it even harder. But as we got ready for bed, it was the little things, like sharing the bathroom and brushing our teeth together, that brought it all home.

He tried once, half-heartedly. "You know, Ab, we could run the shop together. I know it's not your home, but you could get comfortable here."

"Oh, Sunny. It's such a nice idea, but I have to get back to my scene. I am more than comfortable here with you, believe me. That's what scares me."

As I hopped into bed, he joined me, slowly, languorously, enveloping me in his arms, entwining my legs in his. He said, quietly, as he nuzzled my ear, "You always were a little contrary."

We held each other for a while, letting our bodies instinctively respond, little hormonal sparks firing in all engines. We were so well tuned. We didn't spend much time sleeping that night, but near dawn, we did doze off for a while. A murder of crows fighting over something finally woke me. I lay there for a while as Sunny slept on. I looked at him and asked myself once more if I was making the right decision. Sunny was perfect for me — self-assured, funny, independent, cute and strong.

And now as the fish and bleach odour wafts its way upward and I whip up one more shake, getting ready for a day of dodging cars in this dusty city, I find myself asking that question again. Then, as the sun reflects into my living room from the window of the cheese store across the street, my ten classy bikes gleam and beckon to me, and I assure myself that this is my place.

ACKNOWLEDGMENTS

TAKING RAW CREATIVE work and crafting it into a published novel requires tremendous collaboration. I would like to acknowledge some of the people who helped bring *Ragged Chain* into the world. Once again I had the good fortune to have the principled direction of Jennifer Day, my editor for much of the process. Thank you Jennifer, for your ideas, discipline and hard work. I would like to thank Sumach Press for taking on the book and for making the transition to CSPI/Women's Press smooth and painless. Many thanks to Colleen Wormald, the production editor at CSPI/Women's Press for stepping in and taking the reins so well.

Of course, I am also very appreciative of the support and assistance from my friends and family. Special thanks go to Judy Scannell for turning my scrawl into type and I am particularly grateful for the support, patience and silence of my children and spouse during the editing process. Thank you, Smokey, for the bike advice and encouraging words.